The Ticking Ghost

PHIL MILES

ABOUT THE AUTHOR

Phil Miles has been writing screenplays, short stories and novels for over twenty years. He has been a finalist in several major writing contests, including BBC Talent, the Red Planet Pictures Prize, and Scriptapalooza. His first novel *Dark Drive* was a top 100 bestseller in Amazon's time travel fiction chart. His second novel *The Jaguar & The Wasp* is also available on Amazon now. You will soon be able to download his short stories *Teamwork* and *The Voices In The East Wing* for free at www.fictionjunkies.com

THE TICKING GHOST

SATURDAY
00:00

Midnight at Spook Central. Drew Turner had been summoned, by the spirits that dwelt in the shadows.

He placed his phone and his ID in the sliding tray, surrendering them to the Red Bull-chugging ghoul behind the bulletproof glass. The pale-faced entity examined the ID and tapped on his keyboard. He returned the ID but kept the phone, then waved Drew on through to the body scanner. Drew enjoyed its quiet *swish-swish*, and when he stepped out of the pod he felt like he had crossed over. Here, on the other side, there was an impeccably dressed young woman waiting for him. She led him out into the expansive ground floor lobby, where a cleaner, the only other visible human being, was auto-polishing the stone floor. It was now so highly polished that a shimmering distortion of the words *Threat Level: Substantial*, from the display on the wall above, was reflected in it.

They went into a nearby lift. The woman pressed 4. The doors closed silently. Drew studied his reflection in the lift's mirrored walls. He looked exhausted. Hardly surprising. He was clean-shaven, eyes dark brown, red-rimmed and bloodshot. He could afford to dress well, and did, but eyes could never really be dressed, could they? Nor hidden. Not in his profession. Drew looked into people's souls for a living. It seemed only fair to let them look back into his.

The lift doors slid open. They emerged into a warren of white-walled, blue-carpeted corridors, through which the young woman led him at a quick pace, turning corner after corner. Then she ushered him into a small, sparse waiting room with a coffee machine, and disappeared again.

Here, a late middle-aged woman with greying hair sat behind a desk. She wore an old-fashioned white blouse under a beige cardigan. She had an air of professionalism about her that was as intimidating as it was admirable. She glanced up from her laptop and peered at Drew dubiously through her horn-rimmed glasses. The way Drew carried himself was usually enough to make people nervous, but this woman showed no such inclination. It worried him.

"DSI Turner?"

Drew nodded. He got the impression the woman's desk - and the room itself - was hers and hers alone, and had been for a very long time. She was highly trusted within the department, he guessed. A gatekeeper as well as an administrator. But who, or what, lay behind the gates?

"Please have a seat, Detective. Alec will call you in a moment."

"Who the hell *is* Alec? What's this all about?"

Deary me. Someone hasn't had his Weetabix!

There was the voice again. *Shut up, Jenny. Not now.*

"I don't know what it's about," the woman replied simply. "And you mustn't be rude to Alec." She made it sound less like a reprimand and more like an obvious statement of fact.

Drew was tempted by the coffee machine, but before he could act on it, Alec emerged from a side door. He was a small, nervous ferret of a man, slightly older than Drew, but half his size. He had a balding forehead and a long pointed nose under a thick-framed pair of glasses. He wore a white short-sleeved shirt with a tie. The short sleeves revealed thin, wiry forearms that hung there ineffectually, like T-Rex arms. His eyes darted constantly here and there, making but never holding eye contact with Drew. Silently, he beckoned Drew to enter.

Drew followed Alec into his small but very tidy office. There were no paper files on display, nor even any filing cabinets, only another desk, another laptop. Alec closed the door softly behind them. Somehow, without even opening his mouth, Alec had elicited contempt in Drew. But then Alec *did* open his mouth, and once again the balance of power that Drew was accustomed to seemed to readjust itself, tilting unexpectedly away from him.

"I know you didn't want to be here today, Drew," Alec said. "Today of all days." His voice was surprisingly deep for such a small man. Controlled and calm. Commanding even.

Drew sniffed. "That's putting it fucking mildly."

"I know you were already working a case."

"Not *a* case. *The* case."

"Ah yes. *The* case. DCS O'Brien tells me you were too emotionally invested. Too personally involved."

"DCS O'Brien doesn't get it."

"Get what?"

"I'm the only one who can catch that fucker."

Alec shook his head. "A convenient lie you've told yourself. There's no shortage of talent in your team. And besides, CID to MI5 is hardly a demotion."

"No more powers of arrest. That's a demotion in my book."

"Hardly a humiliation, then. Drew, I need you to get this into your head and get it there fast: *that* case was *a* case. *This* case is *the* case."

Drew smirked. "Is that so? What's it all about then? Defence of the realm? Queen and Country?"

"Ah! Glad you mentioned it! *Do* you love your country?"

Drew shrugged. "I love bits of it. I love some of our places, our people, our customs. Even some of our laws."

"Only some?"

"The laws relating to wrongdoing. Not wrongsaying."

"But you yourself enforce those laws."

"Not *those* laws I don't, and I never will. I'm real police, not Twitter police. Look, who the hell are you, anyway? Are you a silverback or a little baby chimp?"

Alec grinned and leaned back in his chair. "An amusing if slightly mixed metaphor. I'm certainly not a silverback, Drew. I'm a lowly case officer, a baby chimp if you will, but a rather unusual one. Most case officers have multiple cases which they have to juggle, just like senior detectives in the Met. Their cases come and go over the years, just like yours do. Most case officers rise up through the ranks, like you have, or they move on to other things. Well, not me. I've only ever had one rank and one case. A case that's been ongoing since I was first assigned to it. Three decades ago."

"You're joking."

"I'm afraid not." He paused to push his glasses back up his nose. "Thirty years ago, somebody wrote to us." He handed Drew a colour copy of a handwritten letter. There was a thick black bar running horizontally across the top right of the page; for some reason, the date had been redacted. But the rest of it was uncensored. Each word was lovingly spelled out with showy, intricate use of a calligraphy pen. Elaborate flourishes made the writing look almost medieval, though the words themselves were contemporary enough.

To whom it may concern,

I'm rather surprised you haven't already caught up with me. You may yet, but you'll have to hurry, because I shall be setting the timer and planting the device later today. I've found the perfect spot for it. London, if not the world, is my oyster. All it needs now is a pearl.

You might be tempted to interpret my actions as being motivated by revenge for what was done to me. A case of sour grapes. An eye for an eye. Let me assure you that this is categorically not the case. For one thing, it would be several million eyes for one eye, which hardly seems fair. But more importantly, the virus developed by your scientists, the virus whose symptoms I am now experiencing, has one symptom in particular that I doubt they anticipated. It's a wonderful *symptom. A life-changing, perception-altering, truth-revealing symptom. Much the same sort of claims have been made in defence of certain psychedelics, but I assure you the effects of this virus are far more profound. The true nature of the universe has been revealed to me, and I now see the fabric of reality for what it really is, with crystal clarity and total sobriety. I am not under the influence in any way. I am not 'tripping'. It is simply new knowledge which has been revealed to me. And what knowledge! Can you really blame me, then, for wanting others to see this profound truth in the same way I have?*

I have enclosed my diary along with this letter, in an effort to show you how I came to this decision, and the things I experienced along the way. It also explains why I have chosen to delay 'detonation' for thirty years, and why I have chosen to tell you about it in advance.

As for the device itself, well, what can I say? I'm really rather proud of my efforts. It's a simple enough thing really. The only hard part was finding a power source that would last for thirty years plus. Initially, lithium thionyl chloride seemed like the obvious way to go, but then I found something even better: atomic batteries. Betavoltaics, to be precise. These are particularly well suited to low-power electrical applications where long life of the energy source is required; implantable medical devices like pacemakers (my forte!) or certain military and space applications (yours, I dare say).

The device itself is a reinforced weather-proof canister containing the power source (a handful of betavoltaic batteries connected in series), the locking mechanism, the timer, a hinged and spring-loaded lid (rust-proof of course) and the payload itself. Payload! What a sinister term for something so apparently innocuous! Something a child could've come up with! Anyway, once the lock is engaged, nothing and no-one can open the canister. It is quite impregnable. Once started, the timer cannot be reset. When the thirty year period expires, the lid opens (the container being suspended upside down, somewhere air can circulate) and gravity does the rest. I shall set the timer for 6pm.

I would've thought thirty years is enough 'forewarning' even for you. I'm dying to know how exactly you 'fail whilst believing you've succeeded', but I don't suppose I'll still be *around to find out. Pity!*

Again, I must emphasise that this is not in any way intended as revenge for what was done to me. Quite the opposite, in fact. This will not be death as you understand it. It will be a gift to you all. The gift of rebirth. An awakening, just as the man said.

Your missing friend, Magnus Hale

Drew glanced back up at Alec. "Missing?"

Alec took the letter from Drew and carefully laid it face down on his desk. "Back then," he said, "Magnus Hale was a test subject at a bio-research facility in Wiltshire."

"Porton Down?"

"Not quite. The two facilities were related, but this one was newer, more secret, and rather more... *fringe*, shall we say. Its scientists were given free rein. No idea was considered too outlandish. No theory too flaky. They developed a... a virus, of sorts. Hale contracted it, shortly before escaping from the facility. He went on the run, first to London, where he planted his device and sent us that letter. Then he went north, to the Isle of Barra in the Outer Hebrides. A remote fishing village called Scarnish. There's a pier there with an old house at the end of it. Dilapidated. Abandoned. That's where Hale spent his last days, alone, in hiding, and slowly dying from the virus. We tracked him down, eventually, but we were too late to question him. He was already dead. To this day, the canister referred to in that letter remains hidden somewhere in London. And if we don't find it in time, it'll open. It'll open and spread that virus throughout the entire city."

"And beyond?"

"Undoubtedly. It's highly contagious and highly deadly."

Drew looked out of the window behind Alec. It overlooked the Thames, but all he could see was the very top of the London Eye; a glowing purple frown in the night. "But you've had thirty *years* to find it," he said.

Alec half-smiled and nodded. He'd anticipated the criticism. "We began with conventional detective work; reconstructing Hale's movements from eye witness accounts and so on. But those leads dried up very quickly. From then on, it was all needles and haystacks. As you can imagine, when we first read that line about 'gravity doing the rest', we thought: tall buildings. Over the years we've searched damn near every rooftop in London, excluding any that were built after Hale sent us his letter. Nothing."

"What about underground? Tube tunnels?"

"Every inch of every tunnel from here to Uxbridge via Epping. And the river tunnels too. Again, nothing."

"Building interiors?"

"Ditto."

"But you can't have looked everywhere."

"Indeed we haven't. London's just too damn big. And then there's the term itself. *London.* Notice how he didn't say 'Central London' or 'West London' or even 'Greater London'. Just 'London'. I mean Christ, define London! Where does it start? Where does it end?"

"How *did* you define it?"

"Initially, we went on the assumption he'd choose somewhere central, somewhere symbolic and very public. Once those locations were searched and eliminated, we gradually worked our way out. That was in the early days. As the years went by, the search became more systematic. New technologies came along. New strategies. 3D laser scanning. Lidar. That sort of thing. We scanned countless building exteriors and interiors looking for any kind of container that had no rightful business being there. We found plenty, but they all turned out to be something innocuous. 3D scanning was a failure. Then later, quite recently in fact, WAMI came along."

"WAMI?"

"Wide Area Motion Imagery. You might know it as *Argus*, or *Gorgon Stare*. Tech developed by DARPA in the States, and loaned out to us. Essentially, it's a cluster of ultra high-resolution cameras stuck to the underside of a modified reconnaissance drone. Each camera set at a slightly different angle to cover a very wide area. Wide as in city-wide. Ours captured every damn rooftop in London. Central *and* Greater."

"And?"

"We did a systematic grid search. We had a

whole team of analysts looking for anomalies. Again, we found many, many anomalies. And once again they all turned out to be something harmless."

"Maybe it was nothing more than a threat? Maybe Hale never even built the thing?"

"It was tempting to reach that conclusion. To my superiors who authorised and set aside funding for the project, it was *very* tempting. Still is, in fact. I have daily battles to fight with those people, and the thing I always emphasise to them is this: the WAMI dataset covered the entire city, sure, but only from one angle: above. What if Hale's device was shielded from view by an awning? Or stuck to the underside of a balcony? There's CCTV of course, but those cameras are only as good as their arc of rotation. Great for street level coverage, but not much else."

"What about Google? Their street mapping cars take photos from every angle."

Alec nodded. "A dataset we finished searching four years ago. The long and the short of it is, we've been buggered for thirty years, and we're still buggered now." He pushed the glasses up his nose once again. "All except for this..."

Alec reached inside his desk drawer and pulled out a battered old brown leather diary, which he passed to Drew. "This is the diary Hale mentioned in the letter."

Drew took it and flicked through the pages. The writing ended less than halfway through. At that point, a single page had been torn out. "Something's missing."

"Indeed. If that missing page is up in Barra, hidden somewhere inside that house, it may hold the key. Hale clearly didn't want us to read it. Perhaps because it revealed the location of his device."

"That's quite a long shot."

"At this point, I'm afraid, long shots are all we have left." Alec leaned in over the table towards Drew, holding eye contact for the first time since they'd met. "We want you to go up to Barra, Drew. We want you to search the house where Hale spent his final days. If that missing diary page is there, we're confident you'll find it. And if there's any other clues to be had, we're confident you'll find those too."

"But you must've searched the place already, surely?"

"We searched it when we recovered Hale's body. But we may have missed something, and you, I'm told, are the star detective who notices things others miss."

"So it's a mop-up exercise. Doesn't Five have any mops of its own?"

"We used to. A man called Baines. He went up there two weeks ago. As soon as he arrived, he vanished."

00:18

"We have no idea what happened to Baines," Alec said, "but whatever it was, we doubt it was accidental. That village near the house. Scarnish. There's something going on up there that we don't fully understand. The locals don't like outsiders poking their noses in. I mean *really* don't like it. Talk to them by all means, but be careful. And remember: this is a hunt for clues to the whereabouts of the device. It is *not* a hunt for Baines."

"Supposing Baines already found that vital clue? And that's why he disappeared? Or *was* disappeared?"

"There is that possibility, of course. But foul play won't be your only concern. Hale was infected, remember. So there's also the chance of... further contagion."

Drew gave an exasperated sigh. "I'm not doing all this in a bloody hazmat suit."

"Oh, there's no need for anything like that. Transmission isn't biological, nor chemical. We only call it a virus atall because it's analogous to one. But it's actually something rather different. It's... well, it's a phrase."

Drew cocked his head. "Come again?"

"A trigger phrase."

"A *what*?"

"A series of words that induces certain symptoms - *physical* symptoms - in anyone who reads them or hears them said aloud."

"That's impossible."

"I wish it were, but psychosomatic illness is a well documented phenomenon. As is the placebo effect. Sometimes a mere belief in something is enough to make it so. I'm talking about the power of suggestion, Drew. A power those scientists were trying to weaponise. Turns out they succeeded. And then some."

Drew frowned, shook his head. "If it acts like a placebo, then it'll only work on people who believe it will. If they don't *associate* it with harm, then it won't *do* them harm."

Alec grinned slyly. "You would've thought so, wouldn't you? But there's a bit more to it."

Drew raised an eyebrow.

"The scientists began," Alec explained, "in just the way you'd expect. First, they chose a highly suggestible test subject. They told him the phrase he was about to see was special, that it had the power to induce a slight itch on the left cheek of anyone who saw it. And because he *believed* it would, it did. The next day, they showed him a slight variation of the same phrase. This time, they told him his symptoms

14

would be a little more severe. Sure enough, they were, again because the test subject *simply believed* they would be. But they never told him what 'more severe' actually meant. They left it up to his imagination. Well, he imagined alright, and with some pretty startling results. The things he imagined, the things he believed in... let's just say he gave them quite a bit more than they'd bargained for. So much so, in fact, that they had to give him an 'antiviral' - in reality just a sugar pill - to alleviate his symptoms. Nothing but belief had brought them on, and nothing but belief got rid of them. This went on over several weeks. Each time this poor chap was shown a new variation of the trigger phrase, he was told his symptoms would worsen. And worsen they did, until they grew so acute he died from them. In the end, nothing could save him from the wilder excesses of his own imagination. Not a sugar pill, nor even the *true* antiviral they developed from his infected facial tissue. By the time they'd produced that, he was already too far gone."

"Jesus."

"Anyway, now the scientists had their nocebo."

"Nocebo?"

"Like a placebo, but harmful instead of beneficial. However, as you rightly pointed out, the trigger phrase was fatal only to those who *expected* it to be. And that wasn't quite good enough. What they were *really* after was a variant that could make the leap they'd been theorising about. And soon they found one."

"What kind of leap?"

"The leap from nocebo to sinecebo."

"*Sine*cebo?"

"Latin for *I shall be without.* Though I think the concept is better expressed as *I shall be, regardless.*"

"Regardless of what?"

"Regardless of belief. Of association. What those scientists discovered, Drew, was a sinecebo trigger phrase whose viral symptoms are identical to those of the nocebo from which it was derived. Except *this* phrase is even more deadly, because it doesn't need to be associated with anything atall. One is not required to *believe* that hearing it or reading it will lead to anything atall. It functions quite independently, entirely 'without', regardless of suggestibility, and with total efficacy. There is no antiviral."

"And Magnus Hale was exposed to it?"

"Yes. That canister he talks about contains thousands of pieces of paper. Each and every one has this trigger phrase written on it. When the lid opens - during rush hour, I might add - they flutter down over the city, arousing inevitable curiosity, followed by infection, followed by death. Hale calls it his ticker tape parade."

00:25

Drew's natural scepticism, his bullshit detector, was something on which he prided himself. When someone was lying to his face, he sensed it intuitively, and would try and tease out a tell, some tacit admission of guilt, by wearing his scepticism on his sleeve, telling the liar he suspected them. Usually they would squirm or look away or fold in some other manner, but so far it hadn't worked on Alec. Alec just continued to meet his gaze and hold it, blinking slowly, patiently waiting for Drew to look away first.

"If Hale wanted to expose people to this 'trigger phrase'," Drew said at length, "he could've just *said* it. Or written it in the letter."

"He could have, but he didn't. He wanted that thirty year delay."

"But that could've been a ruse. He could still have planted the phrase in the diary."

"He didn't."

"But you must've known that danger was there?"

"Indeed we did. At the time, we thought the trigger phrase consisted of actual words - English

17

language words - albeit words strung together at random. A phrase without any syntax. Without any meaning. That's what the last reports from the testing facility suggested. But when things got out of hand, that facility was bombed. By us. A last ditch containment effort. So we never got to see the *new* progress reports. If we had, we would've realised the scientists had already moved on; from random words to random *letters*. When we first read Hale's diary, we were worried about finding syntax errors when we should've been worried about... words that weren't really words. We should've gone through it letter by letter, not word by word. Even the syntax sweep was flawed, and we knew it. It was dicey, to say the least. But we had to find Hale, and fast. We had to know what he'd written, and fast."

"And who exactly was 'we'?"

Alec broke eye contact and shifted awkwardly in his chair. The way liars did.

Drew went in for the kill. "You got some other poor bastard to read that diary, knowing full well it might've killed them. Didn't you?"

Alec's cheeks flushed red.

Drew sneered. "They never had a clue, did they, because you didn't have the guts to tell them. Who was it? Your secretary out there?"

Alec shook his head ever so slightly. The gesture was so tiny it hardly constituted a denial. He might as well have said 'No comment.'

"I don't work for people I can't trust," Drew

said.

"I'm not asking you to trust me, but I would strongly urge you to accept the assignment."

"Why?"

Alec was suddenly affronted. "Because it's London, for god's sake! An entire city! Don't they deserve to live?"

"The way they vote? Sometimes I wonder."

"Dear oh dear! We were hoping you might put your hard right tendencies on pause for a few days. Hold your nose and save eight million people. That sort of thing."

"It's called a joke, Alec. Or are you too hard left to remember what that is? Like I said, I don't work for people I can't trust. Find yourself another mop. I'm out."

Drew was almost at the door when Alec said: "If you walk away, your career might..."

Drew stopped in his tracks. He turned back to face Alec.

"...take a knock."

"A knock?"

Alec sighed. "We know all about you, Drew. So far you've been unstoppable. Up through the ranks like a rocket. And why? Because you're Drew Turner, of course! The canny, tenacious detective who always gets his man, one way or another. But it's that 'other way' that gets you in trouble, isn't it? Strong arm tactics and all the rest of it. Unbecoming even for a constable, let alone a senior detective.

You're that rarest of beasts: a highly intelligent thug. A thug who's been adopted by the state. Adopted but never tamed, and they're starting to think you're untameable. They were about to let you go, in fact."

Drew's eyes widened. "Bullshit."

Alec shook his head. "DCS O'Brien knows your history, and he knows you can't stand the sight of him. He sees you as a threat, physically *and* professionally."

"O'Brien doesn't do police work. He does PR. I don't want his job."

"Well, he thinks you do. He was all set to get rid of you, citing your numerous past indiscretions. But then this murderer came on the scene. A killer of women. A case tailor made for your 'white knight' sensibilities, so he thought he'd keep you around just a little while longer. And he was right to, wasn't he? You love clip-clopping around London. Sir Drew the white knight! Here to show those attractive but rather uppity young ladies just what they've been missing all through our irritatingly progressive modern age. They're told they're being fed properly, but really they're on a drip, aren't they? A constant feed of nerds, 'allies' and sensitive types. Drip, drip, drip. The only white knighting *those* men do is on social media. But now here's Sir Drew. Here's the real deal. Except... just as you were riding to the rescue, you fell off your horse, didn't you? Fell rather badly, in fact. Your wife, wasn't it?"

Drew snarled: "I could snap your neck like it

was-"

"Of course you could," Alec interrupted. "But you won't. Because now that you're off the case, I'm the only thing stopping O'Brien from cutting you loose altogether."

"Big words from a baby chimp."

"Oh, but the silverbacks are lurking in the trees, Drew. I don't have their rank, but I *do* have their ear. And they're just as willing as you are to use strong arm tactics. If you don't go up to Barra like a good boy, those past indiscretions of yours might suddenly resurface, and if they do, you won't get the chance to white knight ever again. At least not where it counts. You'd be reduced to... *doing it on the internet.* And the kind of man that does that... well, you'd hardly be able to live with yourself. You'd just as soon snap your *own* neck. Wouldn't you?"

Drew stood there, breathing hard in and out. He felt naked, stripped of all autonomy. He was considering murdering Alec just to prove him wrong, when there was a soft knock on the door.

"Come in, Megan," Alec said.

A young woman came in. When Drew saw her, the urge to kill Alec faded abruptly. She was late twenties, he guessed, her black hair tied back in a neat ponytail. Her features hinted at nobility. Drew imagined tossing a coin and seeing her profile when it came up heads. Her skin was very pale. She wore no make-up. The dark circles under her black eyes contrasted sharply with the pallor of her cheeks. She looked very slightly ill, but somehow no less beautiful for it. She wore a white roll-neck jumper over black jeans. She was black and white all over; a convalescing monochrome empress.

Alec's introduction could hardly have been more cursory. "Drew, Megan. Megan, Drew." He looked expressly at Drew and added: "You'll. Be. Working. Together."

Megan caught the whiff of tension. Warily, she said: "Alec's told me all about you."

Drew nodded, then fixed Alec with another threatening stare. "All good, I hope?"

00:30

Megan's imperious demeanour continued to fascinate Drew. It smacked of someone with total confidence in themselves and their abilities. Yet every now and then Drew noticed her expression change, for the tiniest fraction of a second, to one of... what exactly? It was always so fleeting, but now there it was again, and this time he pegged it. It was anxiety. Fear. Borderline panic even. Then it was gone again, and the perfectly poised empress was back.

There was another knock at the door. "Come in Eileen!" Alec said in a singsong voice; the chorus notes from *Come On Eileen*. He was evidently pleased with his little joke, but his smile faded when neither Drew nor Megan laughed.

Alec's assistant - the horn-rimmed matron from the waiting room - entered carrying a tray with three mugs on it. "Tea, anyone?"

"Ooh, yes please!" Alec said keenly, and took one.

Eileen offered Drew a mug. It wasn't coffee, but any caffeine was better than no caffeine. He took one gratefully.

Eileen turned to Megan. "Fancy a cuppa?"

Megan shuddered and shook her head quickly.

Why the shudder?

"It's not poisoned," Eileen muttered. Then she was out the door again, closing it gently behind her.

Alec addressed Drew between carefree slurps of his tea. "Megan will be conducting her own parallel investigation, in conjunction with yours. You'll both be searching for the same thing: clues to the whereabouts of the device, and nothing else. By all means collaborate if you wish, though I dare say your methods will..." he paused, looking pointedly at Megan, "...*differ* somewhat. You might both prefer to work independently. Whatever works best."

"What's best for you, Megan?" Drew asked.

"Independently," she said sharply.

"Why's that?"

"You won't be able to help me."

Ouch. Why so thorny?

Alec checked his watch. "You'd better both be going. There's a car waiting to take you to the airfield. Do try and get on. If you can."

By way of a litmus test, Drew held the door open for Megan and said "Ladies first," prompting Alec to wince.

Megan rolled her eyes and walked through.

The eye roll said it all. She was like a grapefruit, Drew decided; citric and bitter, but nothing that couldn't be sweetened.

"Don't forget this," Alec said. He handed Hale's diary to Drew. "And please don't waste any time. If the information in that diary is correct - and we've no reason to think it isn't - then the canister will open at 6pm precisely, on the eighteenth of this month."

Megan didn't react - she seemed to know it already - but Drew's eyes widened. "That's Monday. Less than three days from now."

"Indeed," said Alec. "I'm told you both work best under pressure. I sincerely hope that's true."

00:48
65 hours and 12 minutes remaining

The roads were never really quiet, not in London, but at that time of night they were at least negotiable at speed. The BMW's flashing blue lights marked it out as an emergency vehicle of some kind, but little else about the dark grey car drew attention to itself. Little apart from the phenomenal skill with which the driver wove his way around taxis and night buses, like a slalom skier zipping past black and red flags.

Drew and Megan sat next to each other on the back seat, the g-forces from the swerves making them lean left, then right, then left. The compelled synchrony almost seemed to bond them slightly, but then the driver ran out of cars to overtake, and the effect wore off immediately.

Drew wanted to sleep, but of course he couldn't. Nor could he focus on the task ahead of him. He'd had no time at all to mentally prepare himself for it, and now all he could think about was the rabbit. The rabbit Jenny had brought home and promised to take care of, right before she was... *Stop. Don't go there.* When he'd left it this morning - no, *yesterday* morning - the rabbit had seemed perfectly content in its hutch in the garden, but now it would have to fend for itself, and who knew for how long? Had he even fed it yesterday? He couldn't remember. Christ, he was tired.

Megan had obviously been briefed far in advance of Drew, and was more prepared. She clutched a small bag full of clothes and toiletries, which Drew now eyed enviously. He didn't even have a toothbrush, let alone a change of clothes. When he mentioned this to the driver, the man reached across to the empty front passenger seat. Without taking his eyes off the road, he grabbed a transparent plastic bag full of men's toiletries and tossed it back to Drew.

"What about clothes?" Drew asked.

"You're fine as you are," the driver replied.

From the corner of his eye, Drew caught Megan's barely suppressed smirk.

They hit the A40, passing Ealing and Greenford, and suddenly Drew knew exactly where they were headed. Not an airfield as Alec had stated, but an air *base*. Ten minutes later, he was proved right. The car rolled to a halt in front of flimsy red and white barriers overlooked by CCTV masts. A blue sign in a pool of orange street light announced their final destination: *RAF Northolt*. The driver flashed some ID at a uniformed guard who sat alone in a little booth. The guard checked his computer, then issued the driver with a temporary pass. The barriers rose, and they passed through to the second line of defence; a pair of tall metal gates, far more intimidating than the barriers. But these too whirred open automatically. They rolled past blandly functional two story brick buildings, car parks, sports facilities, and finally aircraft hangars. There was not a single living soul to be seen anywhere, until the hangars gave way to a wide open vista; the smooth sea of tarmac that was the airfield itself. Here the BMW at last came to a halt.

The aircraft that awaited them was a Bell Griffin HAR2. One of the 'Huey' family of helicopters, it looked like a fatter, almost pregnant cousin of the iconic (and far more svelte) choppers used in Vietnam. This battered old workhorse had apparently been deemed suitable for Drew and Megan. It made Drew wonder how important their investigation really was in the eyes of Alec's superiors.

The pilot was already in the cockpit; a round-helmeted silhouette in a pool of blue-green light from the flight panel in front of him. He was studying a clipboard, checking off pre-flight items one by one.

As Drew and Megan got out of the car, a chill night wind whipped over the tarmac, bringing with it the smell of aviation fuel.

The Griffin's sliding side door, with its two large square windows, was already open for them. Inside the chopper there was seating for eight. Three of the places were already occupied. Special Forces types, Drew guessed. Each soldier wore jet black fatigues under a dark grey bulletproof vest. All manner of pockets and pouches were stitched into their outfits, and all of them were stuffed with small but practical items; torches, pens, handcuffs, flares, handguns, and little canisters full of some unidentified substance; probably an irritant. Drew studied the faces of the three men and guessed at the hierarchy. The biggest of them, a barrel-chested, skull-shaved thirtysomething with a wild brown beard, could not have been first-in-command. He was a little too fidgety, always checking his pouches, making sure he had everything.

The smallest of them, a short, wiry twentysomething with spiky blond hair and performative gung-ho mannerisms, was *definitely* not first-in-command. He was too much like a kid at Christmas. Too new to it all. And that only left...

The one in the middle. The only one with a phone. He was in his early forties, his face craggy, stubbly and lined with small scars here and there. He was big, but not as big as the bearded guy. He sat perfectly still. Only his eyes were restless; irritated glances at the bearded guy who wouldn't stop fidgeting. This one was the CO alright. When he saw Megan emerge from the car, he looked her up and down, but not in the natural way. He was all business, deciding if Megan's outfit was baggy enough to be hiding anything other than her body. Apparently satisfied that it wasn't, he turned his attention to Drew and did the same thing again. When the visual sweep was over, he locked eyes with Drew; something he hadn't done with Megan. Neither man wanted to look away first. Eventually, Drew won out. He'd never been one to shirk a pissing contest.

Drew wondered why such men had been thought necessary for an investigation like theirs. The locals couldn't be *that* dangerous, could they? Then it hit him; perhaps it wasn't the locals these men were here for. Perhaps it was Drew himself. Perhaps they served the same function as a press gang, there to strong-arm Drew in case he suddenly wanted out.

Drew was about to board the Griffin when the CO jumped out onto the tarmac. He patted Drew down expertly.

"What are you looking for? Weapons?"

The CO shook his head. "Phones."

"So you're allowed one, but no-one else is?"

"Correct."

Drew nodded. *The trigger phrase.* They needed a line to London, but no more than one. Phones were viral pathways, after all. But still... "Hale went to alot of trouble to build that device," he said. "To delay the release. He wouldn't have written that phrase down anywhere else. Would he?"

"Hale was a nutter," the CO replied. "He could've done anything."

Fair point. "And if the guy with the phone gets infected?"

"Then kill him as quick as you can, before he uses it." The CO retook his seat, making way for Drew to climb aboard.

Back at the car, the driver was helping Megan unload luggage from the boot; two heavy duty steel carry cases. They each carried one case up to the chopper and passed them up to the soldiers, who heaved them aboard without a second thought. *They already know what's in them.* Then Megan herself hopped aboard. There was no attempt to pat her down the way Drew had been. She took her seat opposite Drew and buckled up, studiously avoiding eye contact with her four male companions.

"What's in the cases?" Drew asked, looking first at Megan, then at the three soldiers. No-one replied. It set off alarm bells in Drew's head, just as the CO heaved the Griffin's sliding door shut and the engine came to life.

They took off and flew north. The CO advised Drew and Megan to try and get some sleep if they could. It was a three hour flight to Barra, he said. It would still be dark when they got there. Drew tried his best, but the poorly insulated cabin made the engine noise insufferably loud.

Halfway through the flight, Megan caught Drew mentally undressing her.

"Nobody patted you down," he said. "You could be carrying."

"Well am I?"

Drew grinned. "Definitely."

The soldiers grinned too.

Megan rolled her eyes. "You're a dinosaur."

"People *like* dinosaurs."

Now the soldiers laughed out loud.

Megan bristled. She cocked her head and studied Drew, like a naturalist examining an insect through a magnifying glass. "Alec told me about your past relationships. With women, I mean." Drew's smile faded. "He said you have a thing for... damsels in distress. I wonder if you're quite so comfortable with damsels in control? Damsels with higher security clearances?"

"He told you about Jenny, did he?"

Megan nodded.

"He told you what happened to her?"

She nodded again, and now she saw the pain in his eyes. She looked suddenly embarrassed. "I'm sorry. That was insensitive." She hesitated before adding: "If it's any consolation, I don't believe death is the end. I think it's a gateway to something else. Like a-"

The CO cleared his throat and stared daggers at Megan. She took the hint and went quiet. Strange, Drew thought. Why had he felt the need to shut her up? Why had she allowed him to?

"It's no consolation," Drew said.

No more was said for a while. But a few minutes later, Megan glanced warily across at the CO. He was staring vacantly out the window, chewing on a glucose bar. Furtively, Megan leaned across the aisle to whisper to Drew. "Does Jenny ever talk to you?"

The question hit him hard. It was so personal, so intimate, so *accurate,* that it almost felt physically invasive. He'd had more than enough unsolicited psychoanalysis for one night; first from Alec, and now from Megan too. "You seem to know an awful lot about me," he said, "but I don't know anything about you."

Megan's eyes were alight with a strange kind of fire. "She does, doesn't she?"

Drew shook his head. "I'd like to get some sleep now." But all he could do was feign it.

They flew on into the night. Megan fell asleep before he did, leaving him awake with the three soldiers, who neither slept nor spoke. Drew longed for a book to read. Reading helped him drift off. Then he remembered he had one. He took Hale's diary from his jacket pocket. As he began to read, he realised the tone of the diary entries was subtly different to the tone of the letter; just as delusional, but less grandiose, and less eloquent. Why? What had induced that shift? The more he read, the more he found himself cringing and grimacing. Hale had been one sad fucker...

January 6th

A new year, a new diary, and already fame beckons! Channel 4 have invited me onto their new talent show. If it goes well I'll soon be saying goodbye to Medtech. Wait until I tell Judy! We are already more than just colleagues, so who knows? Maybe I shall steal her away with me. Be still my beating heart (or I'll be needing one of our own products!)

January 8th

I should be rehearsing every chance I get, but I can't stop thinking about Judy. She's about my age (I think). It's hard to tell as she wears so much make-up. She is quite a large lady (she doesn't walk so much as totter) but I don't mind that. Her dress sense is very colourful and extravagant, which is why she likes the ties I wear. Today she wore a leopard-print jacket over her blouse, and bright red high-heeled shoes. I think women should be obliged to wear high-heeled shoes, at least when they are in the office. I do wish Judy wouldn't smoke so much (her teeth are very yellow and she's always coughing) but nobody's perfect I suppose. Anyway, it's not really her physical appearance that draws me to her. It's her sense of humour, which is similar to mine, if slightly less sophisticated. We have developed a shared banter that's rather flirtatious, and, dare I say, quite risqué! 'The filthier the better', as Judy likes to say. None of the other men in the office pay her any attention, and that's fine by me. As for the women, they are quite catty about Judy, always spreading nasty rumours about her which I'm sure aren't true. I know she can be a bit blunt sometimes, especially with the younger women, but that's just her way. I'm sure there is no truth to this rumour that she told everyone about Sadie's abortion after Sadie had confided in her. And even if she did... well, Sadie should have been more careful, shouldn't she!

January 9th

I have been rehearsing non-stop in preparation for the big day. Today, in the cafeteria, I performed part of my act for Judy. It's always better to have an audience. I did some of the magic tricks and a bit of ventriloquism (I didn't have the dummy with me but I did the voice anyway). I think she enjoyed it, though it drew some funny looks from other colleagues who were sat nearby. I don't think they got the humour. Either that or they are jealous because I'm going places and they're not. Judy certainly did get the humour. Some of it, anyway. I told her it was designed to appeal to both children and adults, but she encouraged me to 'make it more dirty', because it was the rude bits that really made her laugh. Judy is a terrible flirt, but I must admit I like it! She asked me when the show would be broadcast. I told her I didn't know yet, but it would probably be post-watershed judging by how blue my act is about to get!

January 14th

So that was that. I gave it my all, but if I'm honest, the performance didn't go nearly as well as I'd hoped. The show seems to be aimed at a youth audience, and indeed the studio audience was full of drunken young men and women who didn't seem to get the more sophisticated jokes. In fact, they didn't even get the rude bits, which surprised me and threw me off my stride. They laughed in all the wrong places and heckled me. The judges called my act 'mean-spirited and devoid of wit'. As if their show isn't! I gave them a piece of my mind while the cameras were still rolling, but I'm sure they will edit that part out. Afterwards I asked the producer when the show would be broadcast. He said he wasn't sure about the date, that someone from his team would let me know, but the time slot was likely to be around 3a.m. The show is called 'The Sh*t Show' (their asterisk).

January 25th

No-one from the show ever did get back to me with the broadcast date, despite my repeated phone calls. Thank goodness for the TV Times! It's there in next week's listings. Tuesday night. Well, Wednesday morning technically. I am very angry at Channel 4. They booked me under false pretences. The show is described in the TV Times as follows: 'So bad it's good? Or just so bad? Variety rejects are put to the test in this rowdy and riotous late night entertainment show. Who will win the coveted Golden Turd?' Judy keeps asking me what the show is called and when it will be on. I keep telling her it's been delayed because they can't think of a title for it.

January 27th

Judy has been fired after an altercation with Sadie. I didn't see what happened, but I did see the aftermath; Sadie's lip was bleeding when she was called into the manager's office. When she came out she told everyone that Judy had first spat at her, then punched her. For some reason, people were more appalled by the spitting than the punching. Anyway, it serves Sadie right for spreading lies and being a whore. Judy left before I got a chance to speak with her. Ships that pass in the night! Hopefully she will never see my appearance on 'The Sh*t Show'. I never did get her phone number, but something tells me we'll meet again one day. Here's hoping!

February 4th

I am to be made redundant after twenty years with Medtech. Twenty years! They'll regret it when I'm gone. No-one there knows lithium anode cells like I do, and if there's one thing I've learnt in all my time at Medtech, it's this: never share your knowledge!

March 15th

Still no work! I have applied for countless jobs, though I am overqualified for most of them. In interviews, my strategy is to demonstrate how I might be of service by asking them what their internal processes are, and telling them where they're going wrong. You'd think they would be grateful, but no! My money is running out fast. I blame Channel 4. They should have given me the Golden Turd.

March 18th

At the doctor's surgery today I saw an advertisement for clinical trials. They pay well enough, and it has to be less shameful than standing in the dole queue with those awful people. Imagine if Judy saw me!

March 22nd

The trials are being run by the MoD. I will have to sign the Official Secrets Act in addition to all the other release forms. Real cloak and dagger stuff. Watch out Timothy Dalton!

03:58
62 hours and 2 minutes remaining

The Griffin's pilot began the descent into Scarnish. He adjusted his night vision goggles, reducing the sensitivity to counteract the growing glare from the small cluster of street lights below. The adjustment should have happened automatically, but the ATG on the goggles was screwed; a minor annoyance he'd been dealing with ever since Northolt. With the correction made, the street lights were now his best navigational tool. From a distinctive crescent of light that matched a crescent on the map he'd partially memorised, he picked out the pre-designated landing site that lay half a kilometre inland from the pier; a small patch of flat scrubland behind the village.

Once he'd deposited his passengers, a short further flight to RAF Lossiemouth would follow. There, he and his helicopter would both refuel, and he would finally get some well-earned rest before the return flight to Northolt in the morning. He was imagining fresh coffee and a full English breakfast when suddenly, out of nowhere, he was dazzled by a bright green light; a light intensified by the night vision. It induced a sudden stab of migraine-like pain behind his eye sockets, even as it blinded him.

He didn't panic. He screwed his eyes shut and pushed the goggles up over his helmet, keeping the cyclic steady in his other hand. When he opened his eyes again, all he could see was swirling psychedelics. They filled his entire field of vision, crowding out everything else; the cockpit, the street lights below… *You're still descending. Pull up. Buy yourself some time.* He pulled the throttle lever gently up. The Griffin gained some height. Slowly, ever so slowly, the light show playing out on his retinas began to fade.

And then the green dazzle hit him once more, no longer amplified by the night vision, but still intense enough to blind him all over again. *Shit!* Where had it come from? Though he couldn't see, he realised the Griffin's nose was probably still dipped towards the ground, pitched low enough to present an easy target for some kid with a laser pen. *You're gonna pay for this, dickhead.*

A sudden crosswind buffeted the Griffin, and now panic *did* set in. The aircraft tilted wildly. He tried to counteract the rightward roll by nudging the cyclic to the left, but in his literal blind panic he overcompensated. The Griffin rolled nearly a full ninety degrees to the left, cancelling the lift from the rotors and sending the aircraft into an uncontrolled descent. Guided by nothing but his own instincts, he fought with the pedals and the cyclic and the throttle lever, managing to level out the chopper once more.

But he was still blind. He had no idea how much altitude he'd lost, until the auto-warning kicked in and told him: "Terrain. Terrain. Pull up. Pull up."

He yanked the throttle lever up as hard as he could, hoping and praying, already braced for impact. For a moment, it seemed, his prayers were answered. He felt the g-force from the rapid ascent. But then, from above, he heard the ominous grind and crunch of something colliding with the rotor blades. Colliding and staying collided. *Christ, what now?!* The steady *whump-whump* slowed, then stopped altogether. The auto-warning *whoop-whooped* once again. "Engine stall. Engine stall."

The pilot's vision was at last beginning to clear - the smallest of mercies - but then the green light from below dazzled him for the third and final time.

04:01
61 hours and 59 minutes remaining

The three soldiers had rigidly adhered to their training, shouting "Brace! Brace!" like honking geese, bowing forward into their laps with their hands clasped over their heads. Megan too had braced. Only Drew remained bolt upright in his forward facing seat. Megan was opposite him, both of them next to the windowed sliding door. The aircraft's angle of descent - nose down, body tilted left - had finally stabilised, but the eerie lack of engine noise, combined with the extreme leftward tilt, meant that a crash - not a crash landing, but a full on crash - was now inevitable. The tilt was pressing both their sides up against the door's plexiglass window. Though it was dark outside, Drew had seen something through that window; something the others had not. That was why he still hadn't braced. The sight was at once terrifying and reassuring; terrifying because it revealed just how imminent the crash was, and reassuring because it gave him an idea. It was the sight of the Griffin's blinking red anti-collision light reflecting off water below. Not sea water, nor lake or river water. It was a flooded marsh, interspersed with clumps of tall grass rising out of it. The brace position wouldn't save them, he was sure, but that water just might.

He unbuckled his safety belt and stumbled towards Megan, half walking, half falling into her. When they collided, she came back upright and stared at him disbelievingly. When he reached down to unbuckle her belt too, her disbelief morphed into uncomprehending terror. She tried to brace again, but Drew forced her chest back with one hand, feeling for her buckle with the other. For a moment, his groping was almost indistinguishable from a sexual assault. Megan lashed out fiercely, her instincts going haywire as danger piled on top of danger; the real, the imagined and the absurd all melting into one. He took the slaps and the scratches while he found the buckle and flipped it open. The two ends of the belt fell away. The slaps became full-on punches. He caught Megan's flying fist in one hand, quickly readjusting his grip so he had her by the wrist. She continued to land blows on him with her free hand. He had no choice but to take them; his other hand was already on the lever that opened the door.

He pulled it. The door slid open reluctantly, just a little at first; their combined weight was still pressing on it, hampering its movement. The wind came howling inside the Griffin, a sudden intruder that seemed almost as feral as Megan. Drew longed for the chopper to roll right so the pressure on the door would be eased, allowing it to slide fully open.

Instead, the aircraft banked further to the left.

Drew lifted his right leg, aiming to plant his foot on the partition behind Megan's rear facing seat and push away, drawing the door back with him. Megan ducked forward to dodge the foot. Her momentum opened the door a fraction more, but still not enough. The Griffin banked further left still, and now the door became their floor; a sliding floor on wheels. Drew's foot found the partition. He pushed hard on it, keeping the door lever in one hand and Megan's wrist in the other. At last the door slid back the rest of the way.

They fell out into the night.

04:03
61 hours and 57 minutes remaining

They separated in the air. No sooner had Drew let go of Megan's wrist than he was in the water, his rib cage shattering the surface tension like it was a thick pane of glass. There was an audible *crack* when it happened. Had he broken something? As he sank limply into the freezing, murky shallows, he remained hyper-conscious, eyes wide open, grimly swallowing down the gritty marsh water he'd ingested before remembering to hold his breath. He came to a gentle rest on his back in the silt layer at the bottom of the marsh. Its soft embrace would have been welcoming but for the fact that long strands of... of *something* were now alive in the water, wrapping themselves around him, clinging to him like amorous snakes. One of them flicked across his face, and he saw them for what they were: not snakes, but long tall blades of underwater grass. He wriggled and writhed and flailed until he was free of them. Then, his lungs bursting even as the panic subsided, he swam to the surface.

He emerged gasping, coughing and treading water. *Ribs can't be broken. I would've drowned if they were.*

He looked around for Megan. There was no sign of her. The night sky glowed orange from something just over the horizon. Kerosene fumes tainted the air.

At last Megan too emerged from the water, gasping and thrashing wildly about. She could barely seem to tread water, let alone swim. Soon she went under again. *Damsels in control.* Drew swam over and caught her round the waist, heaving her up onto one of the little hillocks jutting out of the water. Together they lay there for a while, spluttering and shivering, until their strength returned.

Where the hillocks began, the shallower outer edges of the marsh began too. They waded through them until they were out of the water altogether. Then they sat down again in the tall grass, checking themselves for injuries. Drew had a large bruise running down his right side, presumably from where he'd hit the water, but that was all. Megan had a small gash on her leg from where she'd clipped the edge of the Griffin's sliding door. Together they improvised a tourniquet and tied it tight around the wound. Megan got to her feet gingerly. She was in some pain, but could walk well enough. Curiously, neither of them were yet feeling the cold, but Drew knew this was a dangerous illusion. Once their bodies ran out of adrenaline and the shock subsided, the cold would hit them with a vengeance. Exposure and hypothermia would swiftly follow if they didn't find shelter soon enough.

They traipsed through the long grass towards

the wreckage. Though debris was scattered over a wide area and still burning here and there, the Griffin's fuselage was largely intact, upright, and already burnt out. Drew peered into the cockpit through the gap where the windshield had once been. The pilot lay slumped forward over the instrument panel, his face hideously blackened and blistered. His helmet was still on, and he was still strapped into his seat. Drew tried to check his wrist for a pulse, but the charred, peeling skin was still too hot to touch. That gave him his answer.

He went around to the side of the fuselage, nearly tripping over another body as he went. It was unrecognisable, having suffered a similar fate to the pilot. Megan had already clambered inside the twisted metal shell, through the gap where the sliding door had been ripped away. She was crouched over two more blackened bodies, her hand over her mouth, but not flinching from the horror. She was looking for something with grim, stoic determination. The body of the third soldier?

"The last one's out here," Drew said.

But Megan only shook her head and resumed her search. The body she was now examining lay in an odd, semi-crouching position. As Megan heaved it away to one side, Drew saw why. Underneath it were her two steel carry cases.

"Help me out here, will you?" Megan said. She passed the cases out to Drew one by one. They were heavier than they looked.

46

"You'd better bloody need these," he said.

"Oh, I do."

The body Megan had moved aside had a phone tucked into a shoulder pouch. *The CO.* Drew removed the phone - the *only* phone - and examined it. The screen was shattered, its hard plastic casing warped and burnt. He tried to power it up anyway, but of course it was dead. There was nothing else to be salvaged from inside the wreck, so they both clambered out again. Drew walked around the surrounding debris field, looking for anything else they could use. He found two pocket torches that still worked, and Hale's diary, all of which he retrieved. The diary was battered but still hanging together. He flicked through the pages. They were sodden but just about readable. He also found a small emergency ration tin, dented but still intact.

And there was one other thing he found. It wasn't useful in any practical sense, but it *was* instructive. Instructive and worrying. It was the mangled remains of a small, four-pronged drone. The kind of drone that people flew in parks for fun. Its propellers - all but one - were missing from the end of each prong, but it was otherwise intact. Something so small couldn't possibly have brought down the Griffin, could it? Unless perhaps it had found its way into the rotor mast and got jammed there, hindering the movement of the blades. And if it had been used in conjunction with something else, like a-

"That's Scarnish," Megan said, interrupting

47

his thoughts. She was pointing at a small cluster of street lights in the far distance. Without waiting for a reply, she lifted one of the cases and began the long, difficult walk across the undulating marshland towards the lights.

Drew now recalled Alec's ominous warning: *They don't like outsiders poking their noses in. I mean* really *don't like it.*

Yes, he thought as he picked up the second case. *It sure seems that way.*

04:33
61 hours and 27 minutes remaining

Weighed down by the cases, Drew and Megan traipsed along the only thoroughfare. The village appeared to Drew like a painting; impressionistic and vague in the night, its palette consisting only of blacks, greys, and muddy smears of orange from the sodium lamps, the outlines of buildings rendered only as gloomy shapes that lacked all detail. There were few cars parked in the street, and those that were looked battered and weather-beaten. The fishing boats they passed looked equally neglected. There were none in the water. All were either propped up on wooden beams, or tipped to one side on the waterfront's volcanic gravel beach.

They arrived at the pier. Entry to it was barred by a couple of two-metre tall Heras fencing panels; wire mesh barriers held upright by sturdy cement feet, but easily unclippable, easily moveable. A token health and safety effort. A red sign on one of the panels read: *Danger of Death - Do Not Enter.* Someone had turned the three 'o's into eyeballs with a marker pen. The house at the end of the pier could not be seen. It was shrouded in the orange-tinted fog that hung low over the sea. The pier itself appeared solid enough near the fencing, but quickly tapered off into the mist, like the ghost of some ancient road.

"This is it," Megan said.

"We need provisions first," countered Drew. *Like a triple Scotch for starters.*

"We've got the ration tin."

"It won't be enough."

They were both shivering. Megan acquiesced. They kept walking, towards the dimly lit pub up ahead. It was open, apparently, at an hour when most pubs would have been closed, but no sound came from within. Drew looked up at the hand-painted sign above the entrance. It creaked as it swung gently in the wind.

"Don't tell me," Megan said. "The Slaughtered Lamb."

Drew studied the sign. The painting was flaked and smeared with bird shit. It portrayed a tartan-shawled man stood on the edge of a cliff, staring down into the abyss. Above the painting was the name of the pub: *The Crofter's Fate.*

"I wish," Drew said. Then he shrugged and put a hand on the door handle. "You never know. There might be a ceilidh going on."

They went inside, dragging the cases behind them.

There was no ceilidh going on.

The pub was almost empty. The décor was

blandly functional. A basic bar with four ales and lagers on tap, a few plain wooden tables and chairs dotted about; barely enough for a gathering of ten. Instead of the crackling fireplace Drew had been hoping for, there was a single portable halogen heater in one corner. No paintings or ornaments lined the walls. They were entirely bare. Peeling, tobacco-stained wallpaper provided the only texture. Drew couldn't remember the last time he'd walked into a pub that stank of cigarettes.

Two young lads, eighteen or nineteen, sat in one corner. They were drunk, smoking, and laughing into their sleeves. They both wore Adidas hoodies over striped tracksuit trousers and trainers. One had a thick curly mop of jet black hair and a thin pencil moustache. The other was clean-shaven, pale and spotty with fine, wispy blonde hair cut short. He seemed to be balding prematurely; *very* prematurely. There was a teetering wooden Jenga tower on the table in front of them, but they seemed to have lost interest in the game. Instead, they now stared at Drew and Megan, eyes bugging out of their sockets. Then they looked at each other and sniggered once again.

"Angus!" Moptop called out to the barman, who was polishing glasses with his back turned. The barman looked back over his shoulder. Moptop cocked his head in Drew and Megan's direction. "Blow-ins."

Angus was in his mid fifties. Curly grey hair over big red ears and a red-veined nose. The face reminded Drew of a troll he'd once seen in a story book. But the fairytale resemblance ended there. From the neck down, Angus was wholly unremarkable; a green checked shirt, unbuttoned, over a plain grey t-shirt. He'd been staring at a wall-mounted TV while he polished the glasses. The sound was turned way down, but Drew recognised the show. It was an old *Monty Python* sketch; *the funniest joke in the world.* The joke that was so funny it killed people. But Angus hadn't died laughing. He looked numb. Immune.

The TV itself looked ancient. The picture was fuzzy in a way that reminded Drew of his childhood. He looked at the shelf below the TV, and sure enough there was an old VCR with several hand-labelled cassettes stacked up next to it. Drew pictured Angus scrolling through Netflix thumbnails with a baffled expression, the way Egyptologists must have puzzled over hieroglyphs before they found the Rosetta Stone.

Drew and Megan dragged their cases up to the bar and perched next to each other on rickety bar stools.

"Triple whiskey," Drew said.

"Same here," said Megan.

Drew had been expecting another snigger from the two lads the second he opened his mouth, but none came. Their choice of drink, it seemed, commanded respect, even if nothing else did. Angus poured the drinks without a word. Drew downed his in one. Megan took her time.

There was a phone behind the bar. An old Seventies style finger dialler. Discreetly, Drew flashed Angus his Met ID. "I need to make a phone call," he said. "It's urgent."

"Phone's out of order," Angus replied.

Now the two lads in the corner *did* snigger, and loudly.

"*Your* phone then," Drew said. "There's been an accident. A bad one."

"There's no signal here," the barman said. "No internet."

Again the two lads sniggered.

Angus seemed to guard the phone behind him, shielding it from Drew.

Megan glanced warily across the room at the two lads. They were both eyeing her hungrily, making hushed, lurid comments into their sleeves. She pulled her coat tighter around her shoulders.

The barman went back to staring humourlessly at the TV. Drew studied him. *He doesn't seem to care about the accident. Why not?*

"I s'pose you'll be going up to the house at the end of the pier," Angus said, without taking his eyes off the TV.

"That's right," said Megan.

"I wouldn't if I were you, Miss. We've seen your people come and go. No good ever comes of it."

Megan shot Drew a questioning glance, mouthing 'Baines?' at him.

Drew shrugged. *Your call.* He wondered why on earth she was deferring to him.

"Why's that then?" Megan said to the back of the barman's head.

At last he turned to face them again. "Pier's dangerous," he said. "And the house too. Prone to collapse. All of it built by some daft Victorian aristocrat from London. More money than sense. Didn't know what he was doing. All he did was pile bricks on top of the pier. No foundations."

A clattering noise came from across the room, followed by more laughter from the two lads. By way of illustration, one of them had collapsed the Jenga tower.

"That's no way to build a house," the barman continued, "and everyone knew it except him. They all tried to tell him, but he wouldn't listen. It's a wonder it hasn't come down already. Every year we place bets on how much longer it'll last."

"Did the aristocrat ever live there?"

"No. He put furniture in, mind. Some, anyway. In the end his brother talked some sense into him. They abandoned it, went back to London. No-one ever bought it, of course. It was unsellable. In the end it was just left to rot. A few years back it was up for demolition, but then the council ran out of money. All they did in the end was put hi-viz jackets on the cherubs. Someone's idea of a joke."

"Did anyone else ever live there? Besides the aristocrat?"

"No." Angus turned back to the television. Story time was over.

Megan gave Drew a sceptical glance. *That's only half the story.*

Drew nodded. *And he knows it.*

Drew continued to study the barman, trying to read his movements, his body language. Every time Angus passed a certain photo on the wall behind the bar - a photo of two pretty young teenage girls standing together in a sunny garden - he would glance at it. Only for a split second, but he could never quite manage to *not* glance at it. A short while later, he crouched down out of sight behind the bar. Drew heard a creaking sound, followed by footsteps which faded into nothing. He peered over the bar and saw a trapdoor lying wide open, wooden steps descending into a dark square hole. A minute later, Angus re-emerged and kicked the trapdoor shut again.

Drew turned his attention back to the two reprobates in the corner. He caught the tail end of their latest exchange. The blonde one was putting on a deliberately whiney, irritating voice. "Please sir, I need to use the phone! There's been a *terrible* accident!"

His friend, Moptop, smirked. "Stop *droning* on about it." Their sniggering erupted into howls of laughter.

Drew's ears pricked up at the drone pun, but he opted to ignore it for now, at least until he'd finished steadying his nerves. He ordered another double and sipped it slower this time. Megan was still finishing her triple, keeping a wary eye on the cases at her feet.

And then, from out the corner of his eye, Drew saw a bright green light, dazzling in its intensity, which quickly disappeared again. It had come from the pair in the corner. He spun round to see what they were up to. Moptop was clearly hiding something under the table. He caught Drew looking at him. He was struggling to keep a straight face.

Drew slammed his whiskey down on the bar. Megan put a restraining hand on his forearm, but he brushed it away. He got up and strutted over to the pair in the corner, forcing a smile as he went. The smile that meant: *You don't scare me.* He pulled up a chair and sat down opposite them. "Alright lads? Where d'you get the laser pen?"

"Mind your own business," Moptop said. This one was the leader. He was by far the more confident of the two. Or maybe just the most drunk.

Drew flashed his badge. "Police."

"Mind your own police business." They both laughed again.

Drew didn't react. He kept his eyes firmly on Moptop. Then Blondie piped up. "Anyway that's a London badge," he said. "You're out your jurish - jurish-" He was slurring badly.

"Jurisdiction? It's nationwide, son. As of yesterday."

At the bar, Megan raised an eyebrow. *Bullshit.*

"Scotland's a different country though," Moptop said.

Drew leaned in over Moptop, dwarfing him. He cracked another smile and ruffled the lad's hair. "Think you're clever, don't you?" Then his smile faded. His hand moved swiftly from the top of Moptop's head to the back of it. "Four people are *dead*." Hard and fast, he brought the lad's face down onto the table. The bridge of his nose caught the rim of a heavy porcelain ashtray. Blood gushed from his nostrils into the ashtray. Cigarette ends swam in the blood.

"Jesus Christ!" Blondie said, his eyes crater-wide.

Megan was on her feet now, sizing up where to go, what to do.

Drew forced Moptop's head back up again. "I'm arresting you on suspicion of manslaughter."

Quietly, Angus said: "Detective?"

"You don't have to say anything-"

"Detective?"

"-but it may harm your defence if you don't mention when questioned-"

"*Detectiiiive!!*" The barman's piercing, unholy yell brought the whole room to a standstill.

Drew let go of Moptop. He turned to face Angus.

"Where you gonna take him?" Angus said. "There's no police station here. No phones. You don't even have a car, let alone a helicopter. Where you gonna take him?"

Drew paused, mulling it over. *Shit*. Then: "I'll-"

A sudden scrape of chairs interrupted him; Moptop and Blondie scarpering for the door. "Oi! Get back here!"

But they were already outside. Drew followed them out, staggering as he ran, the whiskey blunting his reflexes. He stopped in the middle of the road, looked left, then right. They were gone. Lost in the night mist. He went back inside and stood there, breathing hard in and out. He picked up Moptop's pint glass and threw it against the wall. It popped and shattered.

Megan winced. She turned to Angus, hands raised in a placatory gesture. "It's alright. It's alright. I am *so* sorry. Just give him a minute." She fished inside her wallet and thrust notes at him. "Please. For the damage."

He took the money without hesitating.

Sheepishly, Megan added: "Also...we'd like a room for the night."

"I don't know about that," Angus said, eyeing Drew warily.

"Please. We've been in an accident. We just need to rest." She still had the wallet open. There were plenty more notes inside.

Angus made a swift mental calculation. "Aye, okay Miss. You've got yourselves a room."

"Thank you." Megan looked over at Drew.

He was still breathing hard in and out, consumed with impotent rage. She turned back to Angus. "Actually we'd like two."

04:57
61 hours and 3 minutes remaining

That morning, in a small, sparsely furnished room above the pub, Drew fought another losing battle for sleep. The twin stresses of the crash and the altercation in the bar should have exhausted him, but his reserves of adrenaline ran deep. Too deep for his own good. So he gave up the fight, and instead read more of Hale's diary.

April 3rd

Today we - the twelve volunteers - were driven by bus to the facility. The others are all younger than I am. I have little in common with any of them. I was expecting Porton Down to be our final destination, but instead they drove us onto Salisbury Plain; a vast, featureless expanse that stretches for miles in every direction. We carried on into a small forest in the middle of the plain. It was certainly not a natural feature; the trees were planted in long, regimented rows. Soon we emerged from the trees again, arriving in a large clearing surrounded by forest on all sides. Here at last was our facility, enclosed by outer and inner perimeter fences, each topped with barbed wire. Two security checks later (one for each fence) we were in. The bus pulled up outside a row of Quonset huts; our sleeping quarters for the foreseeable future. Aside from the huts, all I could see was a two storey brick building (an administrative hub?) and a couple of warehouses. I was expecting a busy military hospital; nothing as sparse and quiet as this. I have been told that everything of any note happens underground, which might explain why, at ground level, the place feels like a ghost town.

April 5th

I am settling in to my new routine. They feed us well enough, and we are looked after in most other respects too. When we are not undergoing trials (mine have yet to begin) we are encouraged to exercise or read or watch television, but always alone in our own quarters, never together. The interiors of the Quonset huts have been carefully designed to ensure we remain physically separate from one another. Many are finding the social isolation - the lack of camaraderie - quite difficult, but not me. I live alone anyway. Daytime television does bore me though, and I didn't bring enough books to read, so writing this diary keeps me sane. I'm sure it will be confiscated when I leave, but that's to be expected. Official secrets are official secrets.

April 7th

Trials are underway for everyone... except me. They can't decide if I'm a 'type A' or a 'type B' personality, and this is causing a delay. They tell me this must be determined before my own trials can commence - a safety protocol, apparently - but don't ask me how these two personality types are defined, or how they relate to safety (and whose safety? mine or theirs?). I have no idea. I just wish they would make their minds up and get on with it. Listen to me; jealous that others are being experimented on while I am not. What a thing to envy!

April 9th

At last! This morning I was escorted to one of the underground testing rooms, where I was met by a doctor. In the middle of the room there was a blackboard with a sheet over it, which he sat behind, while I sat in front of it. The board was set within a fixed metal frame and bolted to the floor, so it could not be repositioned. The doctor said he was about to reveal what was written on the board, and warned me not to say it out loud. At this point, I noticed he had a syringe next to him on his desk. I don't know if this was intended for him or for me. Anyway, he removed the sheet to reveal the phrase 'Shiver me timbers'. He remained behind the board the whole time, as if he were afraid to see the phrase himself. Tomorrow, he said, I would be shown a variant of this phrase; a variant with a special property. Reading it, he said, would induce a slight itch on my left cheek.

April 10th

The new phrase was 'Shivver me timbers'; the same as yesterday, but with one additional 'v'. This time the letters were further apart from each other, and the second 'v' looked different to the first 'v', as if someone else had written it. When the doctor asked me if I was feeling the itch on my cheek, I told him I was - perhaps - but only very slightly; so slightly, in fact, that I now suspected the whole exercise to be nothing but an attempt to measure my suggestibility. He looked a little awkward when I said that, but he was adamant that tomorrow's phrase variant would be more powerful, and the effect on my cheek *more severe.*

April 11th

Today, the phrase on the blackboard was 'Skivver me limbers'. The 'k', the 'l' and the additional 'v' were slightly offset from the rest of the phrase, as if each letter had been 'dropped in' while the surrounding letters were still covered up. The itch on my cheek was barely there atall. Things are not going the way the doctor intended. It's as if he is trying to pull off a magic trick, but being a magician myself, I'm not falling for it. Still, he insisted that tomorrow's phrase variant would be far more powerful, and my symptoms correspondingly more dramatic. I asked him why an entire day had to be left between each exposure; why we couldn't just progress to the next variant right away. He told me it was a 'scheduling issue', but I didn't believe him. I think that giving me twenty four hours to dwell on what might happen next is all part of the plan. It allows time for ideas to form in my head; ideas which might make me more suggestible. The trouble is, I already know what they're up to, so it's never going to work! That said, there is one thing that gives me pause for thought; every time my doctor pulls that sheet from the blackboard, his other hand goes to the syringe. He seems terrified I'm about to say the phrase out loud, and convinced that if I do, only the syringe will save him.

April 12th

Today the phrase was 'Skivveg lo limbay'. Again, the new letters looked like they had been somehow 'dropped in'. And yet again, the symptoms on my cheek stubbornly refused to appear. This is getting embarrassing! Tomorrow, my doctor intends to show me video footage of a previous test subject reacting to a further variant of 'Shiver me timbers'. He thinks this might finally induce a physiological reaction in me. But I doubt it will.

April 13th

The video was disturbing, to say the least. Though the doctor's trickery hasn't yet worked on me, it clearly did work on the previous chap. The rash on his cheek was like something out of a horror film. It seemed to have driven him slightly mad; he was babbling about ghosts, claiming he'd been sensitive to their presence before the experiments began, and insisting that the rash had only increased this sensitivity. Tomorrow I am to be shown the same phrase variant that this poor man was shown.

April 15th

I am writing this on board a train whose destination - I think - is London. I didn't care to check which train I was boarding at that little rural station. Nor did I purchase a ticket, for fear the transaction might alert the authorities, who must surely by now have discovered my unauthorised absence from the facility. But I'm getting ahead of myself.

Yesterday all hell broke loose. I was in the room with the doctor, about to be shown the new phrase variant, when someone - another test subject, I think - appeared at the soundproof window, banging his fist on the glass, trying to get my attention. He kept looking back over his shoulder, as if he knew he wasn't supposed to be there. He had a wild, half-crazed smile on his face. But the thing that really disturbed me was that he had what I can only describe as 'stalks' growing from a reddish cavity in his cheek. These stalks seemed to *writhe about, moving independently of one another. I made eye contact with the man and he mouthed something at me, but I couldn't read his lips or hear him through the thick glass. The next thing I knew, his brains were all over the window.*

10:00
56 hours remaining

The alarm on Drew's wristwatch didn't so much wake him as filter through into his dream, polluting it with toxic reality. He sat up in the too small bed, and Hale's diary fell to the floor. He'd fallen asleep reading it. The tiny, threadbare-carpeted room was freezing. There was no shower, only a washbasin, and he'd lost all his toiletries in the crash. He got up and washed himself as best he could, then got dressed in the same torn, filthy and still damp clothes he'd worn yesterday. He went to find Megan, knocking on the door of the room adjacent to his. There was no answer.

He went downstairs into the bar and found her talking to Angus. Her clothes were just as torn and filthy as his. Somehow it made him like her a little more. She was haggling with Angus for food and water. Angus put up a fair amount of resistance, wanting rid of them as quickly as possible, but Megan was admirably persistent. Eventually Angus re-emerged from the kitchen with some frozen bread rolls, a hunk of hard white cheese wrapped in clingfilm, and three large bottles of water, all in a plastic carrier bag. Drew placed the diary, the ration tin and the torches he'd salvaged from the wreck inside the bag too. Megan paid Angus in cash. She seemed to have an endless supply of it, but from now on there would be no-one to buy from and nothing to buy.

They went out the door, Megan dragging one case behind her, Drew carrying the other, plus the carrier bag. Angus watched them leave from behind the bar, polishing glasses that were already gleaming before he picked them up. He had a sullen, mournful expression on his face; like a teacher with lofty ideals his pupils had chosen to ignore.

10:24
55 hours and 36 minutes remaining

Scarnish by day was just as impressionistic as Scarnish by night. Instead of dark grey, the fog was now bright and white, but just as murky and thick, the air still cold and damp. Visibility was about ten metres, just enough for Drew and Megan to navigate back to the pier. As they went, Drew glanced up at the first floor windows of the houses they passed. More than once, he saw curtains twitch.

They heard the waterfront before they saw it; waves sloshing gently on the gravel beach. And then they were back at the fenced off entrance to the pier. Beyond the fencing, the pier's wooden planks looked rotten, uneven and very unstable. This, presumably, was the 'danger of death' referred to in the warning sign.

Drew unclipped one of the Heras panels and pulled it aside, then stepped through. He planted the metal case he carried heavily, almost carelessly, on the first plank in front of him. It held.

"Careful!" Megan protested. "That stuff's valuable."

"So am I." He stepped onto the pier and repeated the manoeuvre, shoving the case in front of him with each further step, using its weight to test the stability of each and every plank. Megan followed closely behind.

Their progress along the pier was comically slow. They were like two shuffling pensioners struggling with their luggage. Here and there, entire sections of wood were rotted away, exposing the foamy grey waters below. They weaved their way around the holes, nudging their cases forward. Soon the mist began to clear, and Drew caught the first hints of hazy sunlight coming through the clouds; just enough to illuminate the bay and the heath-covered hills behind the village. Enough to throw little sparkles onto the perfectly calm water surrounding them. And now the house at the end of the pier gradually revealed itself. It was one of the most incongruous sights Drew had ever witnessed. He had expected something akin to an old wooden cabin, or at best a bungalow. But *this...*

The first thing he saw through the mist was a row of bright yellow hi-viz jackets floating high in mid air. Mottled grey heads poked up through the jackets; toddlers' heads, and the outlines of their bodies too, three stone cherubs lined up on the roof, expectantly awaiting a game they'd been falsely promised. A game called Demolition. Each cherub stood at the apex of a red brick gable with a window set into its centre. The three triangles formed a crown to the facade of a small but imposing Tudor style house, complete with a sloping grey slate roof and a chimney. Drew's eye went further down the facade. The front door had been boarded up. Surrounding it was a grand sandstone archway (sandy yellows and rusty reds predominated) with a short flight of sandstone steps leading up to the doorway. Either side of it were two large bay windows, cracked but still intact, framed by sandstone buttresses.

It was the kind of house one would expect to find on some Millionaires' Row in Hampstead; yet the entire edifice rested seemingly on nothing more than rotting wooden planks. It was just as Angus had said; bricks piled directly on top of the pier itself, with no apparent foundations of any kind. Drew went to one side of the pier and leaned out over the water, craning his neck to see what lay beneath the square section of pier supporting the house. Underneath that platform, there was a dense forest of wood and iron beams. Most were vertical, but others were diagonal or horizontal. An improvised mesh of supporting structures, thrown together haphazardly and held in place by nothing but rivets, optimism, and a deep - *please god, let it be deep!* - half burial into the sea bed.

At last they reached the front entrance. It was boarded up with wooden planks nailed into the door behind. Furtively, Megan opened her case and took out a flat-blade screwdriver. She used it to prise out the nails one by one, until at last the boards fell away. Behind them was a tall wooden door, painted in what must once have been a cheery, welcoming red. But it had darkened over time, and was now the colour of dried, clotted blood. A phrase of some sort had been crudely carved into the wood.

Drew leaned in closer, about to try and read it, and suddenly Megan's hand was covering the letters. Drew mentally kicked himself.

"I'm gonna reveal it one letter at a time," Megan said. "If it doesn't spell anything you recognise after seven or eight letters, *look away*."

Drew nodded.

Letter by letter, Megan moved her hand aside, revealing first a D, then an I. Here she paused, swallowed, then carried on. The next four letters completed a word they both recognised. Now they relaxed a little. Letter by letter, word by word, the message revealed itself. There were three words in all. Three words Drew knew well:

Divide and conquer.

10:52
55 hours and 8 minutes remaining

Drew studied the words etched into the wooden door. "I was hoping for *Home Sweet Home*."

Megan didn't smile. "He means us," she said. "Divide and conquer *us*. He was trying to demoralise us before we even got started."

The front door was locked, but the mechanism was rusty and hanging loose inside a rotten frame. Drew had little difficulty in forcing entry. The door opened into a wide hallway with a wooden staircase at its centre. The walls - even the *inner* walls - were red brick, just like outside. Red bricks with worryingly thin layers of mortar inbetween them. The hallway was unfurnished except for an ornate but battered old wardrobe. The two windows either side of the front door were so thickly covered with grime that barely any daylight seeped in through them. Yet the hall was only sporadically dark, even with the front door pulled to. There was another source of natural light, and it came from below; vertical shafts of daylight piercing the gloom here and there, each one sharply delineated. Drew looked down at the floorboards and immediately understood. They were not really floorboards atall, but simply a continuation of the same wooden planks they had already traversed outside on the pier. And here, inside the house, those planks were no less rotten, no less hazardous. The shafts of light came from holes in the planks where the wood had rotted away. He leaned into one such shaft and peered down into the hole. Sure enough, there was the sea, churning and foaming and hissing just a few metres below. "Cosy," he muttered.

Megan said nothing. She was stood stock still, staring dead ahead, her eyes wide. She was breathing a little too fast.

"You okay?" Drew asked.

She blinked twice and took a deep breath. "I'm fine."

"Are you sure? You look-"

"I'm *fine*," she insisted. Then she grew indignant, adding: "I'm not your fucking damsel in distress, okay?"

Drew was about to let the comment go unchallenged, chalking it up to anxiety or whatever the hell she was feeling, but then she twisted the knife: "Yours never survive anyway."

The jibe sent him reeling. It was unexpected, unnecessarily cruel, and worst of all partially true. But what had made her say it? Insecurity? Misandry? Or was she just testing him? He pretended to let it go. He opened the wardrobe next to the front door and looked inside. "Oh my god."

Megan inched closer, trying to peer over Drew's shoulder. "What is it?"

"I don't know, but whatever it is, it's been hidden away for years. Forgotten. Mothballed. It looks like... Oh my *god*. It's..."

"What?!"

"...your femininity!"

Megan bristled again. "Not funny." Drew was smirking as she elbowed him to one side and looked inside the empty wardrobe. "Not fucking funny."

Either side of the staircase were two doors, one leading left, the other right. Drew went to the right hand door. It opened into a small room with a round wooden dining table, cobwebbed and dusty, two elegant but equally filthy dining chairs, Victorian or maybe Edwardian, and a glass-paned crockery cabinet leaning out from a wall. The panes were smashed, but there were still china plates stacked neatly inside. On the wall opposite the crockery cabinet was a large oval mirror, its glass covered in a thick coating of grime. The room was a sort of Victorian kitchen/dining room combo, though Drew would have felt safer eating halfway up a mountain, for it was the same story here as in the hallway; more vertical shafts of daylight from holes in the floor. More deathtraps. In one corner there was a discarded sleeping bag. Had it once belonged to Baines, or Hale, or someone else altogether?

Drew opened the cabinet's drawers and found

some dirty old cutlery and a few candles. He held one up to show Megan. "We'll set these up around the house for when it gets dark." A sudden howling draft came up through the holes in the floor.

"I wouldn't bother," Megan said.

They went back out into the entrance hall, tiptoeing carefully around the light shafts. Drew tried the door to the left of the staircase. It opened into a living room of sorts, but it was empty except for an old fireplace beneath a chimney flue. There were fewer light shafts in here, but the fireplace posed its own unique danger. There had clearly once been a metal grate around the fire - its holding brackets were still attached to the adjacent walls - but the grate itself was no longer there, and it was alarmingly obvious where it had gone. It had simply fallen through the floor and into the sea. Now, the fireplace was alight once again, not with fire, but with daylight; a wide shaft angled directly up into the flue. It seemed impossible that the entire chimney stack had not already collapsed down into the hole, since it appeared to be resting on nothing, but there it was. When night fell, the light from the fireplace would of course go out, just when it was needed most.

That was the ground floor in its entirety. The house was much smaller than it had looked on the outside; a sort of Tardis in reverse. The elaborate facade had been just that. Some kind of forced perspective illusion. What worried Drew most was that the front door was the only way out of the damn place.

He went back out into the hallway. Megan was already halfway up the stairs. He followed her up. There were two more doors leading off the first floor landing. The first was directly in front of the staircase. Megan went into this room while Drew checked the second door on the right. This one led into a bathroom, if it could be called that. An old free-standing tin bath, unconnected to any plumbing apparatus, was its centrepiece. Up against the wall there was a sink and a toilet with a flush handle hanging off a chain. These too were unconnected. Drew examined the ceiling, which slanted upwards at a forty five degree angle. No attic, then. Nothing above but the roof itself. There were no light shafts in here, no holes in the roof or the floor. Nor had there been any on the landing. Upstairs, it seemed, the house was better protected from the rot. *Then why was the sleeping bag downstairs?*

Drew went back out onto the landing, and into the room at the top of the stairs. He found Megan inside. Once again she was standing stock still, in front of an old grandfather clock, seemingly perturbed by something. But she quickly snapped out of it when she noticed Drew. While Megan studied the clock, Drew studied the only other item of furniture; a large four poster bed. Its wooden frame was blackened and petrified, little round nubs protruding here and there, as if the whole thing had been hewn from a tree in some dark fairytale forest.

The mattress was hidden beneath mouldy pillows, sheets and covers that looked about a hundred and fifty years old; a bed lovingly prepared for a guest who had never arrived, and never would.

He turned his attention to the tall, ornate grandfather clock. Compared to the bed, its various components seemed quite modern. The oak casing housed a fine example of late Victorian craftsmanship and precision engineering. Roman numerals stood out sharp and clear on the pearly off-white clock face. Below, three cylindrical brass weights hung low from their chains, all of them still shining brightly behind the glass frontage. The middle weight was slightly larger than the two either side of it, creating a perfect symmetry.

When Drew had first entered the room, he'd assumed it was something about the clock's appearance that had transfixed Megan. Now he realised it wasn't the look of the thing, but the *sound* of it.

It was still ticking.

11:01
54 hours and 59 minutes remaining

Megan's voice was hushed, reverent, like the whisper of an awestruck tourist in some vast cathedral. "Explain that, Detective."

Drew ran his fingers over three little holes in the clock face. "These holes are where you insert the crank key to wind up the clock. One hole for each of the three weights. When you wind the clock, you raise the weights."

"Then they gradually drop, and the movement of the chains powers the clock."

"Right."

"It runs on gravity."

"Right. Only I don't see a crank key anywhere. And those weights are hanging way down already, so pretty soon it'll stop ticking. Clocks like that need winding at least once a week, and as far as we know, no-one's been here since Baines disappeared."

"That was *two* weeks ago."

"Right. So it must've been wound recently, in the last week or so, and not by Baines."

"Who then? An intruder? Someone from the village?"

Drew shrugged. "Maybe. But why bother coming all the way out here just to wind a clock? And the front door was boarded up when we got here. Boarded up from the outside. Which could mean our clock enthusiast did it himself when he left. Or it could mean..." He froze, chilled by his own thought, and lowered his voice to a whisper. "...it could mean he never did leave. What if someone boarded up that door while he was still inside? What if he's still in here right now?"

Megan shook her head. "We've looked everywhere. This place is an empty shell. There's nowhere to hide."

"As far as we know."

Megan took a deep breath. She seemed hesitant to say what was on her mind. Then she swallowed and said it anyway. "There's another possibility too."

Drew shot her a quizzical look.

Megan sighed resignedly. "Come downstairs," she said. "It's about time I showed you what's in those cases."

11:06
54 hours and 54 minutes remaining

Drew looked on as Megan heaved the two steel carry cases up onto the dining room table. She flipped open the catches and pulled back the lids to reveal various electronic items, each one snug in its own custom-shaped nook cut out of the protective foam padding. One by one, Megan removed the items and placed them on the table. The first was a regular laptop. It was battered and old, and personalised with numerous little stickers. Drew studied them; leftist slogans and memes he didn't agree with, campaigns with reasonable sounding names and hidden, unreasonable agendas.

Next came two 12 volt power inverters; portable batteries inside heavy duty plastic casings with power sockets and on/off switches.

Then came a small cardboard box, which Megan upended. Hundreds of small round sticking plasters scattered across the tabletop. First aid for minor cuts and grazes. But these plasters weren't any natural shade of skin colour. They were perfectly white. Drew picked one up to examine it. Each plaster had a 'nipple' in the centre; plastic, translucent and dark green, like an unlit Christmas tree light. Surrounding it, on the flat part of the plaster, were five tiny metallic squares, arranged in a circle around the nipple and connected to it by ultra thin wires, each one barely wider than a human hair. Drew prided himself on his ability to speculate about almost anything, but the purpose of these 'plasters' was utterly beyond him.

Megan was nowhere near done. The case was like some elaborate chocolate box interior, with a second, deeper layer of items beneath the first. It had to be deeper, because the next item was bulkier than even the laptop. It was also the most incongruous. Drew couldn't help but laugh out loud when he saw it. It was a bear. A brown and white teddy bear dressed in blue denim dungarees, with a chirpy but gormless expression on its face. Megan set it down on the table with a soft, muffled *clunk*; the bear had electronic innards of some sort.

As Megan began to unload the second case, she glanced up at Drew. Though she didn't smile, he was quite sure she was enjoying his baffled reaction. She removed a small plastic wand with a rainbow fan of green, yellow, orange and red stripes. Each stripe led to a correspondingly coloured LED light at the tip of the wand. Drew recognised the gadget immediately. "That's an EMF meter," he said.

"Uh-huh."

"Electricians use them to find hidden wiring."

"Uh-huh."

"But there's no electrics in this house. There never were." Realisation dawned on him like sunlight through parting clouds. "You're not a spy atall, are you? You're-"

Megan pushed a button on the EMF meter. It gave a brief, high-pitched squawk. "An independent parapsychologist."

"A ghost hunter."

"If you like."

Drew shook his head in disbelief. "Christ, they must be desperate."

Megan put the meter on the table and fixed Drew with a hard stare. "Detective work is your field. Parapsychology is mine. I'm not a detective, so I'd be a fool to dismiss it out of hand. I'd be grateful if you could extend me the same courtesy." She picked up the teddy bear and felt around in its fur for a switch. "But yes, you're right. They *are* desperate. Of course they are. This late in the game, how could they be anything else?" She found the switch and flicked it. The bear's eyes lit up and its mouth fell open.

Drew stared down at the bear. The toy. The fucking *toy*. And then he was out into the hallway and out through the front door, slamming it violently behind him. The house was prone to collapse, he remembered. The slam could have brought the entire house crashing down on top of Megan.

For a moment, he wished it had.

11:29
54 hours and 31 minutes remaining

The door to *The Crofter's Fate* was locked when Drew tried it. He peered in through a window. The pub looked empty. He went around the side of the building, found another window, one that wasn't visible from the nearby houses. He tapped on it, but no-one appeared. He searched the gravel pathway for a big enough stone. He found one, removed his jacket and wrapped the stone in it to muffle the sound of breaking glass. When the deed was done, he put his jacket back on and reached in through the shattered pane to open the latch. The window opened just wide enough for him to squeeze in. He hopped down off the sill into the eerily quiet pub.

He searched the downstairs bar and the kitchen. There was no-one around. He went upstairs, checked the two guest bedrooms he and Megan had stayed in. These too were empty. Aside from the bathroom, there was one other door at the end of the short carpeted corridor. He knocked, but nobody answered. He tried the door. Locked. To most people, this would have been a signal to leave well alone. To Drew, it was a positive invitation. He forced the door open with two well practiced kicks.

The room was a small open plan studio with a kitchenette, a sofa, a bed and a desk. No computer, no TV, not even a radio, just a bookshelf lined with empty liquor bottles and a few tattered old paperback novels. Nothing really stood out, except...

Oh, Angus. Everyone needs a hobby, but this?

It was a crucifix. A painted Christ figurine glued to a cross suspended from a hook on the ceiling. There was nothing unusual about the figurine, but the cross itself... the cross was made of phones. Dozens of them - a few iphones but mostly vintage Nokias and fliptops, and even a few landline handsets - all glued or gaffer taped together. There was no finesse to it, no artistry. It was all cobbled together quite haphazardly, forming only a rough approximation of a cross, and the structure wasn't rigid either. It sagged. There was something faintly obscene about it. *Tate Modern would love you.*

He counted the phones; about thirty in all. About the entire population of Scarnish. *They were theirs once, weren't they? Did they offer them, or did you take them?* Optimistically, he tried to power up each phone in turn, but they were all dead. He searched the room for chargers, but didn't find any.

He went back downstairs, to the landline phone behind the bar. An *Out of Order* sign hung from it, but when he lifted the handset he heard the *brrr* of a dial tone. Was this the only phone in Scarnish that still worked? Almost certainly. It would explain why Angus had been so damn protective around it. He dialled a short number, and a female voice answered. "Directory enquiries?"

"Security Service. Thames House."

"Hold the line please..... Connecting you now, sir."

A series of clicks and beeps followed. *They know I'm calling from Barra, and it's triggered some kind of telephony alarm. They're rerouting my call, bypassing the main switchboard.* A recorded message said: "Please leave your message after the tone, then press 1 and hold the line until your call is answered." *Hold the line while our software analyses your words. To make sure they* are *words.*

The tone sounded. "Alec, it's Drew. Pick up." He pressed 1.

A long pause. Then: "Please leave a longer message after the tone, then press 1 and hold the line until your call is answered." *Of course. Too many proper nouns, not enough common nouns. Their software isn't that smart.*

The tone sounded again. "For god's sake, Alec, I'm not infected. Just answer the bloody phone." He pressed 1 again.

A further pause, this one longer still. *The software's done its job, told them the message is safe to listen to. Now one of them is. One of them is making a judgment call. Deciding whether to answer. Taking their life in their-*

"DSI Turner?"

Eileen. She sounded nervous. Who wouldn't

be, knowing what she knew? She was too damn loyal for her own good. Drew pitied her, working for that weasel. In Alec's eyes, Eileen was expendable. Not Alec though. Alec was *far* too important.

"I need to speak to Alec."

"Just a moment."

She placed him back on hold right away, no doubt breathing a sigh of relief the moment she had.

At last Alec answered. "Drew?"

"You lied to me, you snake."

"Excuse me?"

"A lie by omission. The worst kind there is. Wasting my time with your paranormal Scooby-Doo bullshit."

"Calm down, Drew."

"I don't blame Megan. Megan's delusional, in more than ways than one, but *you*... you knew exactly what you were doing. How the hell did you get sign-off? Does your boss even know?"

"Alright. Let's say it *is* Scooby-Doo bullshit. So what? No-one's asking *you* to hunt ghosts. All I'm asking *you* to do is the same job you've always done."

"Then why didn't you *tell* me?"

Alec sighed. "Because your psych profile predicted just this kind of reaction. You never would've agreed to go in the first place."

"My psych profile wouldn't tell you how I feel about ghosts."

"Actually it would. It did."

"How?"

"After your wife died, you visited a medium."

Drew reeled. "How did you... I never told anyone."

"You didn't have to. We already had you in mind, so you were already under surveillance. At first we thought: well, he's perfect. He won't object because he already believes. But you only ever went once, didn't you? And when you came out after that first time, you had a face like thunder. Like you'd been cheated. We spoke to that medium soon after you left. Discovered she was fraudulent right after you did. We thought that experience might have made you sceptical. Turns out we were right. But seeing as you're already up there, you might as well get on with it. Do your work while Megan does hers. She's going to try and contact Hale's spirit, get him to reveal the location of that device. Please don't ridicule her. Don't undermine her. Assist her in any way you can, and she'll do the same for you."

"Assist her with what? A séance?"

"If she makes contact, then yes."

"For fuck sake!"

"If it helps, don't think of it as a séance. Think of it as... a police interview."

"A police interview. Brilliant. Tell me, Alec. Am I the only sceptic on the whole damn team? Or are you one too?"

"I'm strictly agnostic."

"Of course. Spoken like a true weasel." Drew sighed, his anger finally spent.

"So you're back on board, I take it?"

"Sure, why not? Nothing else to do on Barra."

"That's the spirit! Oh, and Drew?"

"What?"

"Don't ever accuse me of wasting time again. Especially not when *you're* the one wasting it. You know what's at stake, so get back to work, or you'll be the first one to hang for treason since Lord fucking Haw-Haw."

The line went dead.

Drew realised he hadn't even told Alec about the crash. Would anything have changed if he had? His hands were shaking. He took a small bottle of whiskey from the shelf behind the bar, opened it and took a slug from it. He was about to replace it, then changed his mind. He stashed the bottle inside his jacket. And though he hadn't smoked in years, he suddenly felt the urge for a nicotine hit too. He searched the bar for cigarettes, but found none, only a cheap plastic lighter, which he pocketed.

He knew Alec was right. The call *had* been a waste of time. But since he was already right next to a phone, and wouldn't be again until... The temptation was too strong. He promised himself he'd be quick about it. Just one last little bit of unfinished business. Business from the other case.

The case.

*

The killer's MO was simple. A bogus 999 call made at night - always at night - from a barely traceable dumb phone, and when the officer showed up... *Boom*. Shot in the head the moment they stepped out of their vehicle. All three victims to date had been patrolling alone. All three had been female.

Every crime scene was a CCTV blind spot. This in itself was not unusual; street criminals routinely avoided the cameras whenever they could. What *was* unusual - especially for such a built-up area - was the ongoing lack of witnesses. Reconstructions revealed that the killer was carefully pre-selecting his firing positions, each one chosen for its absence of any line of sight to the windows of neighbouring houses. He liked alleyways with high walls either side of them, or, even better, tunnels and covered walkways. So no-one ever witnessed a shooting in progress, and the few eye witness reports that did filter through - reports of a hooded man fleeing the scene on foot - were all but useless, because he always kept his face down and well hidden by the hood. They knew he was white, but that was about it. Since his escape routes were so poorly lit (and likely chosen for that very reason) the clothing descriptions were equally sketchy.

They had of course profiled the killer. He would likely live in the same area he killed in; somewhere in East London. He was a highly territorial operator, never straying too far from well known, well trodden streets. He was very methodical, a planner; these weren't crimes of passion, at least not in the usual sense. He was probably a narcissist, because only a narcissist could commit such high risk crimes and hope to get away with them. He probably thought he was too clever for the police. Probably even thought he was a genius. As for motive, the profilers said he might use the sort of anti-police rhetoric that was prevalent in some sections of the media to justify his actions to himself. So he would be more likely to watch certain TV or Youtube channels, read certain newspapers. He clearly had a grudge against the police, probably springing from perceived persecution by them at some point in his life. Perceived or possibly actual, but more likely perceived. He was in denial, they said. His true motivation was probably misogyny arising from sexual rejection, hence the exclusively female victims. Those rejections would likely have been due to his own weakness, whether moral, physical or intellectual, and of course he would be in denial about this too. It always came down to weakness in the end.

Drew was confident, as usual. He always got his man. Always. One way or another. The man they were hunting was smart, but Drew was smarter. The man they were hunting was weak, and Drew was strong. Drew would find him and nail him three times. First out in the world, then in the interview room, and finally through his testimony in court. He would nail him primarily for Jenny of course, but also for Claire and for Fran, because those brave young officers would have expected nothing less from a man like Drew.

The first breakthrough came relatively quickly. Since the scumbag was targeting female constables, and since only a third of the Met's patrol officers were women, Drew realised that for every bogus 999 call which resulted in a kill, there should have been two more that didn't. Two more occasions when a male officer had shown up, and the killer had simply slunk away, disappointed. So they went back and listened to *every single* hoax call, hoping to find their man in amongst them. But the strange thing was, they didn't find him in *any* recordings other than the three that were already linked to the murders. And that raised an interesting question: was it just luck that each and every time he'd called, the unfortunate first responder had been alone and female? Surely not. Surely he would be looking to minimise the number of calls he made, to minimise the risk of being caught. So he had to somehow know in advance which areas the lone females were operating in, and when, so he could position himself accordingly. And surely the only way to know *that* was to eavesdrop on police radio chatter.

Back in the Eighties, anyone with the right equipment could listen in to the police; radio hams, crime reporters looking for a scoop, or just a kid looking for a thrill. But these days it was all encrypted. So how was he doing it? This was the first line of enquiry for the detectives under Drew's command. The online hacking community provided a raft of potential suspects. Drew's team made subtle, cautious enquiries, usually undercover, posing as up-and-coming hackers wanting to crack the police code for their own nefarious reasons. This entailed co-ordination with the NCA and GCHQ, who both happened to be doing much the same thing at much the same time, though for different reasons. Drew's team was looking for a serial murderer. The NCA was looking for child sex traffickers. GCHQ was looking for talent. In the end though, they came up empty.

The second line of enquiry was a more traditional one. Though the killer always retrieved his spent bullet casings, he obviously never retrieved the bullets themselves. Their calibre, combined with the telltale rifling pattern - striations carved into the lead during their passage through the barrel - was usually enough for Ballistics to identify the make of gun, or even the individual weapon, from which the bullets had been fired. Sometimes, a NABIS database search could reveal that weapon's previous history - other crimes in which it had been used - and from there, perhaps, a chain leading to its current owner might be established. This line of enquiry was still ongoing, but Drew knew from past experience that any such chain was only ever as strong as its weakest link.

The third and final line of enquiry was the most promising. The killer's bogus 999 calls always came from a cheap (and stolen) 'burner' mobile. He never used the same phone twice. Such calls could still be traced, by triangulating from the three nearest network masts, but that took time, and he never stayed on the phone for quite long enough. In addition, he was anticipating and easily fooling the Met's highly fallible voice recognition system (put in place to alert them to a call from the killer) by simply putting on a different voice each time he called. These 'impressions' weren't very sophisticated, but they didn't need to be, because the system wasn't either. So Drew's team went beyond mere voice recognition. They began to analyse the killer's speech patterns and sentence construction, from the recordings of his previous calls. This was the purpose of a new kind of software called *Linguamatch*. Once installed on the dispatchers' computers, it analysed the phrasing patterns and grammatical quirks of each and every caller, and would immediately flag up any matches it found to Drew and his team.

But *Linguamatch* had come too late to save Jenny. Jenny Turner, née Taylor, a sergeant in the Met. They were newlyweds. Drew's first wife after a lifetime of loneliness. Drew had always been an introvert. A tough, good-looking introvert, sure, but an introvert nonetheless. His looks made people assume he was an extrovert. It was funny how that worked. While his introversion never hampered his self-confidence, it did hamper his compatibility with extroverts; the personality type he was most attracted to. So his relationships with gregarious, sociable women always broke down in the end.

But then he met Jenny, and everything changed.

And then she was murdered.

Jenny was Drew's first wife, and the killer's third victim. After Claire and Fran died, Jenny had led her remaining constables fearlessly and by example, until she too was killed in the same way: one shot to the head from a hidden vantage point, the second she stepped out of her vehicle. No time to radio for help, nor even to see her killer, let alone provide a description. Drew had been informed by one of the constables under Jenny's supervision. He was glad it had come from someone who looked up to Jenny rather than down on her, someone who knew and respected her, and was therefore almost as devastated by the news as Drew was. Almost. At least that way the initial pain had been shared, the burden eased, if only a little. He was glad the call had not come from some higher-up whose words of consolation would have inevitably rung hollow. He was especially glad the call had not come from DCS O'Brien.

After her death, Drew was given two weeks' compassionate leave while the killer remained at large. He came to accept the fact of Jenny's death very quickly. There was none of the denial that grief psychologists always obsess about. But then Jenny started talking to him. Not literally, of course. Not in any real sense. But sometimes little phrases of hers would pop into his head unbidden. *Don't be an idiot, Drew* was the most common one. In life, she'd never said it in a disparaging way. She wasn't the henpecking type. Quite the opposite in fact. When Jenny told him *Don't be an idiot*, it was always because

94

Drew was doubting himself in some way. Feeling unnecessarily guilty about something. Jenny had always had faith in him, even when he hadn't. *Don't be an idiot* was Jenny's way of reminding Drew that she loved him. On rare occasions though, she would lose respect for him, and this was when her favourite linguistic game came into play. She would choose the name of some famous actor and adapt it into a puerile schoolyard pun, then use it as a playful insult to launch at Drew. He'd been called so many of these names over the years - *Tom Wanks* ("because you're acting like a tosser"), *Marlon Dildo* ("because you're acting like a prick") - but Jenny always did it playfully. Drew gave as good as he got too - he'd been especially proud of *Sigourney Beaver* - and Jenny always took the insults in the right spirit.

Usually when these phrases popped into his head, they came in his own voice, a surrogate for Jenny's, but sometimes, just occasionally, he would hear *her* voice echoing in his mind. This happened more frequently in the first two weeks after her death. Drew didn't believe in ghosts or the afterlife or any of that nonsense, and continued to not believe in them even as Jenny's voice grew more persistent. But he did believe in psychology and psychologists, and decided it might be time to pay one a visit. Then, at the last minute, he changed his mind, figuring (correctly) that such visits would have to be recorded on his medical record at work, and could be used against him, planting the seed in the mind of DCS

O'Brien that Drew Turner was mentally unstable. That, of course, was the last thing Drew wanted. And so, against his own better judgment, he went to a medium instead.

The house in Gunnersbury wasn't hard to find. An average semi-detached house in an average West London suburb. The only thing that distinguished this house from a thousand others like it was its proximity to the North Korean Embassy, itself hardly any different to the residential properties surrounding it. Save for the flag, it hardly looked like an embassy atall.

Alarm bells should have been ringing from the moment Drew stepped into that living room. Every spiritualist cliché in the book was present and correct, from crystals and wind chimes to Native American dreamcatchers. The topics of the various books strewn about the place were just as stereotypical; feng shui, spiritual healing, psychic healing, crystal healing and so on. There was no sense of specialisation to any of it, just a litany of all things vaguely 'alternative', as if the medium had found a section marked 'Spirituality' in a department store and emptied the shelves in a bulk buying frenzy. Alarm bells should have been ringing alright, but somehow they weren't. Drew's usual cynicism was on hold, displaced by a pathetic, desperate hope.

The medium was late middle-aged with long grey and white hair, the white being carefully dyed highlights that vaguely resembled streaks of lightning.

Her name was Stormcat or Thunderchild or something. She'd told him but he'd already forgotten, and didn't care that he had. He was relieved to note that Stormchild didn't require any props to do her thing. The trinkets that lined the walls and the mantelpiece remained mercifully untouched.

"She's here," Thundercat said. She had a placid smile on her face. "Jenny's here with us now. You can talk to her."

"Jenny?"

"She's listenin'."

"Jenny, it's Drew. How... how are you?"

Stormy Daniels put a hand to her forehead, as if she'd just felt some sort of twinge there. "What's that, darlin'?" There was a long pause. Then she smiled and nodded. "She says she's fine. She loves you, she misses you, but you mustn't worry about her. She's happy where she is now. She's perfectly at peace."

Drew nodded warily. *Give me a reason to believe you. Give me specifics.*

"What's that, darlin'? She's sayin' somethin' about... have you got a... a pet of some sort?"

In spite of his scepticism, Drew felt suddenly elated. "Yeah. A rabbit." *You just gave her the answer, you daft-*

"That's right. She wants you to take good care of... is it... Flopsy?"

Shit. "No."

"It ain't comin' through very clear, say it again

97

darlin'... Thumper?"

"No." The thin sliver of hope he'd been holding onto now slipped from Drew's grasp like a wet bar of soap.

"Sorry, it's hard to... one more time, darlin'. Sounds like... Oreo?"

"No." His cheeks grew hot. A heady cocktail of anger and embarrassment. The urge to play along, to say 'Yes, Oreo!' if only to spare this woman's blushes, was strong. But then he remembered that charlatans didn't have any shame. She would have been incapable of blushing.

"Bunny?"

Drew stood up and glared down at Thunderclap. "We'd only just got it," he said. "We never gave it a name."

"Oh. I'm sorry, love." Quickly, she added: "It might not've been Jenny after all. Sometimes the spirits-"

"Forget it," he snapped, already heading for the door.

When he got home he googled 'top ten rabbit names'. Flopsy, Thumper, Oreo and Bunny were all on the list. He was tempted to go back there and show the woman his badge. Intimidate her. Teach her a lesson. Instead, he burst into tears. But when he was done crying, a name for the rabbit popped into his head. A name that made him laugh.

Two days later he was back at work. There had been no real breakthroughs in his absence.

O'Brien wanted him re-assigned to a new case, because the personal angle would 'cloud his judgment' and all the rest of it. Drew argued that it would in fact do just the opposite. It would focus his mind, make him work harder and longer than anyone else. It was true, and O'Brien knew it. O'Brien caved.

DCS O'Brien spoke in a calm, measured way that most people found reassuring. When seated, he would articulate his thoughts with fingertips pressed gently together, the very embodiment of civility and decorum. But Drew wasn't fooled. Too often, O'Brien's responses to Drew's questions and challenges would take the form of an evasion, especially when Drew quizzed him about guidelines issued by the College of Policing. Drew thought the institution was too mired in woke ideology, but O'Brien seemed to venerate it as if it were a source of profound wisdom. According to the College of Policing, ongoing defunding of the Met was an inevitable fact of life. Something to be accepted and adapted to, not fought, heavens no... imagine the fuss it would cause! Imagine the protests! According to the College, two person patrol units were a thing of the past, lone officer patrols were the way forward, and since women were just as physically capable as men, it followed that lone female officer patrols were nothing to worry about either. O'Brien had his eye on a Commissioner role, Drew was sure of it. O'Brien wanted to tilt away from detective work, away from police work altogether, and move into the realm of public relations, with the College's guidelines forever tucked under his arm like a script he could instantly retrieve and recite to the media.

On the night the ongoing animosity with O'Brien finally caught up with him - the night he was re-assigned to Barra - Drew was cruising around East London in his unmarked car, listening in to the chatter between Dispatch and the patrol officers. He should have been fast asleep at home, but his insomnia had worsened. Besides, the killer was a night stalker, and Drew wanted to be there when they made the arrest. He wanted to see the expression on the fucker's face and savour it like Beaujolais.

It was a bait and switch operation. When *Linguamatch* gave Dispatch the heads-up that this latest caller was their man, it would also alert both Drew's team and SCO19, the Met's firearms unit. PC Debra Frost was tonight's 'bait'. If and when the killer made his call, Dispatch would instruct an apparently oblivious PC Frost to respond to it alone as, regrettably, there were 'no other units available'. This was a scripted lie intended to reassure and reel in the eavesdropping target. In reality, PC Frost would already be alert to the danger, via instant text alert from Drew's team. In reality, PC Frost would be (to use her own expression) 'backed up as fuck'.

Drew knew Frost well. Though they'd never worked together, they often worked out of the same building. She was in her twenties. Her quick smile and chirpy Essex tones had endeared her to him immediately. She loved her job, her colleagues, her life. More than anything, she loved a foot chase followed by a taser deployment. Drew had never seen her with her hair down out of that bun, though he'd often imagined it. She was obsessed with *Fifty Shades*. She called him 'Sir' when she didn't have to, and he liked that.

Drew checked the clock on his dashboard. Eleven twenty p.m. The night was coming alive, and the radio chatter with it.

"November four-seven from Kilo Sierra."

Drew's ears pricked up. November four-seven was Frost.

"Kilo Sierra, this is November four-seven, go ahead."

"November four-seven, be advised, the incident you're proceeding to is code purple. Repeat, code purple. Confirm no more units needed?"

Code purple. Inside the killer's patch.

"Kilo Sierra, that's correct. I'm aware it's code purple."

"Backup available if you need it."

"Kilo Sierra, I say again: *Negative*. If I need backup I'll ask for it."

Frost was pissed off, and rightly so. This was a regular callout, not a *Linguamatch* alert. Kilo Sierra, the dispatcher, was sticking his nose in where it didn't belong. But now he seemed to realise his faux pas: "November four-seven, apologies, we're just looking out for you. Out."

Was this guy new? Who did he think he was?

Twenty minutes later, Captain Chivalry was at it again. "November four-seven from Kilo Sierra, confirm your location."

"Kilo Sierra, I'm on Elm Avenue heading west. Is your map on the blink or something?" Frost's location should have been right there on the dispatcher's screen. There should have been no need to ask.

"Negative, November four-seven. We're just looking out for you."

Jesus.

"Kilo Sierra, that's sweet, but please *stop*. Out."

Drew heard nothing more from Frost or Kilo Sierra for another three or four minutes. Then: "November four-seven from Kilo Sierra."

Frost's tone was already abrasive. "Kilo Sierra, this is November four-seven, go ahead."

"Reported domestic at three-one-two Harding Lane, code purple. Can you deal?"

Drew's phone rang. He glanced down at the screen. *Fuck.* It was O'Brien. He turned the radio right down and took the call.

"Sorry to call so late, Drew. I'm afraid- are you *driving?*"

"Yes sir. Couldn't sleep."

"Fried, are we?"

"Scrambled."

"Well, you're about to be poached too. You're

off the case. The spooks want you."

11:42
54 hours and 18 minutes remaining

Now, as Drew stood behind the bar in *The Crofter's Fate*, he made his second phone call. The call he'd been dreading, despite the compulsion to make it. When DCS O'Brien finally answered, his voice was like an intrusion of drab reality into a bizarre parallel world. A *Twilight Zone* episode placed on pause while the bins were emptied.

"O'Brien."

"Sir? It's Drew."

"Oh." A hint of apprehension in O'Brien's voice. "Aren't you meant to be-"

"I am, sir. But I had a spare moment, and I just wanted to ask... how it's going."

"How what's going?"

"Linguamatch. Any results?"

O'Brien sighed and said: "It went bad, I'm afraid."

Drew stiffened. "Bad?"

"Dispatch took a call they thought was genuine. Linguamatch didn't flag it because the caller wasn't our suspect. He must've paid that lad to make the call for him. And when our officer showed up... I'm sorry, Drew. He's killed another one."

Drew swallowed hard. "Who was it?"

"PC Frost."

Drew pictured his last exchange with Frost, her eyeing him cheekily while they bantered about *Fifty Shades*. Half banter, half flirtation, with a mutual affection as well as a sexual charge underlying it all.

"How many times have you read that book, Frost?"

"Lost count, sir."

"You don't have to call me sir."

"I know, sir."

Would Jenny have minded, so soon after? He felt a twinge of guilt mixed in with the now familiar sense of sudden, painful loss, and he turned it outward, directing it at O'Brien. "If you'd left me in charge it never would've happened," he said.

"Now hold on a minute, how can you possibly-"

"You're a dead man," he snarled, and hung up, instantly regretting the threat. To compensate, he brought his oft-repeated mantra to mind; the ego boost he gave himself when no-one else would. *I always get my man. Always. One way or another.* But the words rang hollow. A weak pitch from a dodgy salesman.

Don't be an idiot, Drew, Jenny whispered. *Of course you'll get him. And no, I wouldn't have minded. I want you to be happy.*

He appreciated the pep talk, but he doubted it

all the same. Not least because, by threatening O'Brien, he'd almost certainly just ended his career on the spot. Alec's string pulling wouldn't save him. Not now. The Met might have worked with Five, but it didn't take orders from them. He searched hard for a silver lining, but there was no light behind the cloud. Jenny was gone, Frost was gone, and the man who'd killed both of them was no longer his to get.

11:44
54 hours and 16 minutes remaining

Drew opted to pretend he was still a police officer. Since the Security Service had clearly lost its mind, what other choice was there? He left the pub and went door to door. There were no more than twenty houses in the village, and he knocked persistently at the door of each and every one. No-one answered, though he saw numerous upstairs curtains twitch. What was it? Suspicion? Fear? *Who's strong-arming you people? Who's gagging you?* He gave up - for now - and went back to the house at the end of the pier.

Megan had been busy. She'd placed the little white sticking plasters all over the walls, in every room, so they were evenly spread throughout the house. Drew still had no idea of their purpose, and he was grateful for the curiosity that now arose in him. It edged out other, more painful emotions. Megan barely acknowledged him when he came in to the dining room. She was busy attaching a video camera to a tripod. He sat at the table and watched her work. He had to hand it to her; she certainly seemed to know what she was doing. He admired competence in anyone, even if their chosen field was littered with steaming piles of bullshit, as Megan's clearly was.

"Why don't you talk me through your kit?" he suggested, keeping his tone as non-judgmental as he could. For the first time since they'd met, he felt an obligation to try and get her onside, perhaps because he was fast running out of allies.

Megan glanced up at him from the tripod. "Don't you have police work to be doing?"

"Humour me."

Megan shrugged. "Alright."

She talked him through all of it, item by item, warily at first, but with growing passion and confidence once she realised he was actually listening, and no longer dismissing everything out of hand.

The camera was a full spectrum digital video recorder, for capturing footage in infrared, which lay to one side of the spectrum of visible light, and ultraviolet, which lay to the other. She used full spectrum for two reasons: one, to record in the dark, and two, to capture spirits that could not be seen by the naked eye alone.

The talking teddy bear was something called a 'boo buddy'. It was loaded with atmospheric sensing equipment; a thermometer calibrated to detect sudden, dramatic drops in temperature ("Brrr, it's cold in here!"), a barometer to detect sudden changes in air pressure ("Hey! That tickles!"), and a motion sensor which worked by detecting changes in nearby optical, microwave and acoustic fields ("Would you be my friend?"). The bear was apparently so lonely it would try and befriend literally anything that moved. It also doubled up as a sound recorder. On playback, its motorised mouth would move in time with any noises it had recorded. Drew looked on as Megan demonstrated it for him. She recorded the sound of a chair as she dragged it across the floor. On playback, the staccato clattering noise emerged from the bear's mouth, perfectly in synch with its chattering lips. The effect was oddly disconcerting.

And then there was Zenaframe; a program on Megan's laptop which only worked in conjunction with the cameras and the little round nodes that looked like sticking plasters. This was the tool Megan seemed most proud of. The program captured spirits in action - spirits that would otherwise have been invisible - rendering them onscreen as animated stick figures. Drew asked her how it worked, and she gave him a long but evasive answer about quantum entanglement, which, she claimed, would take about three hours to explain adequately; three hours she just didn't have. Her speech amused him, but he noted with some disdain that a long, clever, assertive evasion was still an evasion. "Just give me the gist of it," he persisted. "As if you had to explain it to a ten year old."

"I feel like I already am," Megan shot back.

Drew was learning to anticipate these unnecessary little provocations from Megan, though he still wasn't sure what motivated them. She was like a wounded animal lashing out at a potential rescuer. But how had she been wounded? He smiled patiently and said: "Please. Continue."

Megan paused for thought. Formulating the concept in a way Drew could understand was apparently no mean feat. Finally she said: "Spirits aren't really spiritual. They're physical, just like everything else. They're like... invisible human beings. They move just like we do, interact with their surroundings just like we do. They can't fly or float in mid air, and they can't be in two places at once. We've got reams of Zenaframe data to prove it."

Then why aren't the world's scientists all over it like ants on jam? But he didn't ask her. Not yet. He wanted to see how far down the paranormal rabbit hole she was willing to go. "So they're... here but they're not here?"

"Mostly not here. They inhabit a different realm. We call it the shadow world. When people die, their spirits leave their bodies and cross over. But there's only a thin veil between the two worlds, and sometimes spirits that cross over retain a kind of... emotional connection to the world they left behind. That connection allows them to step back through the veil. Back into *this* world. And sometimes they listen in on us. They eavesdrop."

"So you think Hale's spirit is here? You think he's listening to us right now?"

She shrugged. "It's possible. I haven't detected a presence yet. But that's just the half of it."

"Oh?"

"Okay. So you know how gravity is the weakest of the four fundamental forces?"

"Uh-huh."

"Weaker than the strong nuclear force, the electromagnetic force, and the weak nuclear force?"

"Uh-huh."

"And string theory has some ideas about *why* it's so weak, but no-one really knows for sure?"

"Uh-huh."

"You didn't know any of that, did you?"

Shit.

Megan rolled her eyes and carried on, warming to her subject. "Now, apply that same question to poltergeist activity. Why? Why is most of that activity so weak? So small-scale? I mean, moving coins or toys or car keys around a house? It seems trivial. Inconsequential. Why even bother?"

"Why indeed?"

"Well, here's the thing. The more you try to answer that question, the more disturbing things get. People who live with minor phenomena like that... when they describe the spirit, they use words like 'playful', or 'child-like', or 'mischievous'. It bugs them, sure, and it mystifies them, but it doesn't *scare* them. On the other hand, when it's *major* phenomena we're talking about, when *furniture* starts moving by itself, well, people who live with that kind of thing describe the spirit in very different terms. They stop using words like 'playful', and they start using words like

111

'scary'. 'Creepy'. 'Evil'. 'Demonic'. In other words, there seems to be a correlation between strength and malevolence. The more 'evil' the spirit, the more powerful it gets. And why? Because the source of that power is *fear*. We call that type of spirit a feeder."

"Because it feeds on people's fear of it?"

"Correct. Think about that."

Drew thought about it. "It might turn into a feedback loop. It might snowball."

"Right. Exactly. And then there's the questions we haven't even *begun* to answer. What's the true nature of the shadow world? The true nature of the veil between our world and theirs? Does that veil exist in our own universe, or in some parallel dimension? What does it look like? What's it *made* of?"

Megan's eyes were shining again, the way they had when she'd asked him about Jenny. Was it mere passion, or something more dangerous, like fanaticism?

Drew cast his eye over the array of equipment laid out on the table. One item was still in its cardboard box, which was square and flat. There was no need to even ask. With a knowing grin, he said: "Ordered pizza while I was out, did you? Hope you saved some for me?"

His clever bollocks attitude seemed to at once amuse and annoy her. "Sorry," she said as she stashed the box away under the table. "I scoffed the lot of it."

13:14
52 hours and 46 minutes remaining

Drew went to work, searching each and every room systematically, looking for small anomalies he might have missed first time round. He finished his sweep in under an hour. Nothing stood out. He was at a loss.

And then he realised there was one factor he hadn't taken into consideration: the walls. They were brick, but that didn't preclude the possibility of cavities behind one or more of them, especially the interior walls that backed onto another room. So he went back to his starting point - the downstairs living room - and began a new search, this time looking only at the walls. Almost immediately, he noticed a brick that was sunk further into the wall than its surrounding neighbours. Only very slightly, but still... He went over and tapped it. *Well I'll be...*

It wasn't a brick atall. It was a thin piece of plywood, cut and painted to resemble one, held in place only by its snug proximity to the real bricks surrounding it. Drew prised it out with his fingernails and looked inside the cavity that lay behind. It was the height and width of a single brick, but it was three bricks deep. More plywood lined the interior, but the cavity was otherwise empty. He was about to move on when he noticed that the cavity's dusty floor had a dust-free rectangle in the middle of it. Something had been hidden here alright. Hidden and then removed, fairly recently, since the dust hadn't had a chance to re-settle. Something about the size and shape of a paperback book.

Drew took Hale's leather-bound diary from his jacket pocket and placed it over the rectangle. It was almost an exact fit. The diary was just a couple millimetres longer and wider. Had its missing page been hidden here? Drew studied the outline in the dust. One long edge of the rectangle was well defined and perfectly straight, but the other was fuzzy and jagged. That confirmed it. *Hale clearly didn't want us to read that page*, Alec had said. *Perhaps because it revealed the location of his device.* So he'd torn out the page - the jagged edge was the torn edge - and stashed it here in the wall cavity. Years later, just recently in fact, someone else - probably Baines - had found it and taken it. But Baines had disappeared before he could report back. Had someone killed him? Who? Why? Where was the body? And more importantly, where was that missing page?

Drew deliberated, wondering which line of enquiry to prioritise; the diary page, or the mysteriously ticking clock. Even if he found that missing page, there was no guarantee its contents would yield anything useful. But the clock on the other hand... Megan had implied that it might indicate some unusual poltergeist activity. A clock being wound by a ghost. Hale's ghost. This was obvious bullshit. Instead, Drew wanted to eliminate the possibility of an intruder hiding somewhere inside the house. Someone hiding and emerging only to wind the clock, for reasons yet to be discovered. He suspected there might be other wall cavities, other hiding places like the one he'd just found, only bigger. Much bigger. Yet he'd seen nothing else quite so obviously out of place as that fake plywood brick. A really thorough search would entail poking and prodding at each and every brick in the entire house, and that would take time. *Alot* of time. With just fifty two hours until Hale's canister opened, could he really afford to spend so much time on a single line of enquiry? And a pretty tenuous one at that?

Fuck it. Just work fast.

And work fast he did. He went about it methodically, using a black marker pen to mark off every brick he checked. Outside, the wind was picking up, whistling through the holes in the floor. For a while, the whistles seemed to coincide with each stroke of the marker pen, as if the elements themselves were cruelly mocking his efforts.

20:15
45 hours and 45 minutes remaining

Megan sat at the dining room table, hunched over her laptop, with only the boo buddy for company. It was getting dark outside. Soon the only light in the room would be coming from her screen. Not that she minded. It was just the kind of light she was most comfortable with. Drew was in another room, drawing lines on bricks with a marker pen. Lines on bricks! Was that the best this supposedly talented detective could come up with? Surely there was something more useful he could be doing? But of course if she said anything he would react badly, like the snowflake he presumed her to be. His masculinity was so toxic, his white fragility so brittle, that he would probably either shatter entirely or, like an alien with acid for blood, melt a hole in the floor. And there were more than enough holes in the floor already, thank you very much.

So the real work was to be left to her, then. Fine. Whatever. At least she had the right kit for it. She had two full spectrum cameras mounted on tripods. She'd placed one here with her in the dining room, and the other upstairs, in the bedroom with the grandfather clock in it. She wasn't sure why she'd chosen to focus on these two rooms in particular. Instinct, perhaps. The gut feeling she'd had when she first walked into them. A subtle sense that these were the two rooms Hale had dwelt in the longest. The feeling had been fairly strong here in the dining room, and *very* strong in the upstairs bedroom. A small but persistent voice in the back of her head told her that, in that case, the bedroom, not here, was where she should be right now. It was the voice of reason. Professionalism. But she'd ignored it. Why? To save time, perhaps? After all, her equipment had already been unpacked here on the dining table, and she had at least felt *something* here, so here was as good a place as any to start. Yes, that was it. A time saving measure, when time was of the essence. Nothing to be ashamed of, and definitely not a decision based on...

Don't go there. Stay focused.

The nodes she'd stuck to the walls throughout the house fed a constant stream of data to the Zenaframe program on her laptop, but so far the only moving frames they had detected were hers and Drew's. So she switched to a new tab that brought up the live camera feeds from both rooms on a split-screen display. Both cameras were set to thermal imaging; warmer spots (like humans or animals or electrical items) were rendered as oranges, yellows and whites, cooler spots as purples and blacks. If a spirit

117

was captured, it would appear onscreen as a black figure on a purple background. Spirits were cold, not warm.

The dining room camera was up against the wall behind her. She swayed from side to side in her chair, noting the tiniest of delays before she saw the corresponding movement on the screen. When she watched the dining room feed, she was literally watching her own back.

Now, grudgingly, her eyes flicked across to the other half of the split-screen; the upstairs bedroom. The four poster bed was visible in the frame, but the grandfather clock was not; a mistake she would have to rectify at some point. Here, purples and blacks predominated. The only yellows came from the nodes stuck to the walls. The bed frame was rendered as black against a dark purple background. There was something about that gnarled, blackened old bed that worried her, made her reluctant to linger on it. Her eyes flicked back over to the dining room feed, whose yellows and oranges seemed more cheerful by comparison.

But the more she stared at these twin feeds, the more her imagination got the better of her. Her eyes began to flit about ever more rapidly. She was forever thinking she'd caught some kind of anomaly here or there, only for it to retreat back into her imagination when she focused on it. She was hyper-alert, her heart racing, yet nothing out of the ordinary had happened. *You're being unprofessional. This isn't like you.*

She closed her eyes and took long deep breaths, forcibly slowing her heart rate. After a while she felt calmer again, but she was still afraid - *afraid;* there, she'd said it - to open her eyes, in case she saw something onscreen that hadn't been there before. Something lurking in the background in the dining room or the bedroom. *Please god, not the bedroom.* It was an odd thought to have, since she wasn't even *in* the bedroom. She imagined something terrifying in the dining room instead. A voice, or an apparition, or some heavy duty poltergeist activity. The table skittering, or even flipping over entirely. Wouldn't that be something! Such thoughts might have spooked an amateur, made their heart race faster still, but this was Megan's favourite trick. A sort of psychological insurance policy. Over the years she'd learned that, when the activity finally came (if it came atall) it always came in ways that took you by surprise. Never in ways you had already anticipated. By pre-envisaging terrifying scenarios, like the table flipping over by itself, she was ensuring that this particular scenario would not occur. And somehow that helped to relax her.

She leaned back in her chair and finally opened her eyes. She saw nothing unusual. Then, somewhere very close, a voice said:

"Brrr."

It startled her, made her jump in her chair, but then she recognised it and laughed. *You twit!*

"It's cold in here!" the boo buddy complained in its cutesy *Teddy Ruxpin* voice. The bear had noticed the drop in temperature before Megan had, but now she realised she could see her breath in the air. This was no big deal in itself. Sometimes temperature drops were a sign. Sometimes they weren't. And in a house as dilapidated as this, it was only to be expected. Shivering, she pulled on her padded jacket and zipped it up.

She looked down at her screen. The dining room feed. Her body glowing orange. Still nothing unusual. Keeping her eyes on the feed, she stretched and yawned, again noting that tiniest of delays.

Then she froze.

From the bottom of the frame, two black spectral hands had appeared, emerging from the purple void behind her, seeking out the warm glow of her back. They advanced slowly, trembling with... with *something*, still a few feet out behind her. *But the delay-*

Icy fingers closed around her waist.

20:22
45 hours and 38 minutes remaining

Megan was on her feet in a flash. The fingers relinquished their hold. She whirled round. There was no-one behind her. She turned back to the dining room feed. The hands were already gone. Now she studied both feeds, dining room and bedroom, looking for dark blue or black humanoid shapes in amongst the purple. Nothing.

She clicked on the Zenaframe tab. It brought up the same two camera angles but without the thermal imaging filter, only natural light, which was almost nil. But Zenaframe didn't require natural light to produce its CGI stick figures. All it required was movement, disturbances in the atmosphere. There were no stick figures in the bedroom feed, and the only one in the dining room feed was her own; a wire frame superimposed over her body, shifting and adjusting its posture in perfect tandem with her movements. Nothing out of the ordinary.

But the boo buddy wouldn't shut up about being cold (each "Brrr" denoted a further drop in temperature), and now the EMF meter was sounding too, emitting random squeaks and squawks as its rainbow of LED lights went on and off and on again. Her tech was picking up anomalies everywhere. There was too much data to process.

*

Drew had almost finished checking off the bricks in the living room. He was pleased with his efforts, thinking he would have the whole house covered before long. But then he heard Megan's urgent shout.

"Drew! Get in here, quick!"

Stepping gingerly around the holes in the floor, straining to see them in the dark, he passed through the hallway and into the dining room. "It's *freezing* in here."

"No shit." Megan pushed her laptop aside, keeping the screen vertical to illuminate the table. She reached under her chair, took the Ouija board - a real antique - out of its 'pizza' box, and placed it on the table top.

"I fucking knew it," Drew muttered.

Megan ignored him and placed the carved wooden planchette on top of the board. The Victoriana contrasted sharply with the sleek laptop that illuminated it. An old Arthur C Clarke quote popped into Drew's head: *Any sufficiently advanced technology is indistinguishable from magic.* The planchette resembled a mouse, he thought, the Ouija board a keyboard. Perhaps the Victorians had once been visited by a time traveller with a computer. After he left they'd tried to replicate it, and the Ouija board was the result.

"Sit there," Megan ordered. "Put your fingers on the planchette. Lightly."

"I know how this goes," Drew said. "We push it around the board, but so gently we don't even realise we're doing it. Then-"

The planchette slid over to *No*. Drew jumped. Neither of them had yet touched it.

Megan beamed. "You were saying?"

But Drew was already smirking again, trying to figure out how the trick was done.

Megan cleared her throat and raised her voice, addressing the room itself. "I'm talking to the spirit that's here with us now." Each mini exhalation hung in the air like a wispy little phantom. "If you have something to say, please use the board to communicate, like you did just now."

They waited. Nothing happened.

"I suppose it's occurred to you," Drew said, "that your ghost, if it's real, might opt to infect us both by spelling out the trigger phrase?"

Megan shrugged. "You'd better hope it's all bullshit then, hadn't you?"

Drew frowned. *He* thought it was bullshit alright, but did she? She claimed not to, which left only three possibilities: Megan Mallory was either a liar, very courageous, or very reckless.

Megan addressed the room again. "Please tell us who you are."

Now the planchette moved by itself once

more, a little slower this time. It went to *H*. Megan and Drew glanced at each other, both with knowing expressions, both knowing different things. Then their eyes went back to the board. The planchette went to *A*. Then *L*. Then *E*.

"We're in business," Megan whispered.

Drew's eyes darted feverishly over the board and around it. *How the hell is she doing it?*

"Hale?" Megan said loudly. "Magnus Hale? Is that you?"

The planchette went to *Yes*.

"Magnus, my name's Megan, and this is Drew. We'd like to ask you some questions. Is that alright?"

Drew still couldn't find a rational explanation for any of it, though he suspected he was simply watching a highly skilled magician at work. It felt that way too; more entertaining than frightening. *But the cold...*

The planchette hadn't moved.

"Magnus?" Megan repeated.

There was no answer.

Drew's patience came to an abrupt end. "Alright dickhead, stop playing hard to get. Tell us where the device is, or we'll summon Keith Harris and tell him you broke Orville's wings."

Megan eyed him furiously.

"He'll sic Cuddles on you," Drew added.

Still there was no response.

"Great," Megan sniped. "Thanks alot, Drew."

But suddenly the planchette was sliding across

124

the board again, quicker this time, stopping at various letters. It spelled out *G-O-D-C-O-P*.

"I think he means good cop," Drew said.

"Who's the good cop, Magnus?" Megan asked. "Me?"

The planchette slid over to *Yes*.

Drew nodded. "So I'm the bad cop, am I?" He was starting to enjoy himself now. It was more fun when you played along. But then the planchette went to *No*.

"I'm not?"

The reply came immediately: *G-U-I-L-T-Y-C-O-P*.

Drew's smile faded. The association formed in his mind. *Jenny*. Fury rose in him. He upended the board. "Okay, that's *enough,*" he hissed at Megan. "What the fuck are you playing at?"

"Nothing! I'm not-"

The Ouija board flipped over, righting itself. The planchette made its own small jump, from the table back onto the board. And then it was moving again, slowly at first, but gradually gaining speed. It spelled out *T-I-C-K-T-O-C-K*. Then it repeated the sequence: *T-I-C-K-T-O-C-K*, faster still now. The message repeated over and over - *T-I-C-K-T-O-C-K-T-I-C-K-T-O-C-K-T-I-C-K-T-O-C-K* - faster and faster, the planchette darting from letter to letter, its contours a blur. Then it shot off the table altogether, flying up and away towards...

Crack! Megan screamed. The sound had come

125

from the mirror on the wall close behind her. The planchette clattered on the floor and stayed there.

Drew looked at the mirror. It was cracked, but not shattered. *Okay, that was impressive.* He went and picked up the planchette, placed it back on the board, eager for more.

Megan swallowed hard to regain her composure. "Magnus, would you like us to leave?"

More words came: *N-O-T-Y-O-U*. A pause, then: *J-U-S-T-H-I-M*.

Drew shook his head. "I'm not going anywhere."

The planchette remained still.

Megan was breathing in and out, in and out, ever slower, ever deeper. Drew studied her. Fear like that couldn't be faked, could it? But if she was such a pro, why was she so afraid?

'Hale' still hadn't responded.

Drew looked at the wall mirror again. There was something on its surface that hadn't been there a moment ago. Not the crack. Something else. Scratches. Letters. Seven words crudely etched into the glass. Had 'Hale' grown tired of the Ouija board? Was he showing them he didn't need it?

Now Megan noticed it too, averting her eyes as soon as she had. "Careful," she said as Drew approached the mirror. But this time he knew the procedure. He placed his hand over the message without looking at it, then revealed the letters one by one. It was a variation of a phrase he'd seen before, in

126

Hale's letter to MI5.

They shall fail, believing they have succeeded.

SUNDAY
02:07
39 hours and 53 minutes remaining

The temperature in the dining room had returned to normal; if an indoor temperature that matched the outdoor temperature could be called normal. They'd heard nothing more from 'Hale'. He'd gone stubbornly quiet, despite Megan's continued efforts to communicate. Drew had stayed with her, trying and failing to spot hidden mechanisms or other telltale signs of trickery. It was late. They were both exhausted.

Drew was about to head off to find somewhere to sleep - somewhere without wind whistling through holes in the floor - when Megan called after him: "Drew?"

At the door, he turned back to face her. Her usual frosty demeanour had evaporated. Now he saw a vulnerability in her eyes that made him warm to her, if only a little.

Hesitantly, she said: "You *are* having trouble believing all this... aren't you?"

Strange way of putting it. Hopeful, almost. "You

could say that."

"Right, so... if I told you we're dealing with a feeder... that it's drawing power from my fear of it, but your *lack* of fear, your scepticism... if I told you your disbelief is the only thing keeping it in check... would you believe *that*?"

"Of course not."

She gave a nervous little smile. "Good."

"You really *are* scared, aren't you?"

She nodded.

"Then maybe we shouldn't be sleeping alone." He cringed even as he said it, realising how it sounded, how Megan would choose to interpret it, though he hadn't meant it that way.

Sure enough, the vulnerability in her eyes evaporated, and the hard suspicion returned. "You know what?" she said. "You're right." She picked up the boo buddy and tossed it to him. "Don't cuddle him too hard. He's expensive." Then she was out through the door and up the stairs, taking her sleeping bag with her. At the top of the stairs she went into the first room she came to - the room right in front of the staircase - and slammed the door shut behind her.

*

Megan was pleased with her 'Don't cuddle him too hard' line; she'd taken Drew down a peg or two, getting any ideas he might have had out of his head. As a result, she'd been on a high as she went up the stairs, and she'd walked into the room without really thinking about it, more concerned with making a

129

suitably assertive exit than with where she was actually going. But as the door slammed shut behind her, and despite the reassuring presence of the Zenaframe nodes glowing green on the walls, she suddenly felt profoundly cold and alone. She couldn't leave right away, not without losing face in front of Drew, so for now she would have to stay where she was: alone in the bedroom with that incessantly ticking clock and the nasty, grizzled old bed.

She forced herself to sit on the mattress. It was too hard for her liking, but worse than that, there was something sticky and cloying about the feel of the sheets, something unsavoury about the musty smell of the mould-spotted pillows.

Don't be a fool. It's not the first time you've slept in a room with a vibe.

With her instincts screaming at her to leave - *Get. Out. Right. Now.* - she laid her sleeping bag on top of the bed. She got half undressed, then shuffled into it and zipped it up. She screwed her eyes tightly shut, fervently willing sleep to come, knowing it never did when she thought like that... and still doing it anyway.

*

In the end, Drew opted to sleep downstairs in the dining room. He had no option but to use the sleeping bag left behind by god knows who. The boo buddy, the toy, (he was still convinced it was little more than a toy) remained mercifully silent. With the sleeping bag pulled up over his head to keep out the bitter cold, he shone a torch onto Hale's journal, flicking through the pages, trying to recall where he'd left off. There had been the experiments, followed by the dramatic interruption. The man in the window with the thing on his cheek. His demented expression, and the words he'd tried to say. His abrupt death; shot in the head by a guard, presumably. Drew found his spot and read on.

My doctor saw the man die just like I had. He told me to stay where I was while he opened the door with his key. The second he peeked out into the corridor, another shot rang out, and he fell back onto the floor, blood trailing from a hole in the breast pocket of his white coat. Terrified, I went over to him, but I didn't know what to do. Before he died, he gave me two pieces of advice: "Don't read anything," and "Cover your ears." I took the bunch of keys from his belt. I had no idea if the shooter was still in the vicinity, but eventually I mustered enough courage to look out into the corridor. It was empty. I ran down it, hoping the keys would open any doors I came to. They did. As I turned into yet another gleaming white corridor, I saw someone - another test subject - running ahead of me, away from me, but he quickly disappeared around a corner. I followed him, thinking he was running from danger, not to it. An emergency alarm began to sound throughout the underground warren. That was when I noticed the writing on a nearby wall. The ink was blood. The letters still dripped. Remembering the doctor's warning, I carefully avoided reading those words. I looked down at the floor as I passed that ghastly graffiti, and there I saw the source of the 'ink'; another doctor, who now lay dead in a spreading pool of blood. He too had been shot through the chest.

I tiptoed carefully through the blood and carried on my way, leaving a trail of red footprints on the polished white floor. I turned another corner, only to be met by an even more alarming sight. An armed guard was trying to keep a pair of earmuffs clamped over his ears, while a test subject - the man I'd seen running - tried to remove them. It was a fierce struggle, but strangely neither one of them seemed to care about the pistol holstered at the guard's waist. The fight was over the earmuffs, not the gun. Now I recognised the test subject from the bus journey; a gambling addict, if I recall. I hadn't liked him much on the bus, and I liked him even less now. I saw my chance and I took it. Took the pistol, I mean. The gambler saw me and got two syllables out before I shot him. Then I shot the guard too. I had to. Everyone had gone mad. But I would be lying if I said I didn't enjoy it. I put on the guard's earmuffs and the alarm faded almost to nothing. I dropped the gun, but only when I realised I'd used all the bullets. Then I took a lift up to ground level.

Once outside, I made for the perimeter fence. The compound was even quieter than usual; I think the guards had all rushed below ground to try and contain the emergency. On the way to the fence I passed my Quonset hut, and went inside to retrieve my possessions. Not everything, just some essentials; wallet, house keys, the diary, all of which I stuffed into a small satchel. Then I went back outside, where I now heard the occasional far off gunshot. The panic had evidently spread to the surface. When I reached the inner perimeter fence, the gate was unmanned, because both guards lay dead next to it, both shot to death. But two more guards still manned the outer gate up ahead. I passed through into the sandy strip of no-man's land between the two fences with my hands raised. They already had their weapons trained on me. All I could think to say was: 'It's alright. I'm not mad.' I kept saying it and kept walking, even as the two guards yelled at me to stop. They didn't seem to care who I was. Whatever procedures or protocols they'd been taught were already long forgotten. All that mattered to them now was the expression on my face and the tone of my voice, both of which I was at pains to keep calm and level, and nothing like the demented shouts of those who had already gone mad. For that reason alone, they waved me past. Or rather, one of them did. The other one took the earmuffs from my head as I went. Our eyes met, and he smiled a strange, unnatural smile that I will never forget. And then he said the words right to my face; the phrase that began with the same two syllables the gambler had gotten out before I shot him. It sounded like a foreign language. Then he began to laugh, and I realised this one too was mad. He'd been suppressing his fervour until now. His companion looked just as alarmed as I must have. I panicked and ran out through the gate. Behind me I heard a gunshot which stopped me in my tracks. I thought I had been shot, until I looked back and realised the mad one had been shot dead by the sane one. Then the sane one turned the gun on himself and pulled the trigger, and he too fell. A kind of sanity, I suppose.

I ran into the forest. Once hidden from view, I looked back at the compound. That was when I heard the whoosh of a jet engine from above, followed by loud explosions as the first of the Harrier's bombs rained down hell. Within a minute, the entire facility was engulfed in an acrid ball of fire and smoke. I ran further into the forest, trying to outrun the spreading flames. Several trees were already alight. As I went, I began to notice *something strange. My fear subsided, replaced by a strong sense that the forest around me was not really a forest atall, but a sort of curtain painted to look like a forest. A curtain I might easily have pulled back to reveal something radically different. Eventually I-*

Drew's torch light went out, plunging him into darkness. *Damn battery!* He shook the torch in frustration. He'd been eager to continue Hale's story, but he had no other light source to hand. The nodes on the walls shone faint beams of green light around the room, but they weren't bright enough to read by. Then he remembered the lighter he'd stolen from behind the bar in the pub. It was in his jacket, which he'd hung from one of the dining room chairs.

He was about to unzip the sleeping bag when the boo buddy piped up. "Hey! That tickles!"

02:39
39 hours and 21 minutes remaining

That tickles. The bear had detected a change in air pressure, and a change in air pressure usually meant a change in the weather. That was the true purpose of a barometer; not to warn you that a ghost was coming, but that a storm was. Drew wished that instead of a barometer, the bear had come with a reading light.

He unzipped the sleeping bag and clambered out into the darkness, taking the dead torch with him. He stumbled blindly over to the table and chairs, dropping the torch on the table. The beam flickered back on briefly, then went out again. He felt for the jacket he'd laid on top of a chair. He found it and reached inside the pocket for the lighter.

"Drew?"

"Jesus!" The voice startled him. It was Megan. "Try knocking?" She was somewhere in the room with him, but he still couldn't see her. Couldn't see anything. The left jacket pocket was empty. "Got a torch? This one's fucked."

"Drew. Listen to me. *I want you.*"

He froze. Three little words were all it took.

His desire was instantaneous, all-consuming.

"Right now, Drew. *Now*."

He went towards her voice. When he found her, he put his arms around her waist, and he realised she was naked, her back turned, her warmth an oasis in the desert of the cold room. He kissed the back of her neck, pushing his erection hard up against her. She shivered. His hands caressed her belly, then went up to her breasts, but she took them and guided them back down, down between her legs. All the while he kept kissing her sweet-scented neck, even as his fingers slipped easily inside her.

Soon his lips sought the side of her mouth. He wanted her to turn and face him so he could kiss her full on, but she wouldn't. What was it? Inhibition? A kink of some sort? He was about to force the turn when his lips registered something strange. Something on her cheek that was hard and elongated where it should have been soft and smooth.

A sudden howling draft came up through a hole in the floor. It sent the torch rolling off the table and onto the floorboards. The beam came on again, illuminating their clinch from a low angle, casting tall shadows over Megan's nakedness.

She was facing the wall mirror, Drew looking over her shoulder at the reflection. His lips had come to rest on the black-headed tip of a stalk growing out of her cheek. One of many, all emerging from a pink, fleshy cavity bored deep into one side of her face. The stalks were the colour and consistency of dead skin, yet they writhed like probing antennae, their pulsing black ends exploring Drew's lips, pushing in between them, seeking out his tongue.

He recoiled, his ardour turning to revulsion, quick as water into steam on a red hot hob. He staggered backwards and fell against the dining table, tripping on the torch as he went. The light went out again, darkness swallowing the room whole.

The realisation hit him right after the shock; a one-two punch. The thing on her cheek. It was the infection. The same viral symptoms Hale had described in his diary. Somehow she'd been exposed to it. Driven crazy by it. He scrabbled about on the floor, groping blindly for the torch, knowing that the thing inside Megan was still there with him, still wanting him.

At last he found the torch. He shook it and shook it until it came on again. He swept the beam all around him in a quivering three sixty arc. He swept it across the floor, the walls, the ceiling. Each time it told the same story. She was gone.

He recalled the sensation of Megan's body against his. Her warmth the oasis, the cold room the desert. The metaphor felt true to what he'd experienced, yet it was also back to front. Warm was cold and cold was warm. It didn't make any sense, unless...

...unless the oasis was not an oasis, but a mirage.

03:15
38 hours and 45 minutes remaining

Megan lay on the four poster bed, cocooned in her sleeping bag. Sleep still eluded her. The beams emanating from the wall nodes criss-crossed the room at every conceivable angle; a mesh of translucent green lines, like some high tech bank vault in a Hollywood movie. If something - *anything* - passed through them, the time and position of each 'break' would be recorded and converted into the final digital product; the telltale stick figure she'd been waiting for. The more she stared at those beams, the safer she felt. She was like a diver in a shark-proof cage, surrounded by lurking predators, but protected. The analogy relaxed her, allowed her to finally fall asleep.

A short while later, something woke her. She sat up, and the sleeping bag fell down around her waist, exposing her to the cold. The bad kind of cold. The darkness was near total, the Zenaframe beams providing only the faintest ambient green light. She could hear the grandfather clock ticking away steadily in the corner. An oddly comforting sound. The clock was something wholly physical, purely mechanical, reassuringly predictable.

But there was another sound too. Something organic. Something human. Someone out there in the dark was breathing heavily. Megan stiffened, her fear growing, gaining momentum. Snowballing.

"Drew?" A hoarse, feeble whisper was all she could manage. There was no answer, but the breathing grew louder. Closer. It was somewhere near the centre of the room - an area criss-crossed by the green lines - but when she looked, their faint glow revealed nothing. The breathing grew louder still. It was a man, she was sure. Each breath sounded heavy, laboured, urgent.

A short section of one of the beams, one that was very close, blinked out for a half second, as if a shadow had walked right through it. And then she felt the warm breath on her right cheek, accompanied by a powerful stench of rancid halitosis.

Megan recoiled, gave a panicked shout. The sudden noise made the presence diminish, shrink back into the dark. She felt blindly for her torch, found it, switched it on. Trembling, she shone the beam into the centre of the room, illuminating the wall opposite the bed. It was bare. She swept the beam slowly around the rest of the room, dreading whatever might suddenly reveal itself. But nothing did. She let the beam fall lower and did another sweep, this time searching the floor. That was when she saw the clothes. A man's clothes, lying scattered across the floor, as if they'd been hastily removed.

Each item of clothing formed part of a trail leading from the door to the bed; diamond patterned brown socks, a dirty white shirt, a brown pair of trousers, underpants - an old style that nobody wore anymore - and finally, on the bed itself, just inches from her sleeping bag... a discarded bandage. The stain on the inside of the bandage was unusual; not bloodied, but marked instead with little black ink spots.

Megan controlled herself as best she could, swallowing the scream back down even as she screwed her eyes shut. When she finally found the courage to open them again, the bandage was gone. So too were the clothes.

07:22
34 hours and 38 minutes remaining

To some within the Security Service, Alec and Eileen were affectionately known as 'the three percenters'. Alec and Eileen believed a viral cataclysm to be inevitable, if nothing was done to avert it, but those who had given them the nickname - their seniors - saw things differently. Their seniors believed there was only a *three percent chance* of said cataclysm occurring, even if nothing was done. Over the years, as numerous ever more sophisticated operations had tried and failed to locate Hale's device, the probability of its existence had decreased. Not the *true* probability, but the probability as determined by low level analysts who arrived at any damn percentage number they were *told* to arrive at. It was gut feeling disguised as maths. A judgment call dressed as a science project. Every time Alec's department came up empty handed, the reliability of the source intel - Hale's letter and diary - was re-assessed and downgraded. Though Alec and Eileen's nickname stuck, the number itself - three percent - did not. It was constantly revised, without their knowledge or input, from three to two to one, and so on. As the years passed, newer, more plausible threats emerged. Priorities and resources moved elsewhere. Accordingly, Alec's department was gradually downsized, until only he and Eileen remained. They were like two frogs being slowly boiled, regarded with less and less affection, seen more and more as kooks clinging desperately to the outer fringes of the intelligence community. And so, paradoxically, the nearer the world came to a viral cataclysm, the more the imminent apocalypse was ignored. Denial was *so* comfortable. And the higher one went, the more comfortable it became.

*

Alec was at his desk promptly at seven that morning, while most Thames House staff were still at home fixing breakfast or out for their morning runs. He was surprised to get a call from his section chief at that hour, though he knew his boss worked long hours too. Her name was Patricia Simmons. A recent promotion. Though he'd met her once or twice, he knew her primarily as a disembodied voice on the phone. It wouldn't have done her any harm to visit them in person now and again. Alec had always preferred face to face meetings rather than phone chats (even a video call would have sufficed) and Patricia's office was only one floor above his. But he appreciated the woman was busy. Not that Alec wasn't.

"In early again, are we Alec? Well done, well

done."

"What can I help you with?"

"Oh, nothing, nothing." *Then why call?* "Just... I had a chat with the DG yesterday. He's a bit worried."

"About what?"

"About your department. You and Eileen. I stuck up for you, of course. Told him how hard you both work. How loyal you are. But still, he's concerned you're not really... providing value."

"Value?"

"He's worried your results aren't really justifying your budget. You know what he's like."

"We're trying our best."

"Of course you are, of course you are, and I for one fully support you." *For one?* "But I just wanted to give you a heads-up. About the sort of language he was using."

"What sort of language?"

"He called your operation in Barra a dog and pony show. He tends to use that phrase when he's not too impressed. When he's thinking about... well, you know."

Alec did indeed know, and the thought of it terrified him. "He's aware we're less than two days away from a potential-"

"Of course, of course. He's well aware of that, as we all are."

"Then what the hell is he thinking? I take it you gave him my recommendation?"

Alec's recommendation had been a dramatic one, to say the least. He'd made it two weeks before bringing in Drew and Megan, right after Baines had disappeared. His recommendation had been that the DG put a word in with the Home Secretary about initiating a COBRA meeting with the Prime Minister, his cabinet, and the joint intelligence chiefs. A COBRA meeting whose subject was to be the evacuation of central London.

There was silence on the other end of the line while Patricia tried to formulate her answer. All she could seem to manage was a heavy sigh.

"You did *give* him the recommendation?"

"I did, I did. I'm afraid he wouldn't take it any further."

"You're joking."

She sighed again. "He doesn't trust your judgment, Alec. Not since you got this woman Mallory involved. The parapsychologist." She said the word as if it were her least favourite profanity. "He called her a mumbo-jumbologist."

Alec was shaking. He tried hard to suppress his anger enough to give a reply that was measured, diplomatic. He failed. "In that case," he said, "the DG is a bloody irresponsible idiot who's about to have an unprecedented amount of blood on his hands."

Patricia's tone went up a notch. "Now look, I've tried to defend you as best I can, but you're not doing yourself any favours by-"

"I know. I spoke out of turn."

"And the rest!"

"But what if he's wrong? What if you're *all* wrong?"

There was another long pause. Another heavy sigh. "Then we'll just have to rely on your dog and pony show up in Barra, won't we?"

08:17
33 hours and 43 minutes remaining

The memory of the previous night's encounter was sharp and clear in Drew's mind, like the memory of something very real. And yet now, as they sat together at the dining room table, sharing their meagre breakfast of bread, cheese and water, there was no sign of any infection on Megan's cheek. He could tell from her raw looking eyes that she too had barely slept. *Parasomnia, perhaps?* He bit the bullet and described the events to her in detail, including the fact she'd been naked, though he censored his own arousal, his own complicity.

"I think I'd remember something like that!" Megan said defensively, as if he'd cast some kind of aspersion on her character, which of course he had. "I never came down here all night. Not once."

"You're sure?"

"Of course I'm sure!"

"Any history of parasomnia? Sleepwalking?"

"No."

"Sexsomnia?"

"Definitely not."

"So you think I dreamt it."

"Probably. Unless..."

"Unless?"

"The stalks. Was there something... *black* on the end of them? Like an eye?"

Drew nodded grimly.

She told him what she'd seen in the bedroom. The clothes. The stains on the bandage. The 'ink' spots. He didn't want to buy any of it - it was all too grotesquely outlandish - but his own story was just as wild.

Megan opened her laptop and brought up the Zenaframe footage of the bedroom. "Let's see what we can see," she said, and spooled through the recording at high speed, until she found the point where she'd climbed into the sleeping bag and lain down on the bed. Then she slowed it a little, though it was still on fast forward. They both looked on as the wire frame stick figure superimposed over Megan's sleeping body shifted in synch with her tosses and turns. And then a second stick figure appeared in the frame. Megan hit pause, then adjusted the playback to normal speed. The second stick figure had no accompanying human form. It stood in the middle of the room, apparently watching Megan while she slept. Its posture was stooped, hunched over. It crept closer to the bed, warily at first. Then, seemingly satisfied that Megan was still fast asleep, it lay down on the bed, very close beside her.

Drew studied Megan as she watched the two

147

stick figures lying there together, almost intertwined. Her hand was over her mouth, her eyes wide. If she was play-acting, she was damn good at it. Now the footage showed her abruptly sitting up on the bed, spooked by something. As she did so, the second stick figure got up off the bed and shuffled away into the middle of the room. But it didn't retreat entirely. It lingered there, loitering, waiting.

Megan rewound the footage and replayed the incident. "Look at the way it moves," she said. "Like a frail old man."

Or Hollywood VFX. A pre-rendered CG animation, dragged and dropped into last night's footage. But he bit his tongue. The more suspicious he appeared, the more on guard she would be. Instead he said: "Hale wasn't that old when he died."

Megan shook her head. "Doesn't matter. We're not looking at his physical form, we're looking at his spirit. The way it moves is determined by how powerful it is. Here, it's weak and slow. It hasn't had enough fear to feed on. Yet. But it's getting there. Most spirit frames I've seen are too weak to even move. They just stand there, then they fade away. Not this one."

"But why would it lie next to you like that?"

Megan hesitated. "Spirits don't stop feeling what they felt in life. They still have all the same emotions, the same desires. Even more so when that desire is frustrated by..." she shuddered at the thought, "...an inability to consummate."

"On account of being dead?"

"Right. I've seen weak spirits - spirits I *thought* were weak - suddenly draw immense power, from their own intense emotions."

"Which emotions?"

"Sexual frustration. Sexual jealousy. Especially jealousy. Trust me, you don't want to be around a feeder when its eyes start turning green."

08:32
33 hours and 28 minutes remaining

After breakfast they tried to contact 'Hale' once more - again with the Ouija board - but without success. Drew wondered why sometimes this 'ghost' communicated and other times it didn't. If Megan was a fraud, orchestrating the whole thing like a magician, shouldn't she have tried to drum up another show for him? To convince him further? For all she knew, just one more apparent miracle might have been the tipping point for Drew; the last remaining peak between the valley of scepticism and the valley of belief. Then again, perhaps their current failure was an equally calculated move by Megan, one intended to introduce an element of realism; because if Hale appeared on demand every time without fail, that in itself would be suspicious. Far better for the ghost hunt to be a hunt like any other; sometimes you caught your prey, sometimes you didn't.

Drew decided to leave her to it. He took Hale's journal and went out into the hallway. Sitting at the foot of the stairs, he found his place in the diary.

April 16th

I have arrived in London. Yesterday I found an abandoned caravan and claimed it. And not a minute too soon, because something had appeared on my left cheek. The cavity was broadly circular, about a centimetre wide, not bloody, but it nonetheless resembled an open wound. The stalks growing out of it seemed to be made of dead skin (though they were clearly far from dead), and at the tip of each one there was a tiny, pulsating black eye. Not a literal eye - there was no iris or pupil - but I really don't know what else to call it. That was yesterday. When I checked the wound again this morning, it had grown larger still; at least two centimetres wider. The stalks are now slightly longer, and they have multiplied. Their movement is noticeable even from a distance of several feet. When I next leave the caravan, I shall have to wrap the wound in several layers of bandage if I am to avoid alarming people.

I do wonder about the purpose of those black-eyed stalks. They seem to act like feelers, reaching out and touching the air, but with a view to finding what? Food? Or something more fundamental, like the fabric of reality itself? I'm only speculating, but something tells me this latter notion isn't far wide of the mark.

April 17th

My insights into the true nature of reality grow sharper every minute, even as the stalks grow longer. And the key insight is this: Imagine a fly hovering close to the eye of a wild elephant. Though both creatures are looking out over the same stretch of open savannah, they each perceive it quite differently, because their perception mechanisms - their eyes - are built quite *differently. Similarly, the lunatic perceives the world quite differently to the non-lunatic. To most of us, the world of the mental patient is nothing but delusion. A fiction. To the patient, however, it is utterly real. So how can we be sure that this so-called 'fiction' is not in fact the true reality, or as true a reality as any other?*

Here, Hale had written *FICTION!* several times over everything he'd written previously; a messy, oversized scrawl that was nothing like the careful calligraphy of his handwriting. This defacing of his own work resembled the scribblings of a madman, yet his thoughts about objective versus subjective reality were sound enough to resonate with Drew. They made a certain kind of sense. As for the tone, it was a world away from the puerile office gossip of Hale's earlier entries. Had the infection caused the shift?

April 18th

I walked through the city for a long time today. Again I had the strong conviction that the shop fronts and vistas I passed were nothing more than painted backdrops, a curtain I could have grasped and pulled back to reveal... what? I didn't know, but I felt sure that whatever I found behind that facade would be far more real, far more tangible, than the facade itself. It was the same feeling I'd had when running through the woods, but now it was more acute. Once or twice I even tried to physically reach out and touch that 'curtain', but whenever I did, passersby would stare at me, and I would give up out of sheer embarrassment. So... conformity guards the veil. Conformity is the enemy of truth.

This too resonated with Drew; the idea of a curtain about to be lifted. Once, while scrolling idly through Youtube thumbnails, he'd stumbled across leaked raw footage from a TV ghost hunting 'reality' show. Footage never intended for public consumption. The show's presenter, a young woman, was in some allegedly haunted pub with her co-host, a middle-aged man with an earring who called himself a medium. Halfway through a tour of the pub, he was suddenly 'possessed' by the evil spirit that haunted it. In fact the spirit was more than just evil. It was demonic. The medium gave a convincing and uniquely disturbing performance, apparently scaring the life out of his colleague by threatening to first maim and then rape her. Had the clip ended there, viewers would have been left in no doubt that either the spirit (if they bought into the act) or the medium (if they didn't) must be deeply troubled by a fierce streak of misogynistic sadism.

But when the director called 'Cut', the cameras kept rolling; an act of sabotage perhaps, by a whistle-blowing crew member. And right away - *instantly* - the illusion was shattered. The medium was no longer possessed. His co-host was no longer terrified. Instead, they both looked at their director, asking 'Was that alright?' and 'I thought we nailed it that time, didn't we?' The curtain had been well and truly lifted. Drew had found this sudden, jarring switch from one reality to another far more disturbing than the apparent demonic possession. The truly frightening thing was the deliberate deception. There was something callous about it; a contemptuous disregard for the fans of the show who honestly believed. As it turned out, there were demons in that pub after all. Celebrity demons, caught unawares by a hot mic.

Not for the first time, Drew wondered if there might be a similar 'curtain' or 'veil' surrounding him in the house at that very moment; an equally deceitful web of illusion being spun by Megan Mallory. But if so, what lay *behind* that curtain? What did Megan's true face look like? Was it apologetic and guilt-ridden, or was it cruel and contemptuous, demonic even? And how far was she prepared to go to keep her 'audience' from discovering the truth?

Don't be an idiot, Drew.

Jenny was right. Dismissing the thoughts as paranoia, he shook them from his mind and read on.

In the afternoon I encountered a young street preacher. He must have been in his early twenties, though he had the wisdom of a much older man. His appearance was startling; a milky white complexion, eyes sunk deep into his bald head, thin nose pointing down to a trimmed ginger beard. His cranium seemed to bulge out, as if his brain were still growing when the rest of him had stopped, his skull cracking and stretching to accommodate it. He wore a black sheepskin coat, black leather trousers, black boots. Various occultish trinkets hung around his neck; a pentagram and an inverted crucifix, but also a swastika, and even a hammer and sickle! He was a walking mish-mash of 'extreme' ideologies, both spiritual and political. I began to sense that here, in some respects at least, was a kindred spirit. Conformity - the guardian of the veil - was his enemy as much as mine.

He spoke fervently and compellingly, about life being an illusion, a puppet show; all of us nothing but puppets dancing about on a stage, with some unseen person pulling our strings. He spoke of a great injustice going on behind the scenes, behind the painted backdrop in front of which we all dance, oblivious. And then he locked eyes with me and he said: "Thirty years from this very day, a man who walks among us even now shall inspire a rebirth, a great awakening among the people. Those in power shall be forewarned. They shall try to prevent this rebirth. But they shall fail, believing they have succeeded." Then he pointed at me and said: "It's you! It's you!"

Now, I am well aware that a prophecy by itself doesn't amount to much. A prophecy will not come to pass unless someone first hears it, then believes himself to be the one destined to fulfil it, and finally goes on to do just that. There are many historical instances of self-fulfilling prophecies, and an even greater number that go unfulfilled. I am nobody's fool in this regard, and yet... well, I'll come to that in a moment.

At this point the preacher was approached by a policeman who asked him to 'tone it down', apparently because he was 'scaring people'. The preacher interpreted this as harassment, and objected violently, whereupon he was arrested. I carried on my way.

Later, in a shop window, I saw a poster depicting a ticker tape parade in some American city. And at that moment, everything clicked into place.

I know what I must do. The prophecy shall be fulfilled.

April 23rd

The device is nearly complete. My 'supplier' (also Medtech's supplier!) happens to be located within walking distance of my caravan. Yet more proof, if any were needed, that I am destined to fulfil the prophecy. I have obtained some betavoltaics from their not very secure loading bay. In my previous role, I visited them so often they gave me the four-digit entry code - a code the silly fools still haven't bothered to change! As for the other components, I have purchased a heavy duty waterproof canister from an outdoor specialist, a timer switch and a set of tools from a DIY store, and waterproof paper and ink from a stationers'. Now it's just a matter of assembly. The canister will soon be stuffed full of my 'ticker tape'. Writing out the same little phrase thousands of times is quite a laborious task, but it will all be worth it come the day of the parade!

April 25th

As I write this, I am sat in a café. I wouldn't call it a nice café. I believe 'greasy spoon' is the term. But it is the only establishment I have found that doesn't refuse me entry on account of my appearance; tattered old bandages over an ever expanding wound. So I've been coming here regularly in the last few days. Like me, the décor is shabby and uninviting. Faux leather seats with bits of the 'leather' missing, and yellowy foam stuffing within, which customers have torn and picked at. The sticky formica tabletops are forever stained with ketchup and tea rings. It's a family-owned business run by three generations of women. The eldest, a woman in her early seventies with a milky cataract in one eye, is very proud of her menu, though it consists only of variations on a single theme. Whichever variation I choose - sausage egg and chips, egg chips and beans, beans bacon and two eggs - she always says the same thing: "Oh yes, that is a nice meal!" Her daughter, a capable woman in her thirties, does the bulk of the work around the place. I get the impression she could cope perfectly well without her mother, but her mother seems to derive some meaning and happiness from helping out in the café, even if she does so at an all too leisurely pace. And then there is the granddaughter, who is just three years old. A chubby cheeked, energetic little cherub who rarely cries or complains because she's too busy 'running' the café. She is always scurrying about, pretending to serve customers, giving them menus and 'taking orders'. She's really rather sweet.

But I must get my letter written. Those in power must be forewarned, as it says in the prophecy. I shall set the timer and plant the device as soon as I leave this café. I have found the perfect spot for it.

One day, that little girl will thank me.

And there Hale's account ended. The next page was the one that had been torn out, and the pages after that were all blank. Something else had happened soon after, then. Something either external, out there in the world, or internal, in Hale's own mind.

Something he'd first recorded, then later removed. An act of censorship. But to what end?

09:47
32 hours and 13 minutes remaining

Drew went out onto the pier to clear his head. The wind had died down a little, but storm clouds far out to sea were drifting closer to shore. The rain showers hanging beneath them looked like tornadoes threatening to form, their dark funnels wide and diffuse, but gradually coalescing into something narrower, sharper, deadlier.

Exposure to the elements made him think about the rabbit at home, secure in its hutch in the garden. For a moment he envied the creature, blissfully ignorant and shielded from the weather in its snug little hideaway, until he remembered that it was trapped inside that hutch with dwindling food and water, and no means of escape. When *had* he last fed it?

He thought back over the events of the previous night. The séances, the Ouija board, the planchette moving by itself. Neither he nor Megan had touched it, but that alone wasn't enough to preclude trickery. If he'd had the wherewithal to carefully examine the underside of the board, the planchette, what would he have found? Megan's hands hadn't been on the table, they'd been under it, either in her lap, or perhaps holding a magnet. A magnet powerful enough to move the planchette from below, if the planchette had had an iron strip on its underside.

Then there was his vision of a naked, infected Megan. A vision induced by Hale's ghost? An unusually vivid dream? Or a simple makeup effect?

Perhaps Megan really was nothing more than a professional liar; a label applicable to mediums, magicians... and spies. She'd told him she did not normally work for the Security Service. She'd told him she was an independent parapsychologist employed by them on a one-off basis. Had that been a lie too?

Supposing all of it was fraudulent, then. There was still one thing Megan couldn't possibly have faked by herself: the message etched into the mirror. *They shall fail, believing they have succeeded.* One minute it hadn't been there, the next minute it had. But Megan had never left the table, probably because she was busy manipulating that magnet, deflecting Drew's attention away from... what? Someone etching the words into the glass? No, that would have taken too long, and he surely would have noticed another person in the room. Unless it was done so swiftly that he *hadn't* noticed. Unless the words had been etched beforehand, onto a *duplicate* mirror, and the two mirrors had been quickly switched. Any way you sliced it, it all pointed to the same thing: an accomplice. The same accomplice who'd been winding the clock. A man or woman who'd been with them in the house all along. Watching. Waiting. Hiding. In a space between the walls (Drew was yet to finish his brick marking) or else... the grandfather clock? No. Its housing *was* large enough to hide someone very thin, but the three brass weights and their chains took up the bulk of the space. Under the bed? No, he'd already checked. The space between the floor and the bed frame was far too narrow. Where then?

He glanced down through a hole in one of the pier's rotten planks. Perhaps the accomplice wasn't in the house, but under it. He lay next to the hole and poked his head down into it. From his upside down perspective, he surveyed the pier's underpinnings; the latticework of crossbeams and supporting struts that kept the house above water. Though the forest of wood and iron was fairly dense, it wasn't quite intricate enough to provide a hiding place for anything larger than the sea birds that settled there. And that only left the roof. *The chimney.*

He went back inside the house, into the living room that had once contained a hearth, until its metal grate had dropped through the floor into the sea. Now, daylight shone up through that hole in the floor, only to be swallowed up again by the overhead chimney flue. He lay down as close as he dared to the light shaft, craning his neck out over the hole, trying to bridge the gap so he could look up into the flue.

But the gap was too wide.

There was only one other option. A dangerous one. He didn't like the thought of it, but his urge to find Megan's accomplice was turning into an irresistible itch. He went upstairs, into the bathroom. He chose this room over the bedroom because it was closer to his objective; the other end of the chimney stack. He opened the window and sat on the sill with his back to the open air. The window was set into the face of a gable which, along with two others, formed the crown of the house's facade. Each sloping side of the triangle was a sloping grey slate roof, slick with sea spray and bird droppings. Leaning out backwards as far as he dared, he reached up and grabbed the tip of the triangle where the two slopes met. His hands closed around a join whose surface was thankfully rougher than the smooth wet slates, affording him a decent grip. In front of his hands were the bare feet of a stone cherub, whose featureless eyes stared coldly down at him while its hi-viz jacket fluttered in the wind. Drew stood on the window ledge and straddled the gap between the window and the sloping roof to his left, until his entire body was flat up against the slates.

Inch by careful inch, he shuffled towards the chimney. He was almost there when a slate came loose as his toecap brushed against it. His body twisting, he pedalled frantically to find a firmer footing, and found one as the slate shattered on the pier below. At last he reached the square brick chimney. Transferring his handhold from the apex of the roof to the chimney itself, he heaved himself up over it and peered down into the stack.

The chute was easily wide enough to hide someone. Had it been clear all the way down, the hiding place or even the accomplice himself might have now been revealed. Either that, or he would have seen through the hole in the living room floor, all the way down to the water below. But the chute wasn't clear. It was blocked by something a few feet down; a bird's nest with two fluffy grey and white chicks who now looked up at him, cheeping loudly, their yellow beaks wide open, begging to be fed. They sat snugly together on a woven fabric of twigs and detritus poached from the shore. The parent was nowhere in sight.

Damn it.

He leaned down into the stack, grasping for the nest, but it was an inch or two out of reach. He would have to dislodge it with his feet. He readjusted himself so that his feet were dangling into the stack. Then he lowered himself down, his elbows propped up on top of the surrounding brickwork. His feet felt around for the nest. They found it. *Sorry kids. Your nest is about to turn into a raft.*

And that was when the parent returned.

10:14
31 hours and 46 minutes remaining

The bird, a large and very aggressive seagull, seemed to come out of nowhere. Something slimy and worm-like, food for its infants, fell from its mouth as it settled on the chimney top. Its beak closed, became a stabbing weapon. First it went for Drew's hands, his forearms, pecking and jabbing at them, drawing blood. He wanted to bat the creature away, but if he did he would fall down the shaft, since he was propped up only by his elbows. Praying the creature wouldn't go for his face, he screwed his eyes shut, bowed his head and took the assault. He could do little else. He would just have to ride it out until hopefully...

...but there was no 'hopefully'. The gull was already underneath his bowed head, jabbing up at his chin, his cheeks, his forehead, exploratory taps here and there, looking for a weak spot. Soon it found one. His right eyeball felt the first little stab through the flimsy shield of his eyelid. Only a gentle tap, but the next one would be far less kind. The gull had found its target.

Had he been thinking clearly, his priority would have been to haul himself up out of the chimney. But instinct tends to override clear thought, and nothing triggers instinct like a stab to the eye. He brought both hands up to his face. And then, of course, he fell.

Slowly to begin with, feet first, down into the stack, his extremities scrabbling for purchase against the surrounding brickwork, finding some, but not enough. He tried to lean back, facing upwards so he could wedge himself, but the downward momentum was already too great. Each fleeting attempt at a foothold brought nothing but a painful ankle twist. Each try for a handhold brought only another torn fingernail. And the filthy roiling dust he generated in the process made the task harder still, blinding him even as it clogged the back of his throat. Ever faster he fell, clawing desperately at the brickwork, trying to get purchase and failing, failing.

Now there was light rushing up at him from below, and suddenly, for a second or two at most, he was out in the open. The burst of clean air sharpened his senses, gave him a moment to think ahead, to stop flailing, to adjust his posture and hold his breath. As he'd intended, he hit the water feet first.

The freezing murk engulfed him, but the prior moment of anticipation lessened the shock. He sank fast, then slowed, then swam. He resurfaced, surrounded by cast iron struts and wooden crossbeams. He looked up, saw the hole he'd fallen through, how close it was to one of the beams. He must have missed it by inches. Floating in the water nearby was the seagull's nest, and, bobbing along next to it, seemingly unperturbed by their ordeal, two familiar balls of grey and white fluff. The chicks had found their raft, but they didn't seem to need it.

*

Megan had heard a noise coming from the living room - a brief, muffled scrabbling that sounded like a trapped animal looking for a way out - but when she'd gone in there to investigate, she'd found nothing. Ten minutes later, from her preferred spot at the dining room table, she heard the front door open and close. She went out into the hallway. Drew was stood there, soaked from head to toe, shivering. His rolled up shirt sleeves revealed scratches all over his forearms. *Scratches?*

"Chimney's clear," he muttered, and went upstairs.

She called after him - "What happened? Drew?" - but he ignored her. *What the hell?* She went back into the dining room and sat down again. Not for the first time, she wondered if Drew was losing his mind. Twice now she'd caught him taking slugs from a small whiskey bottle, before guiltily stowing it away again inside his jacket. Then there was his growing obsession with the walls, his closed off demeanour, and now the scratches on his arms... self-inflicted? No. They couldn't be. He wasn't the type. But the possibility of it chilled her, and now she had more than just a feeder spirit to deal with. Now she had that, plus an unhinged colleague who seemed convinced that some mysterious stranger was lurking inside the house, in the walls, emerging only to wind a clock or fake some phenomena, when in reality it was perfectly obvious that Megan and Drew were the only two people in the building.

Then again, perhaps *she* was the one losing her mind? No. Surely not. Given the circumstances, her unease was perfectly rational. She glanced down at the Ouija board, the planchette that stubbornly refused to move. The boo buddy too had been silent for hours on end. Hale seemed to be absent, but why the sudden retreat, just when he was gaining more power? It didn't make any sense. His power couldn't have diminished, because her sense of unease - *call it what it is!* - her *fear* was still palpable. More than ever, in fact, and precisely *because* the spirit was so quiet. She supposed Hale must be marshalling his forces, planning something big, and that was a frightening thought. A teacher had once told her that the fear of something was usually worse than the thing itself. Usually, sure, but not here, not now. Here and now, a different rule applied: if you allowed your fear to snowball, an avalanche would surely follow.

Familiar creaks came through the ceiling. Upstairs, Drew was pacing the floor again. Well, he could pace up and down all he wanted. It got them no closer to their goal. Had he forgotten what was at stake? The urgency of it? He seemed to be all out of ideas, if he'd ever even had any. Either that or... the thought disturbed her, seemed outrageous, yet it rang true all the same: what if Drew didn't care? About *any* of it? What if his mind was still on the case he'd been working before he was poached by Alec? More than anything, Drew wanted to catch the man who'd murdered his wife, but so far the killer had eluded him. He was out of ideas in this case, and probably in that case too, and that would be troubling him. And then there was the incident in the pub. The impulsive brutality for which he'd shown no remorse. Was that standard procedure for DSI Turner? For all his seniority, all his credentials, perhaps he was nothing more than an authoritarian thug who routinely abused his power. He was certainly a right winger, a traditionalist, someone uncomfortable with women who outranked him, or even just knew something he didn't. He seemed to be opposed to everything Megan stood for, yet he chose to live and work in London. London: home of liberals, progressives, multiculturalists. Drew must have felt like an alien down there, surrounded by his ideological enemies.

And then it hit her. What if... *oh god.* It couldn't be, could it? But the more she thought about it, the more it made sense. London was full of his *enemies.* And one enemy in particular: a man he'd so far failed to bring to justice. What if Drew was now sensing an opportunity? A chance to not only 'get his man', but also to punish those who'd shunned him for not believing the things they believed? Those who'd ostracised him, left him all alone, one tiny blue dot in a sea of red? What if the punishment he had in mind was awesome in scale, apocalyptic even?

And to inflict it, all he had to do was do nothing.

10:32
31 hours and 28 minutes remaining

Drew had gone upstairs to be as far from Megan as possible. She never seemed to leave that dining room anymore. She'd claimed it for herself. Fine. He would claim the bathroom then. He closed the door and paced the room, contemplating the illusionist. The fraud. The spy who posed as a ghost hunter, for reasons that still eluded him. Or maybe there was no reason for it atall. Maybe spies simply lied and cheated reflexively, whether deception was necessary or not. They might even lie to their overlords in the Home Office, paying lip service to its nominal conservatism while secretly cheering on its firmly entrenched leftist die-hards, whose telltale signs were the ongoing equality mantras and the 'diversity is strength' Orwellian bullshit. *Strength isn't diversity, you pricks. Strength is* unity. *Remember unity?* Not that Megan would have understood, or even cared. She would be too busy climbing that greasy pole, no doubt given constant leg-ups by some woke as fuck HR policy. Megan would never stop. She was too ambitious. She would go far, and all in the name of equality, or worse, *equity*. Communism in all but name. If they *called* it communism people would smell a rat, so of course they had to give it a nice, reasonable sounding name. That was the key trick. And never mind about the history. Never mind about the famines and the purges and the gulags. Just warn the kids about Hitler and leave it at that.

Drew rubbed his eyes. They burned with fatigue. At least there were no holes in the floor up here. Here he could stretch out properly and finally get some sleep. And sleep he did, as soon as he lay down.

He woke after what seemed like moments, but now there was something subtly different about the light in the room. Daylight still streamed in through the windows, but it seemed brighter, sharper. The other odd thing was that the walls looked different. The bricks were gone, replaced by horizontal wooden slats. He got up and went out onto the landing. There *was* no landing. He was outside. Outside in the camp, surrounded by wooden huts like the one he'd just emerged from. It was snowing again; a fresh covering lay thick on the stony ground. It never seemed to stop snowing in the camp.

The dream about the house at the end of the pier had been a vivid one, but now he remembered where he was, and what day it was, and his heart leapt. He looked out beyond the huts, at the barbed wire fences and the watchtowers. Uniformed women manned the towers, rifles slung over their shoulders, binoculars raised, on the lookout for detainees who weren't where they should have been. Drew wasn't where he should have been. Today was Volunteer's Day, and he had volunteered. Head down, hands in pockets, he trudged through the snow towards the muster point.

Shouts came from the women in the watchtowers. He'd been spotted. "You're late! Get moving!"

He quickened his pace. Up ahead in the exercise yard, a square of open space bordered by more huts, he heard the first shots. It had already begun.

Drew had thought long and hard about whether he should volunteer. Months ago, before he'd been taken to the camp, he would have balked at the idea, actively opposed it, claiming it was... he struggled to recall what he would have claimed it was. Those thoughts he used to have seemed impossibly distant now, like the vaguest of shapes glimpsed only through thick fog. And besides, he didn't especially *want* to recall those thoughts, because they were the very thoughts that had gotten him in trouble in the first place.

His new thoughts were better. Much better. There was a moral clarity about them which he found reassuring, comforting, and Volunteer's Day was the ultimate expression of that clarity. But why then, if it was such a no-brainer, had he pondered so long and hard about it? After all, dinos were sick in the head, everyone knew that, and the best way to cure a dino was to lead by example. Dinos were people who still clung to the old ways. They were few and far between, but they clung tight. So coddled had they been by those obsolete societal structures, so comfortable in their roles as oppressors, that when they'd finally realised the game was up, they'd screamed and screamed like spoilt little children. All power had been stripped away from them, to be distributed more evenly elsewhere. They really hadn't liked that atall. Well, tough. Drew knew he'd been one such child, once upon a time, but he'd grown up since then. He'd been part of the problem, and now he wanted to be part of the solution.

He arrived in the exercise yard to see that the queue of volunteers was already snaking around two huts. In the centre of the yard, at the head of the queue, the work itself was well under way. He found the back of the queue and joined it, waiting patiently while he shivered in the snow. Now that the moment was about to come, he felt elated. It was atonement after all, for his past sins, of which there had been many.

The queue moved quickly. As he shuffled closer to the centre of the yard, he turned and studied the faces of the men behind him. They looked hopeful, proud even. He knew what they were all thinking: *Don't be part of the problem. Be part of the solution.* His spirits were instantly lifted. There was solidarity here.

And then he recognised a face. At first he couldn't quite recall where he'd seen the man before (another shape in the fog) but eventually he did. He even remembered the man's name. *O'Brien. DCS O'Brien.* He couldn't remember what the letters DCS stood for, but he presumed they were the man's initials. Probably a David or a Daniel. O'Brien's eyes met Drew's for a fleeting moment, but there was no recognition in them, only hope and pride. Drew dimly recalled that he hadn't really liked O'Brien much. Why had that been? Something to do with their work. A case. O'Brien had been part of the solution, back when Drew had been part of the problem. Now they were both part of the solution. But still, somehow, the animosity lingered. O'Brien hadn't been a good man, Drew was sure of it. He'd been a bad man. A cowardly man.

He studied the faces of the other men in the queue. What was their collective sin? The thing they'd all done? They'd all made sexually suggestive comments about the guards, of course. Revenge by way of disrespect. But only in the early days, before re-education. These days, none of them would dare, nor even want to. No, there had been a much graver sin. What was it? Something about the way they all looked. Something about who they were... inherently? *Immutably.* Careful! Forbidden word! But what did it mean? He struggled to remember. Something like... unchangeable. Yes! The one thing none of them could ever change about themselves, no matter how hard they tried. *That* was their sin, and his.

For the first time, he noticed something strange about the expressions on the faces of those men. Though they all exuded pride, in a few of them there was something else behind the eyes. Fear. Meekness. *Cowardice.*

The revelation shook him awake. The hope wasn't real. The pride wasn't real. It was all an act. The inverse of what he'd assumed it to be. Could it be possible, then, that Volunteer's Day itself was the inverse of what it appeared to be? Could it be possible that the solution was in fact the problem, and vice versa?

Another gunshot, much closer and louder this time, echoed off the walls of the huts. It seemed to wake him further still, flip some sort of switch in his brain. A new, radical notion occurred to him: if everything was the inverse of what it appeared to be, then perhaps it was his duty to be a part of the problem, not the solution. Yes. That was it.

Be part of the problem.

He broke away from the queue and ran. Sort of. It was the closest thing to a run his malnourished body could manage. A flailing stagger towards one of the watchtowers. Here, the towers lay on his side of the fence. If he could get underneath one of them before the guards noticed, then perhaps he could climb up it and tackle one of the sentries. Seize a rifle. A foolish notion, he knew, but even if he didn't make it, his action might trigger something in the others.

Might just flip the switch in their brains too.

He was halfway to the tower when the first bullet pierced his spine. It came from behind, not from the sentry in the tower up ahead. That one had been slow, but one of the others hadn't. The pain was instantaneous. He staggered and twisted, then fell backwards into the snow. He tried to writhe in agony, but quickly learned that writhing made the pain even worse. Instead he lay still in agony, staring up. Big heavy snowflakes continued to fall. Black silhouettes against the bright white sky. It could just as well have been ash.

And then a human silhouette loomed over him. The guard's rifle was still in her hand, its barrel still smoking. A little out of breath, she peered down at her quarry, excited and curious to see how quickly Drew would die. How much he would suffer, and what his final expression would be. She knelt down beside him and tutted quietly. It was almost motherly.

"When you're shot in the head," she said, "there's no pain atall. Your brain doesn't have time to process it."

Drew read the tag stitched into the front of her uniform: *4079, Mallory, M.*

Very softly, she added: "That's why it's better to volunteer."

*

Enough was enough. She had procrastinated for far too long already. It was time to shift the focus of her investigation to the bedroom, where she knew Hale

176

would be more present. More responsive. *And more powerful?*

Megan shook the worrying thought from her mind. She picked up the laptop, the portable battery, and the connecting cable. She went out of the dining room, into the hallway and up the stairs. The bedroom door was wide open. Murky light from the grimy window lit the room, but just barely. The grandfather clock was still ticking away, reliable as ever. At the threshold, she hesitated. *Just do it.* She went in and placed the equipment on the floor. There was no other surface big enough. Except perhaps the bed... *No.*

She checked the cable connection. It was solid, but the battery was already half drained. She would need the second one. Glad to be out again, she went back downstairs to the dining room. The battery lay on the table. She felt a surreal urge to plug herself into it. She too was half drained. *Fully* drained. She sat down at the table. She fell asleep. When she woke she was still there, but the vibe was different.

She was in a restaurant. A candle-lit restaurant. Drew sat opposite her. He looked handsome in the soft mood lighting. He wore a suit and tie, its finer details hard to distinguish in the candlelight. It was certainly stylish, but was it a suit for work or for pleasure?

She glanced down at her own outfit; a flowing, elegant, shoulderless red dress. Her fingernails were finely manicured, painted a shade of red that perfectly matched the dress.

The cutlery was highly polished, as were the crystal wine glasses. Somehow she knew the bottle of red on the table was an expensive one. The restaurant felt at once cosy and luxurious, intimate and exclusive. It was... Italian? French? This too was hard to discern in the dim ambient glow of the candles.

They were sat by a window. Outside in the street, it was snowing heavily. Red phone boxes, black taxis and theatre lights said central London. The West End. Jolly theatre-goers trudged past in groups. Union Jacks flew from every lamppost.

Now she noticed the same symbol inside the restaurant; on bunting strung up along the walls. The waiter came to the table. A handsome young man in a starched white shirt under a black waistcoat. "Are you ready to order?" he asked with a pleasant smile. His accent was very English.

Megan perused the menu. As she visualised each dish, her mouth watered. This was an exclusive place alright. "I'll have the... how do you pronounce that?"

The waiter cocked his head at the menu. "Fish and chips, Madam."

Slowly, she repeated the words, lingered lovingly over every syllable. "Fish. And. Chips."

"Excellent choice." The waiter turned to Drew. "And for you, sir?"

"Steak and kidney pie."

"Very good."

"The kidney. Is it lamb?"

"But of course! *Young* lamb, sir. The very best."

Megan glanced out the window again. On the other side of the street, she saw a police van pull up outside an apartment building, right next door to the theatre that was still emptying out. Drew saw it too. He looked at his watch. In fact it was more than just a watch; very discreetly, he spoke into it. "Go. Go. Go."

Megan giggled at this. It excited her.

Outside, the van's rear doors were flung open, and a dozen armed policemen jumped out, their rifles at the ready. The last man out carried a small battering ram instead of a rifle. The other officers flanked him on either side as he approached the apartment building. He smashed the door off its hinges with two neatly timed shoves of the battering ram, and then the men were inside, storming up a flight of stairs. The commotion was attracting attention from people emerging from the theatre next door. Some of them lingered on the pavement, watching and waiting, stamping their feet to keep warm, grinning expectantly.

Through the restaurant window, the entire scene seemed to play out like a silent film. The other diners hadn't even noticed the unfolding drama. As the last armed officer disappeared up the stairs, Drew turned back to Megan. His eyes sparkled in the candlelight. "Sorry about that," he said. "You know how it is."

Megan nodded understandingly. "Do you always mix business with pleasure?"

"Only when I have to."

"If I didn't know better, I'd say you were doing it deliberately."

"Why would I do it deliberately?"

Megan blushed. "To impress me."

Drew grinned. "Is it working?"

Megan blushed deeper still, then smiled and looked away.

Their food arrived; little Union Jack flags planted in Megan's fish and Drew's pie. They thought of everything here. It all smelled delicious. Megan sighed contentedly. Drew attacked his steak and kidney pie without hesitation. He speared a piece of kidney with his fork and examined it in the candlelight, admiring its smooth, silvery sheen before popping it into his mouth.

Megan tried to slice the tail off her battered fish, but she couldn't. Either the fish was too tough, or the knife was too blunt. She wasn't sure which. She was about to call the waiter over when renewed activity outside caught her eye. The armed officers were leading an entire chain of suspects out of the apartments and into the back of the van. The prisoners were chained to each other by the ankles, their hands bound together with plastic cable ties, heads bowed submissively. There were young black men in shorts and t-shirts, shivering and barefoot in the snow. There were young Muslim women, some with hijabs, some without. Some were barely even dressed. Two of them carried babies. There were old men in traditional Pakistani dress. Old, young, male, female. People of all ethnicities. All except one. The onlookers from the theatre clapped and cheered as the detainees were bundled into the back of the van.

Drew saw it and smiled. "That's the last of them," he said. "The *very* last of them."

Megan was still trying to slice the tail off her fish. It looked perfectly fresh and succulent. The knife seemed perfectly sharp. Why wouldn't it cut?

"We've won, finally," said Drew. "We're pure again."

She gave up on the fish and beamed at Drew. Her man. Her hero.

Drew speared another piece of kidney, one that was still attached to a thin thread of white gristle. As he chewed on it, the thread slithered up over his lower lip and into his mouth.

Then, at last, he leaned in for the kiss.

*

Drew lay on his back in the bathroom, staring up at the ceiling. Why had he come in here? Why had he lain down? He got to his feet. As he did so he felt a sharp twinge of pain in his lower back. Unusual for him, but the injury, whatever it was, couldn't have been serious; the pain dissipated even as he noticed it.

He tried to recall the last thing he'd been doing in the house. After a moment it came to him.

The chimney. It seemed like just minutes ago he'd had that terrible fall into the water. But his clothes were already dry. He checked his watch. It was late morning. Monday. *Monday?* That couldn't be right. It was Sunday. Wasn't it?

MONDAY
11:43
6 hours and 17 minutes remaining

Megan was sat at the dining room table. She'd been
eating there with Drew a moment ago, but now
someone - Drew, presumably - had cleared all the
dishes away, and the table was bare once more. She
still had a knife in her hand, but it wasn't any sort of
knife for eating with. It was a large, rusty old
chopping knife she must've gotten from one of the
cabinet drawers. In front of her on the wooden table,
there were scratch marks whose length matched the
length of the blade. She'd been trying and failing to
slice something, but she couldn't remember what.
And if they'd just eaten, why was she so hungry?
Perhaps she'd been ravenous. Perhaps dessert was yet
to come. She tried to recall the main course, but
couldn't. The mood had been romantic, but with
something oddly disquieting bubbling away
underneath. There'd been candles and wine, but
outside there'd been a situation of some kind. Some
sort of...wait a minute... *romantic?!* Had Drew slipped
something into her drink?

She stood, just to prove to herself that she still could. She didn't feel dizzy or in any way drugged, just confused, dislocated. She looked out the window to orient herself. The sea was choppy, but at least it had stopped snowing.

*

Drew crossed the landing and went into the bedroom, looking for Megan. Some of her equipment lay on the floor, but she wasn't there. He was about to leave when he noticed the walls. Each and every brick had been checked off with a swipe of black marker pen. The whole point of marking those bricks had been to keep track of where he'd got to, but he was quite sure he hadn't checked *any* in the bedroom. So far, his efforts had been confined to the rooms downstairs. The living room. And he hadn't even finished *that* room. Or had he? Was his memory just shot? He went back out onto the landing. Here too the bricks had all been diligently marked off. He went back into the bathroom. Same story. His heart began to race as he went downstairs. Here, again, on every last brick in every damn wall he looked at, there was the neat little swipe of the pen. He could no longer be sure which bricks had really been checked, and which ones hadn't. *And that's the point, isn't it?*

There was one room he still hadn't looked in. The dining room. Megan's domain. The room he'd been reluctant to enter, because this, surely, was where he would find the culprit. The saboteur.

He pushed the door open warily. Here too the

184

bricks were all marked. Why would she have done it? To spite him? No. Worse. *To gaslight him.* Then he saw her. She was sat at the far end of the dining room table. She looked up, saw him. There was a glazed, distant look in her eye. She stood. She was holding a knife, but she barely seemed aware of it as she shuffled towards him. That was when he realised she was insane.

"Stay back," he said firmly.

She halted, then gestured at the walls with the knife. "I see you've been busy." Now she began toying with the knife, turning it round and round in her fingers. Not by the handle. By the blade. "Did you find your second hiding place?"

"No."

She scoffed. "What a surprise. Killed some time though, didn't it?"

"Ex*cuse* me?"

She resumed her slow shuffle in his direction. Thin streaks of fresh blood mingled with the rust on the blade.

"Stay back!"

She halted again. "Today's the day. Device goes off at six. Not long to go now. Why don't you put your feet up? Read a book or something?"

"What are you *talking* about?"

"You know damn fucking well what I'm talking about." She raised the knife and rushed at him.

She didn't get far.

With both hands, he went for her raised wrist,

caught it, twisted it. The knife clattered onto the table. He forced her onto the table too and pinned her there. "Alright," he snarled, "I've had it with your *shit*." He gestured at the walls. "What am I supposed to think? The ghost did it? Nice try."

"*You* did it!"

"Bullshit. It was all you. This. Everything. Magnets under the Ouija board..."

"What?!"

"Prosthetics on your cheek..."

"*What*?!"

"I want to know *why*."

"You're insane."

"*I'm* insane?"

The stalemate brought them both to silence. Megan looked drained, exhausted, all out of anger. Drew retreated a few paces backwards. Megan stayed down on the table top, but now she raised her head, propping herself up by her elbows. "Ever since we got here," she said, "you've done *nothing*."

"Nothing? What the hell do you think-"

"Nothing *useful*. Nothing like anything a detective would do." She swallowed before adding: "You *want* that device to go off."

"*What*?!"

"You want it to happen because-"

"I do *not*-"

"-because it's the only way you're ever gonna get the man who killed your wife." Now the glazed, distant look was back in her eyes. "And who cares if eight million more die in the process? They're mostly just foreigners." Suddenly the knife was back in her hand. "Just the kind of people you want *dead*." She raised the knife. She hurled it at him.

He ducked left. The knife shot past, inches from his right ear.

And then he was on her, pinning her down once more, spitting words so fierce they barely had any meaning. Her defensive blows barely registered as he slapped her hard across the face, once, twice. Then, fighting the urge to strangle her, he retreated and stood over her, wild-eyed, breathing heavily, waiting for the urge to subside, but it wouldn't. It just wouldn't.

In the end, it was Jenny who saved them both. *Be strong, Drew. Drew? Be strong.*

He forced himself to stay where he was. At last, bit by bit, the rage subsided.

Megan got to her feet, staggering away from the table, away from him. She went to the door, but didn't leave the room. Her bloodied hand just stayed there on the doorknob. Something - he wasn't sure what - kept her there. The empty look in her eye was gone, replaced by something sadder, more despairing. But at least there was *something* there now. Something other than a vacuum.

Drew sat down in a chair, saying nothing, doing nothing, thinking nothing. After a minute, she too came and sat down opposite him, saying nothing, doing nothing, just breathing and staring down at the floor. Why had she returned? He studied her. He watched her tightly knitted brow gradually unfurrow itself. As he did so, he felt his own features begin to loosen and relax. A weight being lifted. A shadow departing. He could no longer remember why they'd been fighting. The same confusion seemed to be present in Megan's eyes too. His breathing continued to slow in tandem with hers. Clouds parted in his mind. His thoughts became clear again.

So too did hers, enough for a new revelation to present itself. "Divide and conquer," she whispered.

Drew nodded vacantly, but the comment barely registered with him. He was already preoccupied with something else, staring past Megan over her shoulder. Staring at the knife she'd thrown. It was buried up to the hilt in one of the bricks in the wall behind her. Impossible, surely? And then he realised the brick wasn't a brick atall. It was another plywood facade.

11:56
6 hours and 4 minutes remaining

Drew's fingers closed around the knife handle.

Megan looked on.

He pulled. The brick-shaped wooden panel remained speared by the knife as it came away from the wall. He dropped it and peered inside the dusty alcove. The diary page he'd been hoping for wasn't there. But something else was. An oversized hardback book. He took it from its hiding place and held it in the light from the window to examine it. It was an illustrated children's book: *The Ugly Duckling*. It was old and dog-eared and time-weathered. The typeface had a dated, retro look to it. The cover illustration depicted the titular duckling after it had just hatched. It sat there inside the cup of the broken egg shell, more bits of shell atop its fluffy grey head. It looked bewildered by the hostile reactions of its yellow-feathered siblings, who were already cheeping in protest at the strange appearance of this new arrival. Mocking it for not being yellow like them.

"Seems like something Hale might've related to," Drew said, "once he was infected."

Megan nodded. "That thing on his cheek. That would've been ugly alright."

"But still... he was an adult. Why choose a kid's book?"

"Maybe it was his when he *was* a kid," Megan offered.

"I don't think so. That typeface is early Eighties, late Seventies at a push. He was already grown up by then."

"Well it must've been important to him. Important enough to hide."

"Right, but why? And where did he get it? Scarnish? London?"

Megan shrugged. "It's just a book, Drew. It might tell us something about his psychology, but that's all. It doesn't tell us anything we can use."

Drew flicked through the book from back to front, making sure there was nothing tucked between the pages. There wasn't. But when he got to the title page at the front, his eyes lit up. "I wouldn't be so sure about that."

"Why not?"

He grinned. "Because it's a library book."

*

Eileen had once had a life outside of work, but the memory of it was hazy and distant. These days, the combined office and waiting room on the fourth floor of Thames House was like a second home to her. A first home even. She'd been hankering for a fish tank, to complete the illusion of a dentist's waiting room. Something for Alec's guests to stare at while they contemplated other, bigger fish. But in recent weeks she'd noticed a steep decline in the number and frequency of Alec's visitors. In a way she was grateful (less vetting) but in another way it perturbed her. Shouldn't he have been seeing *more* people? The work never dried up though. Alec gave her a plentiful supply of it, and these days she barely even had time for lunch. She seemed to subsist on nothing but Yorkshire Tea and Tunnock's Caramel Wafers, and now, once again, it was time for her mid afternoon pick-me-up. Alec would probably want one too. She always liked to joke about how 'in synch' they were. But there were no wafers on her desk, in her special drawer, or anywhere else in her sparse little office. Had she left them in the kitchen?

She finished the sentence she was typing. A long, convoluted sentence. Alec's words. The one that began: *While a pre-emptive tactical strike with a 21 kiloton weapon and a 5.6 km blast radius might* seem *like an indefensible means of containment...* Alec never had been much of a stylist. She stood, stretched, and went out into the corridor, taking her swipe card with her.

As she shut the door behind her, her hand closed around something soft; a small plush toy, suspended from the door handle by a looped ribbon. How adorable! A little gift from their colleagues down the hall? About time too! She and Alec had been working *so* hard recently, in the run-up to the... *Don't think like that. Stay positive.* She reframed the thought.

In the recent busy period. Yes, that was better. She and Alec were always first to arrive and last to leave, but their colleagues in the adjoining offices hardly seemed to notice. Oh, it was all compartmentalised, of course. No one department knew much atall about the inner workings of any other department, even if they did share the same kitchen. It had to be that way for obvious reasons, but interactions with colleagues now seemed inexplicably confined to a terse 'Hello', when previously they had at least included banal comments about the weather. Perhaps the toy was a peace offering, then. Even if no-one else knew (nor should have known) exactly what Alec and Eileen were all about, perhaps word had somehow gotten out that their work was important, vital even. Perhaps the gift was intended as a morale booster. How lovely!

She took the stuffed toy from the door handle and examined it. It was embroidered to resemble a floating white sheet with eyeholes cut out of it. Her heart sank even as her blood began to boil. *Ha bloody ha.*

She went back into her office. *Let's see what Alec has to say about it. He'll raise hell, no doubt. They'll be sorry.* She went to his door, about to knock. She hesitated. *No.* Alec mustn't know. It would only demoralise him, just as it had demoralised her. He was already under *so* much strain, what with the operation in Barra on top of his own investigations in London. Barra, Scarnish, a larg it yandalo mor. Not to mention the 'difficult' new personalities he was handling. The brutish policeman and the silly young feminist. No, she would go above him instead. She would go straight to Patricia.

She went to the phone and dialled a four digit extension number. Patricia answered promptly, but with a sigh that seemed unwarranted considering she didn't yet know the reason for the call. "Eileen."

"Yes, hello. Sorry to bother you. I just wanted to report... I wouldn't call it *bullying* exactly, more..." She went on to describe the toy ghost, and where it had been left. Then she paused. In the background she could hear another voice beside Patricia's. It said something like 'That pair' before it was swiftly cut short.

"Go on," Patricia prompted, her voice cracking.

"Are you alright?"

"Yes, just a... Go on."

"Right, well I suppose it's meant to be a joke, but it's in *very* bad taste, and it shows that people down here have been ignoring protocol."

"Ignoring protocol."

"Gossiping. Someone outside this department seems to know more than they should. It's only a small thing, I know, and-"

"No, of course."

"-and I know we're only the 'three percenters' or what have you. But three percent is three percent, and I just feel-"

"Of course. I quite-" Patricia's voice faltered

again. A frog in her throat. "I quite agree. Leave it with me." She hung up.

Eileen sat perfectly still at her desk. The need for a caramel wafer had passed, replaced by a craving for gin. The voice in the background had been there again at the end, but this time there'd been no words to decipher; only an unrestrained howl of laughter.

11:58
6 hours and 2 minutes remaining

Drew passed the book to Megan. She studied the 'date of issue' ink stamps on the insert stuck to the title page. There were plenty; the first in January 1982, the last in the same month Hale had planted his device. The address of the issuing library was printed at the top of the insert. "Westminster Borough," she said. "London."

"Uh-huh."

"You think Hale checked the book out?"

Drew shook his head. "He was on the run, living off the grid, such as the grid was back then. Joining a library would've been a dumb move. Hale wasn't dumb. Anyway, the issue date's off. April second. Two weeks *before* he came to London. No, I reckon someone else checked it out, and Hale stole it from them. I need to know who that person was." He took back the book. "I need to call Alec."

He went out into the hall. Megan followed. He was almost at the front door when the nearby wardrobe moved by itself. It skittered across the floorboards, juddering violently as it went, before coming to rest in front of the door.

Drew froze. The initial shock of it set his heart racing. Fear and cynicism vied for supremacy within him. Cynicism won out. *More tricks.* But Megan was still behind him. *Then how?* He went closer to the wardrobe, looking for the invisible thread, the wire, whatever the damn mechanism was. When he found it, he would shift the wardrobe and be on his way. There was no time for anything else. Recriminations could come later.

He was within three feet of the wardrobe when someone - someone unseen - pushed him backwards; a violent shove to the chest that was so powerful it actually lifted him off his feet. The book went flying out of his hand. He fell back, hit the floor and stayed there, winded, staring up at the flaking ceiling. Then he sat up and found his breath, eyes darting here and there in search of his assailant. It wasn't the first time he'd been accosted like that. Far from it. Even now, his instinct was to get up and give chase, tackle the fucker and make the arrest. Deploy the chokehold if necessary, or even if not. But there was no-one to chase. No-one to arrest. He'd been pushed by... by...

Megan came and knelt beside him. There was a strange mix of fear and remorse in her eyes. "Drew, I'm sorry, that was-"

"Someone pushed me."

"It was my fault."

She wasn't hearing him. "Someone *pushed*

me," he repeated.

"I was afraid he'd try and stop you," she replied. "That's what gave him the power to do it. It's my fault."

"But there was no-one there." His heart was beating like a jackhammer. "*There was no-one there.*"

Megan seemed to notice something in his tone, something she didn't like, and her expression shifted; a new and terrible realisation dawning on her. "You were right!" she blurted, suddenly panicked. "About everything."

Daylight had been streaming in through the grimy windows, and up in vertical shafts through the holes in the floor. But now it began to fade. Heavy weather outside making its presence known. It was moving in fast. Yet the sound that would normally have accompanied it - the whistling of the wind beneath the floorboards - was absent.

And now there was something else in Megan's voice, her eyes. Something that didn't suit her atall. Desperation. "I faked all of it," she said. "I'm a fraud, Drew."

Her abrupt *volte-face* - a hastily improvised deception - didn't fool him for a moment. He shook his head. "No. No, no, no-"

"It's true. You were right. Magnets under the Ouija board. Makeup on my cheek. And the wardrobe... the wardrobe has a-"

He grabbed her by the shoulders. "I don't care about the wardrobe, I'm telling you someone *pushed* me, and there was *no-one fucking there!*"

Megan's face was a mask of despair. She had nothing left.

"It's real, isn't it?" Drew whispered.

"No," she replied weakly.

Her lack of conviction only fuelled his burgeoning hysteria. "Jesus Christ, it's *real!*"

The room continued to darken. When Megan spoke again, there was a renewed sincerity in her voice. A raw urgency. "This room's his, Drew. Find another way out. *Quickly.*"

"There isn't one."

"There is. The fireplace."

Drew remembered his fall through the chimney stack, how close he'd come to knocking himself out on the crossbeam. "It's a deathtrap in broad daylight, let alone..." He paused. The room had grown darker still. He surveyed the hallway. One by one, the vertical shafts of light disappeared, snuffed out like candles. "...at night."

"But it's not..." Megan's words trailed off as she too noticed the light disappearing, the windows blackening. Whatever lurked outside, it was no thundercloud.

Though the hallway was now almost pitch black, there was still one last hole in the floor with a shaft of daylight shining up out of it. Impossible, but there it was. A literal ray of hope. A way out. Drew went over and peered down through the hole. For a brief moment, he saw the churning waves below, grey and frothing and vivid in the brightness of day. But then that light too was extinguished, the watery scene fading to black like a film coming to an end. The darkness wasn't a shadow of something else. It was a thing unto itself. And it was hungry.

Until that moment, Drew had never been truly terrified. The sensation was far more profound than mere fleeting fright. True terror lay in knowing that the thing that was coming for you could not even be understood, let alone conquered. But a modicum of enlightenment came along with that terror. At least now he understood why Megan had been so afraid when he hadn't. Her fear wasn't a phobia. It was entirely rational, born not from *lack* of experience, but from a *wealth* of it. By contrast, his own relative composure had been maintained only through sheer, blissful ignorance. She'd tried to warn him about the nature of feeder spirits, but he hadn't listened, hadn't understood. Not really. Well, now he did. Now he knew why, just moments ago, she'd tried to change her story. She'd been trying to keep him sceptical, ignorant, and therefore fearless. She'd been trying to avert the very thing that was now happening. *Twice the fear. Twice the power.*

Drew and Megan stood together, perfectly still in the perfect dark.

"He's in here with us," Megan said, "and he's out there too."

Drew nodded. "He's everywhere."

199

12:02
5 hours and 58 minutes remaining

Once, when Drew was staying with friends in Yorkshire, he'd visited a disused coalmine, repurposed as a tourist attraction. He vividly remembered the moment at the bottom of the mine shaft when the tour guide had switched off his head torch, and urged everyone in the group to do the same, in order to give them all a thrill. The darkness had been total. All-consuming. Yet even the pitch black of that mine hardly seemed comparable to the darkness that now surrounded him and Megan. It was like standing submerged in a huge vat of thick, black, magically breathable ink.

Together, they shuffled blindly over to the staircase, avoiding the holes in the floor as best they could. They sat next to each other on the bottom step.

"I don't get it," Drew said. He was whispering, though he wasn't sure why. "I thought he *wanted* me to leave."

Megan's disembodied voice - an equally low whisper - came back at him out of the dark. "He does. Just not with the info you found in that book."

"Well I'm all out of ideas."

They sat there in silence for a moment. Then Megan said: "Okay, this is kind of unethical, but..." She hesitated.

"What?"

When she finally replied, she was no longer whispering. "Fuck it. Everyone in my field knows it, they just won't admit it."

"Admit what?"

"Feeder spirits draw their power from fear. Sometimes that fear - that power - gets out of hand. When it does, you've got two options. One is to leave. Run away."

"We can't. Anywhere we try and go, he'll be there to stop us."

"Option two then."

"Which is?"

"Cut off the power source."

"You've lost me."

"Break open the whiskey is what I'm saying, Drew."

He smiled. The logic was impeccable. He took the small bottle from his jacket pocket. It was already half empty. He opened it, took a slug and passed it to Megan. She took a swallow and grimaced. "That is *rank*."

"Uh-huh."

After that, they didn't talk for a while. They just passed the bottle back and forth between them, each taking long slugs until it was almost empty.

Lazily, Megan said: "Why don't you tell me about Jenny?"

Drew groaned. "Another bloody grief therapist. Brilliant."

"I don't mean the bad stuff. I mean the good stuff. The happy stuff."

Drew shrugged. "She was a wind-up merchant, like me." His mind drifted to another world. One he still yearned for. "We didn't get much time together. Not really. I was always working when she was off, or the other way round. One time we managed it though. Two whole days. And of course the weather was shit. All we did was watch Netflix. It was nice though. We watched some cheesy action film. Jenny got bored. She went out into the garden to feed the rabbit. We never could agree on a name for it. I only gave it a name after she…" He waved his hand, dismissing the thought. "Anyway, she was out there for ages, and it was *pissing* down. She was missing all the best bits. When she came back in she was drenched, but she didn't seem bothered. I asked her what she'd been doing, and she said: 'Thinking'. Imagine that. Standing outside in the pouring rain, just thinking. Then she told me she was pregnant. Six weeks. She was worried I wouldn't be happy about it. God knows why. The thing was, Jenny worked a really rough patch. Gangs everywhere. Not to mention that…" Again he waved the word away. "I didn't want her out there doing that with our baby inside her. Nor did she. So I said look, give 'em a month's notice, then quit. She said 'Yeah, that's what I was thinking about in the garden.' It was no big deal really. I was making good money, y'know? She knew I'd look after her. Anyway, next day she went back to work. Early shift. *Really* early. She was up in the middle of the night. Never woke me up though. She was good like that. That was the night she died."

Megan remained silent.

He didn't mind. When people told him they were sorry, it rarely rang true. And besides, telling the story had felt good. Like a release. "So that's Jenny," he said. "What about you? Anyone special in-"

"No."

Her abrasive tone rocked him a little. "Okay." But now he was curious. "That day we first met, in Alec's office. His assistant. Eileen. She said something to you, something harmless, but it made you flinch."

"I can't remember. What did she say?"

"She said: *Fancy a cuppa.*"

It was too dark to see if Megan had flinched again, but he guessed she had.

Megan sighed. "It's what Charlie used to say."

"Charlie?"

"My ex. He said it-" she spoke through gritted teeth, "-*all the fucking time.*"

"Ha! Too nice, was he?"

"*Way* too nice. He started to creep me out. So I dumped him, but he wouldn't accept it. He seemed to think I *must* be interested, even though I kept saying no. He stalked me for a while. It was weird, like... all along I'd been dating some guy in a mask, and the mask was what I fell in love with, and then one day it fell off, and underneath it was... the *opposite* of the mask." Almost casually, she added: "He tried to rape me." She said it with no apparent emotion other than vague disappointment. As if she'd said *We're out of eggs.* "That's why I'm... the way I am."

"Prickly?"

"I'm not-" She paused. "Alright. Yeah. I suppose. Anyway, Charlie's in jail now. Fuck him."

"Right. Fuck him."

Dimly, Megan remembered there had been some sort of point to all this; to their drinking the alcohol. She stared off into the darkness, hoping her eyes might have finally adjusted to it, but they hadn't. There was nothing to adjust to. Not even the vaguest of shapes by which to orient herself. Normally it would have frightened her; anything could have been out there. But in her present state of inebriation, it wasn't frightening at all. It was only dizzying. Her head found Drew's shoulder, and the dizziness went away.

Drew felt the gentle pressure on his shoulder. He was grateful for it. He stared off into the pitch black hallway. For a moment, he thought he saw movement in the dark, a vague outline of something tall and looming. He closed his eyes. The shape was still there behind his eyelids, but only for half a second before it faded into nothing. *Don't be an idiot,*

204

Drew, Jenny said. *You're just pissed.* He opened his eyes again. Megan's head was still on his shoulder. He was still grateful for it.

"So what did you call the rabbit?" she asked.

Drew grinned. "Starsky."

It took a moment for Megan to get the joke. When she finally did, she laughed. The sound of it surprised him. It was gentle and youthful, sincere and warm.

"He'll need feeding by now," he muttered forlornly.

"You know what?" Megan said. "That reminds me..."

And suddenly there was light. A small rectangle of bright white light, hovering shakily in front of Megan. A handheld device. An iphone.

12:27
5 hours and 33 minutes remaining

Drew's eyes widened. "Please tell me that's not what I think it is."

"Yes and no."

Drew shook his head in disbelief. "Is there a signal?"

She checked the screen. "Yes, but-"

"Give it to me."

"You're not listening."

"Give." Drew took the phone and dialled a number. Nothing happened. The numbers he'd typed didn't even appear on the screen. "It's not working."

"I was trying to tell you."

"How do you... is it Facetime? Messenger? What's the app?"

"There *is* no app. At least-"

"Then how?"

"You can't."

"But there's a signal!"

Megan sighed. "The signal denotes wireless connectivity, but only within a thirty foot radius."

"Thirty *feet*? What use is that?"

Megan took the phone back. "I told Alec I needed my phone to activate certain... *functions*, on those nodes I stuck to the walls. Hence thirty feet. He said no. No phones allowed in case-" she hiccupped, "-in case one of us gets infected, tries to spread the trigger phrase. I told him it wasn't so much the phone I needed, just one app *on* the phone. An app I designed myself. He said 'give us your phone, and we'll copy your app onto a secure device'." She waved the phone in the air. "This is what they gave me. No calls, no texts, no internet, just my app, and a few others they didn't bother to disable because-" she hiccupped again, "-because they're not comms apps. Those are self-contained. Already secure."

"Then we're still fucked?"

"We're still fucked."

Drew groaned, rubbed his forehead. He checked the whiskey bottle. There was still a little left. He took another swig and passed it to Megan.

She downed the last of it, no longer grimacing as she swallowed. "What were we talking about?"

"Your shit phone."

"Before that."

"The rabbit. Something about the rabbit made you think of the phone."

"Oh!" Now she was giddy, excitable. "Okay, check this out..." She tapped an app launcher on the phone. "This thing comes with ten songs. Ten!"

"You're blowing my mind."

"One song for each decade since the

Twenties. This one... the Sixties song... this one is *so* cool." She cued up the track and pressed play. A bass guitar picked out a rhythmic little melody. Soon it was accompanied by a militaristic snare drum. Still clutching the phone, she got to her feet. Lit from below by the screen, she looked at once sinister and beautiful.

Drew knew the song well, though he couldn't recall the title or the band. The lead guitar came in. A sultry, swirling, mind-expanding counterpoint to the snare drum. He watched Megan begin to move, her eyes closed, head swaying smoothly, blissfully. A Woodstock heart born out of time. He stood, wanting to be level with her. Closer.

Lyrics came, Lewis Carroll-infused. Pills. Alice. Rabbits. The woman's voice was ethereal, yet precise and urgent. Megan opened her eyes, found Drew in front of her. Her pupils dilated. She mimed words at him; caterpillars and chessboard men. They drew nearer to each other.

From somewhere out in the dark came the first faint little taps, knocks, rattles and scrapes. They were discordant, arrhythmic, atonal, at odds with the music. But neither Drew nor Megan noticed. The hookah haze that now enveloped them was far too potent.

The song grew louder, more insistent, mushrooms and dormice coming to life in the maelstrom, dancing in a circle around them. He and Megan drew nearer still, hearts racing, scents intermingling. A cocktail of desire and backwards words, lust and lopped off heads.

The taps and knocks grew louder, competing with the music for attention and getting none. The staircase shook. The walls vibrated. Still they were ignored.

The song reached its head-feeding, looking glass-shattering crescendo.

The white knight kissed the red queen.

Their lips parted as the song drew to a close. But the walls continued to shake. Drew retreated a little, wanting to stay swimming in her eyes, but dimly aware now that something was wrong. Behind Megan, the staircase tapered off into the dark. Her smile faded as her ponytail rose into the air, lifted by invisible hands. Drew saw it, reached out for her, but too late. She was already on her back, on the stairs, flailing, screaming, her spine cracking off the edge of each step as the unseen thing dragged her by the hair, up, up, up. The phone was still in her hand, spotlighting her agonising progress. Now she was at the top, on the landing, still on her back, still being dragged, into the black rectangle of an open doorway. Then she was through it, and *Bang!* The bedroom door slammed shut.

12:35
5 hours and 25 minutes remaining

Drew charged up the stairs after Megan.

How was it even possible? They'd weakened it, hadn't they? There'd been no fear, only... *Shit. Of course.* Megan's warning echoed in his mind. *You don't want to be around a feeder when its eyes start turning green.*

He reached the bedroom door, turned the handle and pushed. It wouldn't budge. It couldn't have been locked. There *was* no lock. He shoulder barged it, but someone very strong - stronger than Drew - was pushing back from the inside. He tried a kick and got the same result. He hammered on the door, calling out to Megan. No answer came. He wracked his brains for a solution, remembered something else she'd told him: *They can't be in two places at once.* It was no solution to the *current* problem, but maybe...

Fuck it. Better than nothing.

He called to Megan through the door. "I'll be back soon, okay?" Still no answer came. "Megan?" Silence. "Don't worry, I'll get you out. I promise."

He hurried back down the stairs. In the

hallway, the unnatural darkness was rapidly receding, daylight taking its place, streaming in through the windows and up through the holes in the floor. The front door was still blocked by the wardrobe. Previously it had been guarded by unseen forces, but now, surely...

Yes! The empty wardrobe was easily moveable. He tipped it over and shoved it away to one side. Hale was weak, he realised. Not in the sense of lacking power - he had plenty of that - but in the sense that he had allowed his desire for Megan to distract him, long enough for Drew to escape with the book. But where *was* the book? It had flown from his hand when Hale had pushed him...

He scanned the floorboards, and immediately he saw it. It was right in front of him, teetering on the edge of a hole in the floor. Teetering, because the rotten wooden plank it half rested on was the same plank Drew's right foot rested on. His shifting weight was... *Shit.* He froze in panic. Then, without moving his feet, he crouched down as slowly and smoothly as he could, trying to keep his weight distribution just the same. The whiskey betrayed him. He wobbled slightly, tilting the plank, and the book slid further out over the edge of the hole. It wasn't stopping. *Fuck.* He dived for it. Splinters bit into his wrist as he went, but he caught the falling book by one corner. He rolled away to one side and got to his feet, his wrist stinging, but still clutching his prize. He picked the splinters out of his skin as best he could while he memorised the library name, the last issue number and the issue date. Then he went outside with the book.

The weather was calm, dry and bright. High white clouds overhead. A balmy stillness in the air. It was almost inviting. But when he stepped off the pier and into the village, heading for *The Crofter's Fate*, the sense of being watched was keener than ever. He glanced up at the first floor windows of the houses he passed. No curtains twitched, but only because they were fully drawn back. And in each and every window, someone was there, grimly monitoring his progress; a thin old woman with long white hair, a fat bearded man and his snarling German Shepherd, a sullen little girl with smears of chocolate around her mouth. All of them stood quite still, staring, like Victorians posing for a photograph. *They're not hiding anymore.* Why not? What had changed? He could have knocked on any or all of their doors, forced entry even, but without their phones they were no use to him. That was what he told himself as he nervously picked up his pace.

He arrived at the pub and tried the door. It was unlocked, possibly open for business. It was hard to tell. He went inside. The bar was empty, but the television on the wall was playing, volume down low. It was TV news, a channel Drew hated. A stern female presenter held court, playing two opposing pundits off each other, eager to interrupt the one she didn't like. Drew looked closer at the screen. There was something odd about the presenter's face; black-eyed stalks sprouting from a fleshy wound in her cheek. But neither she nor the two pundits had noticed. They all just continued to talk over each other. Drew screwed his eyes shut. *You're still drunk.* When he opened them again, the woman's face was back to normal.

He went behind the bar to make his call to Alec. He thought he heard a bell ring, but there was no bell anywhere in sight. *Christ, you'll be seeing pink elephants next.* Recalling the voicemail procedure seemed to push the issue number out of his mind. He tucked the phone under his chin while he flipped open *The Ugly Duckling,* looking for the library insert.

Behind him, something went *Slam!* Wood hitting stone. He whirled round. The trapdoor lay open. Angus was already up and out, charging him, a cosh raised high. He brought it down hard and fast, and everything went away.

*

Megan lay perfectly still on the bed. Hale didn't like it when she moved. She'd learnt that lesson the hard way. Until a moment ago she'd been afraid to move even her eyes, but now her courage returned, if only in part. She glanced down at the floor, at the glow of her laptop screen. Zenaframe was still up and running. A live feed from the bedroom. There were two stick figures in the room; hers, horizontal on the bed, and his, standing in front of the door, guarding it while he watched her. She couldn't yet see him in reality, in the room itself, only on the computer screen. He hadn't yet materialised, but it was only a matter of time. She knew this because she could already hear him. He was whistling. An old show tune she recognised. *Get Me To The Church On Time.*

The stick figure began to move. It crept away from the door, towards the bed. Towards her own stick figure. She tensed as it knelt beside her.

Then came the trembling whisper in her ear: "*Ding dong, the bells are gonna chime.*"

She could smell his breath. It was rancid. "Get away from me," she hissed.

The stick figure retreated, but only a little. "It's my breath, isn't it?" the voice said. Its tone was apologetic yet mocking. Gentle yet malicious. "A side effect of the infection. Not much I can do about it." The stick figure stood up again, adopted a thinking pose. "Unless..."

Megan kept her eyes glued to the screen. It was still a partial comfort to her; reality with a frame around it. Reality contained. But now something outside the frame was fighting for her attention. Something that shimmered in the dark, before turning solid and lacklustre. She tore her eyes from the screen and looked.

He was right there in front of her. He looked awful, even worse than when last she'd seen him. His long brown hair was greasy and lank, parted in the middle over his prematurely wrinkled forehead. His skin was a greyish red, eyes bloodshot but still just as wide, just as eager to please.

Her mouth fell open. She shook her head. "No, no, no, no-"

"Alright Meg, chill out. It's only me."

"-no, no, no-"

Though his health had clearly deteriorated, his smile was still the same; intense and desperate, the underlying terror barely concealed. She couldn't believe it. Even now, he was still trying to keep up the pretence. Trying to convey 'happy-go-lucky' and conveying just the opposite. He never stopped trying, did Charlie.

"-no, no, no-"

He came closer, placed a cold, clammy hand on her forearm. "Fancy a cuppa?"

*

The handheld biometric fingerprint reader was the bane of Pawel's working life. Something they'd brought in to make the job that little bit harder, because it just wasn't hard enough already. Back in the day, roll call had been simple; one of the few times when he could let his guard down, at least to some extent, since the prisoners were already locked in their cells. All it used to take was a swift glance through the window, and *Spełniony!* Done. Another name checked off the list. Sometimes he would even exchange a few pleasantries with the prisoners. Only with the more civil ones, of course, and then only briefly. It didn't pay to get too friendly. But at least there had been that human element to it.

Well, now those days were gone, and all thanks to the 'not so magic wand'. In theory it was still a simple enough procedure. Prisoners would extend their hands - palms up - through the door hatches, and wait until they were scanned. The wand's function was to cross-reference the fingerprints it collected with those already on the prison database, thereby ensuring that the right prisoner was in the right cell, and that none were absent. But of course the damn thing kept playing up - buffering and losing its wireless connection to the database - sometimes for a minute or more. It was a constant thorn in Pawel's side, especially when he was under time pressure, as he increasingly was these days.

Now his heart sank as he surveyed the long row of hands poking out through the door hatches, many of them twitching impatiently. Once scanned, they swiftly retreated again. So far so good. But as Pawel approached cell D19, he saw the dreaded circular swirl appear on the screen. "Kurwa," he muttered. *Fuck sake.* Hopefully the thing would soon fix itself. D19's occupant hadn't yet presented his hand anyway. At last the buffering ended. *D19 - Maddigan, Charles Dexter* popped up on the screen. Underneath was Maddigan's date of birth, and a summary of his 'red flag' events since he'd been detained. A red flag event could mean a physical altercation with a prison officer or another prisoner, or verbal abuse, or any otherwise erratic behaviour. Maddigan had no red flag events. So far he'd been a good boy, but still, Pawel didn't like him one bit. He didn't like him because he'd just read the third and final nugget of information: the offences. Though Maddigan was hardly a career criminal - he'd only committed three offences in his entire life - they were just the kind of thing that made Pawel's skin crawl; harassment (two counts) and attempted rape (one count). And the bastard *still* hadn't put his palm out through the hatch.

"D nineteen! Maddigan!" Nothing happened. "Wakey wakey! Eggs and pork." Still no hand appeared. *Kurwa*. Keeping a good metre back from the cell door (he'd learnt that lesson long ago), Pawel peered through the window into cell D19.

Charlie Maddigan was sat on the edge of his bed, upright and perfectly poised, head tilted back, face up towards the ceiling. For a moment, bizarrely, Pawel thought: *Yoga*. But he quickly dismissed the idea. Nothing in Yoga, he was sure, involved rolling one's eyes so far back in their sockets that only the whites remained visible.

*

"Come in, Eileen." Alec said it flatly, without the jokey sing-song lilt. The knock at the door had been hard, insistent. Nothing like her usual gentle tap.

The door opened. It wasn't Eileen. As the DG walked in, Alec couldn't help but gulp. Rather than calling or summoning Alec to his office upstairs, he'd made the trip down in person. It was unheard of. As the door swung closed, Alec caught a glimpse of

217

Eileen at her desk. She looked fraught; dabbing her eyes with a tissue. The DG sat opposite Alec and propped his feet up on the desk. He put his hands behind his head and reclined, as if lounging by the pool, though his face was stern. He was mid fifties, tall, gangly, balding but very fit and tanned. The feet on the desk agitated Alec, but he said nothing.

"I won't waste your... time," the DG said.

He nearly said 'valuable'.

"Your department is obsessed with ghosts, Alec. The stuff of fiction. Stuff we can't afford."

Alec sighed wearily. *Could his timing be any worse?* "More cuts, is it?"

"I don't mean financially. I mean reputationally."

Hours away from a global catastrophe and he's worried about his reputation. "As you're *well* aware," Alec said, "it's rather late in the game, so at this point we're throwing everything we've got left at the problem, including parapsychology. Everything our ever shrinking budget permits. Would you rather we didn't bother?"

The DG bristled at Alec's impertinence. "I'd rather you threw a literal kitchen sink than a ghost hunter. Honestly? It's embarrassing. I'm embarrassed *for* you."

"Then please tell me what we should be doing instead that we haven't tried already. With thirty years behind us, and a few hours left, tell me. What would be *less* embarrassing?"

"Hours left, according to single source-"

"Oh for Christ-"

"-single source *low grade* intel, Alec! Call me conservative, but I'm not inclined to drop a nuke on Trafalgar Square just because some failed magician with mental health issues sent us a scary postcard. I can't be*lieve* you suggested *that.*"

"Evacuate first, *then* nuke."

"Oh, well in that case, my bad! Should we evacuate the pigeons too? Floating signposts in the sky, telling them where to go? How hard can it be?"

"I was simply outlining the only realistic options for containment."

"Sorry, I'm a bit..." He tugged his earlobe. "Did you say *realistic*?"

"I said-"

"You *did*, didn't you?" He leaned in towards Alec. "Now you listen to me, you dangerous little shit. The source intel's been downgraded. Again. You and Eileen aren't the three percenters anymore. You haven't been for years. As of now, you're the *zero point zero* three percenters. Understand?"

"You're making a bad mistake."

"Am I? Well I guess we'll see about that, won't we? A few hours from now, we'll see. In the meantime, there'll be no 'tactical' strike, and no evacuation. Turner and Mallory are all you've bloody well got."

13:22
4 hours and 38 minutes remaining

Drew woke to find himself tied up. The rope was thick and long, wound tight around his chest and the back of the chair he sat on. His arms were down at his sides, held there by the rope. The force of the constriction was immense. It was an effort to even breathe, let alone move.

He was in the cellar beneath the bar. No other place it could have been. It was lit by a single bare lightbulb that swung gently in a draft. Shadows from the nearby whiskey barrels moved across the floor in time with the swinging bulb, shortening then lengthening, like grasping fingers. An empty sleeping bag lay on a mattress in one corner. Was Angus sleeping down here? Why? Next to the mattress, a flight of wooden steps led up to the trapdoor behind the bar. But the trapdoor was firmly shut. Taped to its underside was one end of a length of string, its other end weighed down by a small bell that hung over the mattress. *That* was why. The bell was an improvised alarm, intended to alert Angus when someone up above was on the trapdoor, which you had to walk over to get to the phone. Drew had heard it ring right before Angus had coshed him. But the time before that, when he'd called Alec and O'Brien… that time it *hadn't* rung. This setup was a new innovation, then. A response to his first break-in. A worrying shift in the barman's state of mind.

Now, the shadows from the beer barrels were swallowed by a larger shadow still. The shadow of a man. Angus stood in front of him, cradling a shotgun. "Say it and I'll kill us both," he said.

"Say what?" Drew's throat was parched, his voice rasping.

"Don't pretend you don't know."

"The trigger phrase?"

Angus gave a confused frown.

"The words. The special words."

"Aye. The words."

"I haven't heard them. I haven't seen them."

Angus raised the shotgun. "Liar!" he snarled. "You've been up there for days now. No-one leaves that house without hearing them."

"Then I could infect you just like that. So why haven't I? And why haven't you killed me already?"

Angus lowered the shotgun again. "Because I can't do it without…" he swallowed hard, choking back some powerful emotion, "…without giving you a good honest reason. If I'm gonna take a man's life, I reckon I owe him that much."

Drew nodded slowly. "Tell me." He turned his wrists, testing the tautness of the rope.

221

Angus caught the movement and raised the weapon. "Keep your hands still, mind!"

Drew complied. The ropes were far too taut anyway.

Angus lowered the gun again. "I had twin daughters," he said. "Kayleigh and Bridie. Both seventeen."

Drew remembered the photo behind the bar.

"Kayleigh was sensible. Mature. Bridie... not so much. It was her idea for them to go up to the house, just for a thrill. They weren't there more than half a day, but half a day was all it took. When they came back, Kayleigh was quiet. Sullen. But Bridie was just the opposite. She was... excitable. She kept saying to Kayleigh: shall we tell him? Let's tell him! And Kayleigh kept shaking her head, saying: don't you dare. I didn't know what they were on about. Didn't even ask. There's some things you just don't ask teenage girls, y'know? If they want to confide, they will. If they don't, they won't. Anyway, next day they caught the rash. Both of them had it in the same place, on the face. The cheek. They were itching and scratching, the pair of them, couldn't leave it alone. I tried giving them ointment, creams, everything, but it kept getting worse. Then the stalks came out. Awful black-eyed things. That was when I pressed them to find out what they'd been up to. Kayleigh told me they'd been up to the house, and a man there had... *whispered* something to them."

So Five had been right to worry about Hale

being 'premature'. Thirty years was a long time to wait, even when you were dead. *You just couldn't hold out, could you?*

"I was about ready to go up there myself," Angus said, "find him and kill him, but Kayleigh said it wouldn't do any good, on account of his being... *there but not there.* Then Bridie started up again: 'Shall we tell him? Let's tell him!' But Kayleigh kept saying no."

This too piqued Drew's interest. Kayleigh and Bridie had each reacted differently to the infection. One of them had wanted to spread it, and one of them hadn't. Was this what those scientists had meant by 'type A' and 'type B'?

"And Bridie listened," Angus continued. "She actually listened! Bless her heart for that. For trying hard to be good, not wanting to hurt her da, even though she was itching for me to... *see the light.* But Kayleigh knew Bridie better than I did. She knew Bridie wouldn't last much longer. That urge in her, the urge to spread the words, it just kept getting stronger. So Kayleigh... killed Bridie. God forgive her, that's what she did. And then she took her own life on top of that. God forgive them both. She had to do it, though. She had to. It was the only way to be sure. The only way to spare the rest of us. And now we do it too. Me, the two lads you met the other night, them and everyone else in Scarnish. We've all made a pact. A promise. Kayleigh's Law, we call it. Anyone who goes up to that house, anyone who even tries... that's

223

why those lads brought down your helicopter, and that's why I'm doing what I'm doing this minute. Anything to stop that thing from spreading, because God help the whole world if it does."

Drew swallowed. It hurt. He tried to keep his voice sounding strong. Calm but strong. "What about Baines? The man who was here two weeks ago?"

"Dead for just that reason."

"You killed him?"

Angus nodded. "But it wasn't murder. Not really."

"Was there anything on him? Papers?"

Angus just shrugged.

"Where's the body?"

"That I can't tell you."

"Why not?"

"He was infected."

"But he's dead. He can't spread it when he's dead."

"I'm not willing to take that risk. If you'd *seen* him..." Both his hands were back on the shotgun now.

Drew's breathing quickened. The ropes seemed to tighten even more. "Angus, hear me out. Okay? Hear me out. There's a chance I can end this thing for good, for *all* of us, but to do that... I need to make a phone call."

Angus shook his head. "You've had your good honest reason. That's all I owe you."

"Wait! Just-"

"I'm sorry, Detective. Like I said..." He levelled the shotgun at Drew. "It's not murder." His finger curled around the trigger. "It's containment."

13:28
4 hours and 32 minutes remaining

Drew tipped his chair back a split second before the shot rang out. The deafening report came at the exact same moment the back of his head hit the floor. The effect on Drew was illusory; a light bump disguised as a skull-shattering concussion. Dazed and disoriented, he lay there on his back, still tied to the chair, still sat in it, but now with his feet in the air. The rope around his chest felt looser though. Much looser. He soon realised why. Hard contact with the stone floor had broken the chair's back support; the single wooden slat around which the rope had been tied. The slat now lay in pieces, sandwiched between the floor and his back. He rolled over onto one side, taking the remains of the chair with him, loosening the rope even more. He shimmied out through the loops. He was ready to spring to his feet when the next jarring blow landed on his right shin bone. Tears flooded his eyeballs. He howled.

Angus loomed over him with the shotgun. No more shells, but no matter; now he held it by the barrel, wielding it like a cudgel. Drew rolled aside, dodging the follow-up blow. The butt sparked off the floor. As Angus raised the weapon for a third try, he made a mistake. He planted his feet either side of his supine prey, presenting Drew with an obvious target. Drew brought his leg up hard and fast, his toecap connecting sharply with the barman's groin. Now Angus howled. He dropped the shotgun, doubling up in pain.

At last Drew was on his feet. He picked up the gun, wielding it like Angus had. He circled his whimpering opponent, calculating where best to strike next. He went for a head shot, missed, caught him on the shoulder instead. Angus staggered but stayed upright. Drew swung the shotgun back the other way. This time the butt connected with his ribcage, producing a sharp crack. Still he wouldn't go down. Drew jabbed the butt into his chest. Angus reeled backwards towards the liquor barrels. Drew followed up with another jab, this time to the chin. Angus fell back, knees buckling. He sank to the floor, coming to rest on his backside, slumped against one of the barrels. His head drooped. He was out cold. The barrel behind him was full of holes, having taken the shotgun blast intended for Drew. The comatose barman lay there, showered by the whiskey like a plant under a watering can. The aroma had a smoky tinge to it. Malt infused with gunpowder. It worked well.

Drew took a moment to regain his composure, to recall what his original plans had been.

The sight of the bell hanging from the string jogged his memory.

Call Alec.

He dropped the shotgun, headed for the steps leading up to the trapdoor. The library book's issue number wouldn't come to mind, though he was sure he'd memorised it. If he was lucky - Christ knew he could use some luck - the book would still be there behind the bar. If it wasn't, he would just have to somehow tease those digits out of that dusty corner of his mind. His memory had never once-

A noise startled him.

He froze.

The bell was ringing.

13:30
4 hours and 30 minutes remaining

Muffled voices came from above, the words hard to discern through the trapdoor. Then a shout broke through: "Angus! Angus! You down there?" *Moptop.* He was pulling at the trapdoor, but it was bolted from below, on Drew's side. Their voices lowered again. Stealthily, Drew crept up the short flight of wooden steps. He pressed his ear up to the underside of the trapdoor. Now he could hear Blondie too. The pair of them were up there behind the bar, bickering, rattled.

"There's nobody here," Blondie said.

"Don't talk shite," Moptop countered. "That London bampot's in here somewhere. He'll be wanting to *spread* it, if he hasn't already. You know what needs doing."

"Aye. How though?"

"Cut the wires."

Shit. They're going for the phone. Very gently, Drew eased back the bolt on the trapdoor.

"I've not got a knife," Blondie said.

There was a short pause, followed by a pop and a shatter. A bottle or a glass breaking. "Use this,"

Moptop said.

The trapdoor sagged a little, brushing Drew's ear. One of them was right on top of it. Drew gave it an almighty upward shove. There was resistance, but only for half a second, then the door flew open the rest of the way. He stuck his head out, scanning first left (Blondie lying face down on the floor) then right (Moptop, standing stock still). So it had been Blondie on the trapdoor. The sudden tilt had sent him flying. Moptop was the priority. Drew came running up the steps, willing himself up and out of the hatch before Moptop could get a kick in. But something wasn't right. Moptop wasn't even *trying* to get a kick in. He just stood there, rooted to the spot, hands up over his mouth. He was staring past Drew, down at Blondie on the floor. Drew risked a quick look back at Blondie. It was obvious what had happened. It wasn't pretty.

The improvised cutting tool had indeed been one half of a beer bottle broken in two. Blondie had been holding the lower half near its base when Drew had toppled him. He'd fallen face first, naturally raising his forearms to protect himself. But he hadn't let go of the bottle, and the jagged teeth of its broken end had buried themselves in his face. Even now he held it there, as if still trying to chug back that beer.

Drew turned back to face Moptop. As the shock dissipated, Moptop lowered his hands, revealing a neat row of stitches running vertically down the bridge of his nose. Someone had patched him up well after their last encounter. He bared his teeth at Drew. A feral snarl that crinkled his nose, popping one of the stitches loose. *Or not so well.* He threw himself at Drew.

Drew was just a couple of paces in front of the open floor hatch. As Moptop came at him, fists already flying, Drew fell back down through the hatch. The lad went down with him. They tumbled down the steps, locked in a vicious embrace. Drew fell away to one side. He landed on something soft and yielding; the mattress. Then Moptop was on top of him, lashing out with a fury beyond measure, his arms a blur. Behind him, the bell swung wildly about on the end of its string. It rang sullenly, intermittently; a grim, funereal soundtrack to the desperate struggle. Drew fended off the blows as best he could, stunned by the speed and ferocity of the attack, until at last Moptop's initial fervour began to fade. Now Drew punched back, jabbing twice, three times. Only one of them landed, but it was enough to send Moptop back on his haunches. The bell swung out in front of him. Drew grabbed it, jabbed its metal edge into Moptop's nose. The remaining stitches came loose in a flash flood of gushing crimson. Moptop screamed. Drew came round behind him, got his neck in the crook of his arm. The chokehold. He squeezed. Blood spurted even harder from Moptop's nose, drenching the front of his tracksuit. Soon he would pass out. In the normal line of duty, Drew would have released him as soon as he did. But the normal line of duty was far behind him now. He'd left it for dust. Still, he felt sorry for the lad. Holding him close like that made him realise how fragile he was. How young. "Shh," he whispered. "Shh. Nearly done." The bell was still in his hand, still ringing whenever Moptop jerked and spasmed. He dropped it, oddly disgusted by it. The lad went limp in his arms. Drew kept the hold a minute longer to be sure. Then he laid him gently down on the mattress and went upstairs.

The Ugly Duckling was still on the floor behind the bar. He picked it up, went over to the phone. Hands shaking, he dialled the number, went through the same automated procedure as before.

At last Alec answered. "Drew! Christ. We'd almost given-" He cut himself short. "*Please* tell me you've found something."

"I have. A library book."

"Okay." The disappointment was palpable.

"It's a kid's book. *The Ugly Duckling*. Hale had it well hidden. It was important to him, Alec. Don't ask me why, but it was. Got a pen?"

"Yes."

"Write this down." He gave Alec the library name, the issue date and the issue number. "Got it?"

"Yes."

"Find out who borrowed it. If they're still alive, bring them in. Interrogate them. Don't interview. *Interrogate*. Search their property. Where they live now, and especially where they lived then. Call me back on this number. Do it *fast*, Alec."

"I'll try, but you have to understand-"

"And get some analysts working on *The Ugly Duckling*. Any... I don't know... hidden meanings. Internet speculation. Stuff about the author. Anything that chimes with what we know about Hale."

There was a lengthy pause. "I'll try. Anything else?"

"How long will it take?"

"How long is a piece of string?"

"Three hours, Alec. That's how long a piece of string is."

*

She'd spat and hissed and clawed and punched, but to no avail. The dice were loaded in Charlie's favour. Each time he came at her, stroking and pawing and fondling, Megan would see him right there in front of her. She would feel his clammy touch as surely as if he were actual flesh and blood. But the moment she lashed out in response, he would dematerialise again, her scratches and punches finding nothing but thin air. Even his Zenaframe stick figure would disappear, briefly, before reappearing in front of the door, zealously guarding it. Then it would start all over again. Last time, she'd goaded him, belittling his masculinity, his virility. In response he'd come at her harder still, and for longer. It had taken all her strength to fight him off, to force his retreat. But he just kept coming back. It was turning into an endless cycle of attack, resistance and retreat, the same battle played out again and again, on a horribly slanted playing field. Each time it drew a little more out of her. It was a war of attrition, Charlie trying to wear her down until she was too exhausted to resist. And then...

She shuddered at the thought. As she sat on the bed, knees tucked under her chin, arms wrapped around her legs, she tried to think of a way to break the cycle. A way to not just level the playing field, but to tilt it in her favour. *Come on. You're smarter than him. You always were.*

Her only ally was the laptop on the floor. The Zenaframe feed. It showed her where he was when otherwise he would have been invisible. But she hardly dared look at the thing, fearing he would notice, realise the advantage it gave her, and destroy it. He was certainly powerful enough. Still, she thought, she might as well use it while she could.

Quickly, almost imperceptibly, she glanced down at the computer screen. Charlie's stick figure was still guarding the door. He was already shifting his feet though, getting antsy, gearing up for another pathetically one-sided assault. This time, she decided, she would try a different strategy.

"Charlie? I can't see you. Are you there?"

"I'm here, Meg."

"Charlie... do you love me?"

"Course I do."

"If-" she swallowed, "If I give you what you want, will you do me a favour?"

"Maybe."

"Will you promise me you won't look until I tell you?"

A long pause. "Okay."

"But I can't *see* you, Charlie. I can't tell if you're looking. So you have to really, truly promise me."

"I promise."

She swallowed again and said: "Pinky promise?" She'd always hated the phrase. It infantilised them both. It was his pet phrase, not hers, but occasionally she would use it when she wanted some kind of assurance from him. It had never failed her yet. Not when she said it in a coquettish way, the way she just had, successfully masking her nausea.

"Pinky promise," Charlie said, his intonation weirdly child-like.

Slowly, she pulled her sweater halfway up over her head. She began to unbutton her blouse, keeping the sweater over her face so she could watch the Zenaframe feed through the holes in the loose-knit weave. Watch without being caught. She must have looked ridiculous, but she knew Charlie wouldn't care. In fact the enticement was already working. The stick figure left the door and crept towards her. *That's it, you fucker. Keep coming.*

"Promise me you're not looking, Charlie."

"I promise."

Liar. She undid two more buttons, exposing her bra, taking her time, still with the sweater over her face, surreptitiously tracking his movement.

235

"Still not looking," Charlie said, his stick figure creeping ever closer.

Her fingers left the blouse buttons and moved slowly down to her crotch. She tried to make the move seem sensual. She unfastened a single button on her fly, hoping - knowing - it would draw Charlie's eye. All the while she kept peering through the gauze of the sweater, eyes fixed on the screen. The stick figure was right next to the bed now, its wire neck craning over her in hungry fascination.

"Lie down with me, Charlie." She pulled the mould-spotted bed covers back for him. The stick figure hesitated. Had he sussed her game? No, thank god. He was climbing onto the bed. She pulled the sweater all the way up over her head. She threw it aside, forcing a seductive smile that must have looked more like a grimace. But Charlie wouldn't care. He wouldn't even notice. Never once had. She saw his indentation appear in the mattress. She heard his quickened breathing, very close now, felt the sickly warmth of it on her face. He materialised in front of her, stroking himself through his trousers, his sweating brow furrowed, his expression strained, serious, impatient.

She bolted across the room to the door.

She almost made it.

Then she felt the cold hands around her neck, dragging her back across the room, back onto the bed. They held her there, squeezing her larynx, punishing her. She gagged and struggled, but to no avail.

At last his fingers relinquished their hold on her throat, but only to explore elsewhere. As she gasped and coughed, she heard Charlie's fey, effeminate laugh. "We were *both* looking, weren't we?" he said.

The Zenaframe feed disappeared, the display reverting to a blue screen that spelt bad news. Blocky MS-DOS text conveyed a simple, devastating message: *FATAL ERROR*. Then the screen shattered and the laptop died, plunging the room into darkness.

16:36
1 hour and 24 minutes remaining

An hour to trace the borrower, an hour to interrogate, an hour to search the properties. The timeframe Drew had given Alec was, of course, sheer wishful thinking. But wishful thinking had worked for him in the past. Rarely, but it had.

He'd used the time to patch himself up with plasters and bandages from a rusty old first aid tin stashed under the bar. After tending to his wounds, he'd dosed himself with painkillers and whiskey. *Over*dosed himself. Realising his mistake, he'd collapsed at one of the pub tables in a dizzy, anaesthetised haze. Stupidly, he'd hobbled his ability to even answer the phone behind the bar, let alone rescue the damsel in distress. *Not a damsel in distress, a damsel 'in control'. Fine. Let's see what she's made of.* But still he worried.

And now the three hours were almost up. Alec still hadn't called. Disappointing, but hardly surprising. As the dual effects of the drugs and the booze began to wear off, he was left with the added pain of a headache on top of the pain he'd been trying to alleviate. He checked his watch. Three more minutes. And then he would just have to go.

Outside, rain was coming down hard, tempting him to just stay put. The third and final minute came. It went. Still the phone didn't ring. He fought the temptation to stay put and got to his feet. Everything ached harder than before. He limped over to the door and opened it. The rain outside was biblical. A long peal of thunder sounded overhead; an ominous low rumble, in harmony with a higher-pitched tone coming from somewhere else. A trill that persisted even as the thunder faded. The phone was ringing.

He closed the door on the rain. He turned back to the bar, limping towards it. Behind the bar, a monster came up out of the floor. A bloodied, festering, re-animated corpse. A zombie, albeit a familiar one. Drew cursed his own stupidity. *You should've stayed with him. Made him talk when he came round.* But he hadn't, and now Angus already had the shotgun raised above his head, about to bring the heavy butt crashing down on the phone.

Brriiinngg.

Drew made a desperate, lunging dive over the bar, scattering glasses as he went. He caught the falling butt in one hand. Its downward momentum - combined with his own - carried him off the counter and down into the narrow space behind the bar, where he landed in a crumpled heap. The shotgun landed with a heavy *thunk* on the floor beside him.

Angus kicked it aside and fell on Drew, kneeling on top of him. He clasped his giant hands firmly around Drew's throat.

Brriiinngg.

Drew brought his hands up to try and loosen the grip. The space behind the bar was too damn narrow for anything else. He couldn't roll away to one side. Nor could he move his legs; Angus was on top of them.

The barman's grip tightened even as Drew fought to loosen it. Angus leered down at him, eyes glazed with a distant, unseeing hatred, blood and sweat dripping from every pore. He stank of whiskey. He'd been under the leaking barrel for hours. His shirt was wet with the viscous liquor, his hair matted with it.

Brriiinngg.

Drew's vision began to cloud as he clawed ineffectually at the barman's steely, sinuous fingers.

"The lad downstairs," Angus growled, "the lad you killed. That was my boy." He loosened his grip just a little, allowing Drew a last right of reply.

Brriiinngg.

Drew gagged and gulped down air, grateful for the respite. "I didn't know he was yours," he rasped.

Then the fingers tightened again. "Neither did he."

Drew's vision clouded once more. The world around him grew quieter, more distant. His efforts grew weaker as the last reserves of strength drained out of him.

Angus snarled: "I've always wanted to kill someone from London."

Even now, as Drew continued to fade, the comment riled him. Anger divorced from all power, all agency. A little boy stamping his foot.

Brriiinngg. The sound was barely audible now.

The mist enveloped him fully. The thing that scared him was this: it felt *good*. His arms fell pathetically either side of him, hands hitting the floor like lead weights. No more sights. No more sounds. No more pain. Only a last dwindling sense of touch remained. His left hand lay on top of something small. Something that had fallen from his pocket. He realised what it was, what it might do, if only he had the strength. He remembered a time when he'd *been* that little boy stamping his foot; a regression made more vivid by the sensory deprivation. The act itself, the act of stamping, was comical of course, but the rage inside that little boy, the sense of injustice, was anything but. It was fierce. Brutal. Deadly.

The rage gave him renewed strength. He picked up the lighter. He flicked the wheel. He was still blind, had no way of knowing if the spark had lit the flame, but he held it up anyway, as near to Angus as he could judge.

A moment later, he was gasping for breath, and getting it. Sight and sound returned.

Brriiinngg.

Above and in front of him, a blazing column of fire moved erratically, like a flaming whirlwind. Angus was on his feet, staggering blindly, crashing into the bar.

Brriiinngg.

Drew shuffled backwards on his elbows, putting distance between himself and the flailing, flaming, blackening limbs. He got to his feet, seeking out the tortured face within the flames. Seeking it and finding it. Victory was a sweet, heady rush. He found mocking words to make it sweeter still. "Flame-grilled Angus burger."

The monster fell to the floor.

Drew watched it burn. "London speciality, you cunt."

16:42
1 hour and 18 minutes remaining

Brriiinngg.

Drew stepped over the barman's burning body. The stench was sickeningly familiar. Stripped of its grisly context, he might even have found it pleasant. He looked around for a fire extinguisher. There wasn't one.

Brriiinngg.

He found a soda dispensing nozzle, tried to douse the flames with it, but when he squeezed the trigger nothing came out.

Brriiinngg.

The fire had already set light to a wooden panel forming one end of the bar. Soon the bar's entire length would be up in flames. *Fuck it. Just be quick.* He kept a wary eye on the fire's progress as he went to answer the phone. "Alec?"

"About bloody time! Where were you?"

"Never mind. Just tell me."

"You sound out of breath. What-"

"Just *tell* me, Alec."

The flames continued to spread.

"Right. Well. Your *Ugly Duckling* was loaned out to a business address. A café in central London. CTC raided the premises. Conducted a thorough search."

"And?"

"No device. Nothing."

"Shit."

"I haven't finished yet."

The heat from the fire grew more intense. Drew wiped sweat from his brow. "Go on."

"The book was issued to one Lily Anne Baker, former owner of Lily's Café, Darwen Street, off Piccadilly. She died a few years ago. But it's not the first time we've raided Lily's. Remember the café Hale described? Same place. He never names it in the diary, but we found it thanks to the detail about the old woman with the cataract. Lily's mother. Back then - this was thirty odd years ago - we interviewed her and Lily. They remembered Hale, but they couldn't give us anything useful. We never interviewed Lily's little girl, though. She could barely talk at the time. Well, guess what? Now she runs the place. Name of May. Incredible memory she's got."

The fire was now halfway along the bar, forcing Drew back against the wall in a vain effort to dodge the encroaching black smoke. "And?"

"And nothing. Not yet. But I'm about to interview her. If you hang on a bit longer I might - emphasis on *might* - be able to give you-"

Drew coughed as the first wisps of thick, acrid

smoke entered his lungs. "I can't," he spluttered. The far end of the bar had yet to catch light, though it soon would. Bottles on the counter popped loudly as the fire consumed them.

"What the hell is that?! Drew?"

"Pub's on fire."

"*What*?!"

Drew left the receiver hanging. Trying not to inhale, he went to the flame-free end of the bar and ducked out under the serving hatch. He limped past the tables to the door, opened it and went outside into the downpour. He turned his face up to the heavens, gratefully inhaling the cool, clean air, letting the raindrops splash over his face and trickle down his parched, strangled throat.

And then he was off again, half running, half limping, back down the road towards the pier. Towards a new and deeper level of Hell.

*

Lily's Café no longer resembled the traditional greasy spoon Hale had described in his diary. Gone were the sticky formica tabletops and the torn, foam-padded seats. Now, thirty years later, it was all naked brickwork, austere wooden furniture, and oversized lightbulbs hanging down in bunches. Though the menu hadn't changed as radically as the décor (Full English breakfasts never went out of fashion) the presentation certainly had. Beans still swam in tomato sauce, but now, instead of flooding the entire plate, they were neatly contained in a ramekin. 'Sausage egg and chips' lived on, but now the classic combo had competition from eggs Royale and smashed avocado on artisan toast. The owners had adapted over the years, stayed nimble and receptive to new trends, and the business had continued to thrive. But now, after the raid, tables and chairs lay overturned, plates smashed, cakes and pastries stamped into the floor. Alec was embarrassed by CTC's heavy-handedness.

He sat with May, the current owner, at one of the plain wooden tables they'd set right again. The interview was almost over. May was thirty three years old. She wore blue denim dungarees over a stripy jumper. She had a practical, patient, kindly but world-weary air about her. Even a raid by armed counter-terrorism officers had elicited little more than a 'now this' eye roll. While other café owners would have been justifiably angry, May's attitude was far more understanding. She had even expressed regret that they hadn't found whoever or whatever they were looking for. Alec had already run her name through several databases. She was clean, and her waitressing smile was pleasant enough. He wondered what her real smile was like. May had been living in the same flat above the café her entire life. They'd searched the flat too - including the roof of course - and found nothing there either. When her mother died, May had inherited the flat and the business, running it dutifully if not quite happily.

"I'm so sorry about all this," Alec said.

May shrugged. "That's alright, darlin'." She

winked and added: "One of your lads gave me his number."

Alec laughed. "Every cloud, I suppose."

"Was there anything else?"

"Actually there was one more thing. Does *The Ugly Duckling* mean anything to you?"

"You mean that kids' story?"

"Yes."

She paused to think. "Yeah. It does."

"Oh?"

"Like I said, I used to play in here when I was little, while Mum was serving the punters. I was always running about getting under her feet, giving menus to people, copying Mum, pretending I ran the place. But I had my own little play pen too." She pointed to a corner of the café. "Right there it was. I had colouring books, picture books, all sorts. Some of 'em had words but I was too young to read. Mum was busy all the time, so I used to try and get the punters to read 'em to me. I'd just plonk the book in front of 'em and hope for the best. Most of 'em were like: 'that's nice, darlin', but they wouldn't actually bother reading. But the man I told you about, the man with the bandage on his face, he would. I don't think Mum liked the look of him much. She'd always shoo me away if she saw me with him, but I didn't care. I thought he was nice, and he was the only one who ever read to me properly. So one day I plonk *The Ugly Duckling* down in front of him, and he opens it and starts reading out loud, and I'm stood there listening and looking at the pictures. But then he gets to the bit where the farmer tries to shoot the duckling, and all of a sudden he goes really sad and quiet. Don't ask me why. And then Mum comes over and drags me away, says he's busy."

"Busy?"

"Yeah. He was... writing a letter or something. He had this old-fashioned pen with a big wide metal bit on the end, wider than normal, like a..."

"A fountain pen?"

"Yeah, but bigger. When he wrote with it, the letters came out... old-fashioned like. All fancy and swirly."

Alec nodded. "Calligraphy."

"Calligraphy! That's a good word."

"Did you recognise anything he wrote down?"

"No. I was only three. I couldn't make head or tail of it."

"No, of course."

"Anyway I didn't care. I just wanted to know what happened to the ugly duckling. So whenever Mum was busy I'd go back to him with the book, and we'd pick up where we left off. That went on over a few days. He was a good storyteller. I liked him. But we never did get to the end. One day he left, and he never came back. I got into a right tizzy over it."

"Because he was gone? You missed him?"

May shook her head. "Because the *book* was gone. I missed the *book*." She looked apologetic. "That probably doesn't help you much."

"I don't know," Alec said thoughtfully. "It might." He stood. "I wish I could help you tidy up, but..."

"Don't worry, darlin'. You've got a scumbag to catch."

Alec smiled. *If only.* "Thank you for your time, May. If you think of anything else..." He gave her a plain card with his number on it.

May examined it closely. "You ain't normal police, are you?"

Alec just smiled again. Then he turned and headed for the door. When he was halfway out, May said: "If you're lookin' for that nutter..."

Alec paused in the doorway. "What nutter?"

"The one who's been on the news. For killing them policewomen."

Alec liked May. He wanted to tell her the truth, but of course he couldn't. "That's right," he said.

May nodded. "Well it ain't that man with the bandage on his face. That much I *do* know."

Alec thanked her again.

May flashed him her waitressing smile.

On the way back to the car, fatigue hit him hard. Suddenly he regretted turning down May's offer of a coffee. Though he'd vowed never to do so, he went into a Starbucks. He ordered a strong, large coffee 'to go', thinking the Americanism would help smooth the transaction. It didn't. The barista fired several Italian-inflected words at him, none of which he understood. He asked which one meant 'strong and large', and was met with a blank stare, followed by a finger pointing up at the menu. He chose a coffee at random. They asked him his name and he asked what his name had to do with anything. Then he realised he was drawing far too much attention to himself and said 'Palmer'.

While he waited, he watched a young woman at a table as she scrolled through some kind of social media feed on her phone. Here was another aspect of modern life he didn't partake in, though he knew a little about the psychology underpinning it. The woman scrolled incessantly, hungrily, looking for her next dopamine hit. A barista yelled 'Palmer'. He collected his coffee and chugged it through the hole in the plastic lid. It was neither strong nor large. The young woman sipped a dark green smoothie as she continued to thumb through her feed. They were both slaves of a kind, he thought. Caffeine was his master. The algorithm was hers.

And then he realised why the woman must have caught his attention in the first place. There was something very odd about her face; stalks growing out of a fleshy cavity in her cheek. Stalks built from dead skin, except for the tips which were black. Yet she seemed entirely unconcerned, too absorbed in her screen to pay any mind to her obvious affliction. She was typing now, her brow furrowed in concentration. She looked angry. Offended. No-one else in the café had noticed her disfigurement. There were no stares or hushed whispers. She might just as well have been invisible.

Alec rubbed his eyes. When he looked again, the wound had disappeared. Her cheek was perfectly smooth. Briefly, he wondered if one of the baristas had spiked his drink. Then he put it down to lack of sleep and carried on his way.

*

The ghost was inside her.

Not in quite the way it wanted to be. Not just yet. Its physicality was still too transient, too fleeting, though it grew more constant each time her fear intensified. And for Megan, the sense of invasion was already total; a suffocating forced intimacy, a surrogate for that frustrated lust. It was there in every pore of her skin, every strand of her hair, every cell of her blood. A clammy, clingy, internal caress that explored her vital organs, her nervous system... and her mind. As it did so, it felt the weight of her fear and played with it, willing it to grow heavier. She got the distinct impression this wasn't Charlie anymore. Charlie's spirit would have been just as invasive, but more hesitant, more apologetic. This one was different. There was a sense of arrogance and entitlement about it.

This one was Hale.

She'd fought him as best she could, by fighting back her own fear, depriving him of power, but now, as he continued to explore her insides, terror reasserted itself.

And then something changed. Those hands inside her were suddenly - impossibly - her *own* hands, and her insides were someone else's. Her feelings too were no longer entirely her own. Her fear had evaporated, not because she'd won, but because something alien had taken its place; a selfishness that was cold, callous and calculating, yet gloriously liberating.

So this is what possession feels like.

That thought, if nothing else, was still her own. The thread that Megan Mallory still hung by. He'd claimed her emotions, but not her thoughts. Not yet. The consolation, scant as it was, gave her renewed strength, though her mind continued to tear itself in two. She forced her eyes open. She was still on the bed. The room was not quite pitch black. Though the white light from the laptop was gone, a dim green ambient light persisted. It came from the nodes stuck to the walls, their tiny LED lights glowing like pinpricks of hope. She felt inside her pocket for the phone that - until now - had been no damn use to anyone.

Hale must have sensed he was losing her. His response was to wrap both icy hands around her fast-beating heart. The constriction felt like imminent death. *Not there*, she told him. *Lower. Touch me lower.* The hands left her heart and moved further down inside her, excited by her apparent consent. Distracted.

She took the phone from her pocket and

pushed its only button. The screen lit up, its familiar icons shining like the face of a true friend. She quickly found the app. The app itself was merely the controller. The 'TV remote'. The nodes were the actual TV. She prayed to god she'd built them right. To some extent they'd already proven themselves - with Zenaframe - but their second mode was far more experimental, far more reliant on certain metaphysical presumptions. And if those presumptions turned out to be wrong...

Hale's internal caress worked its way down, pausing to poke and prod at the inner walls of her uterus. She shuddered.

Doubt consumed her. She'd never even tested the app, let alone used it. Car manufacturers had crash test dummies, but there was no such thing as a crash test spirit. Still, it was all she had.

Hale was outside her womb again now, but still fascinated by it. And then, quite abruptly, he was alert to the danger. His half-lustful, half-clinical fascination turned to anger. His cold caress became an iron grip, squeezing her uterus. Megan howled, somehow deriving pleasure from her own agony. But it wasn't masochism. It was *sadism*. Hale was invading her feelings once more, replacing them with his own.

Quickly.

She pointed the phone at the nearest node and launched the app. The app which, in a fit of blind optimism, she had labelled *Counter-possession*.

17:04
56 minutes remaining

The storm raged around Drew. The pier's rotten planks were slick with rain and seawater. He trod carefully. *Almost there.* Another wave came crashing over the side of the pier, battering his left side, but he leaned into it to compensate, retaining his balance. Lightning flashes came thick and fast, their jagged forks skewering the sea. Every step presented him with a new hazard. The gaping holes underfoot were hard enough to avoid in *calm* weather, but now, with the waves and the wind buffeting him here and there, they were deadlier than ever. The wind was strong enough to rock the entire pier from side to side with each gust. Yet somehow the house still stood.

As he finally neared it, another wave - the fiercest yet - came over the side of the pier, smacking him hard. He staggered and fell to the right. His hand shot out to break the fall, but it never found a surface. Only a hole in the decking. The right side of his face followed. Instead of thin air, it found the edge of the hole; a soggy mess of rotten wood which cushioned the blow before giving way completely. And then he was falling.

A plunge into cold water was something he should have been accustomed to by now, but its freezing embrace still shocked him. As before, he sank fast, then slowed, then swam back up. But this time the current hindered his progress. It was like swimming against the tide, but with the tide flowing *vertically down*. He searched around in the murk for one of the pier's iron struts. Something to cling onto and haul himself up by. But his eyes stung so badly in the brine that he was forced to close them. He felt around blindly, ineffectually. *No good. Suck the pain up.* He forced his eyes open again. They burned like never before, and still he saw nothing in the thick, silty murk.

At last his hands fell upon something. Something that had no rightful business being there. A fabric of some kind, cotton perhaps, though it was still hidden in the silt cloud. Then a prolonged, staccato lightning flash, somewhere very close, revealed it for what it was, and the sight of it terrified him beyond measure.

The garment was a hooded top, worn over a human body that stood upright with its hands outstretched towards him. The hood was still up over the head of the... man? woman? There was no way of knowing, not from the face alone, nor from the hands, since both were covered in pale, writhing worms. Some were knotted together like jumbled shoelaces. Others stood to attention, distinct from one another.

Drew gagged on seawater, had no option but to swallow it down. Then he realised what he was looking at. Not worms, but symptoms of the virus. *Advanced* symptoms. Pulsating stalks full of who knew what, covering not just one cheek but an entire face, and hands, and probably the entire body. The victim was dead, but the stalks lived on. He looked closer. The black eyes on the stalk tips were in fact tiny round windows hewn from a carapace of dead skin. Windows that revealed the dark ooze within; the ever probing essence of the virus itself. Something so dreadfully alien that even the fish had steered clear.

The body was weighed down by a chain wrapped around the ankles, the chain's end attached to an old ship's anchor half-buried in the sea bed. Who was it? Hale? No. They'd removed his body long ago. The face and the hands revealed little, but the clothing... dirty blue trainers, grey trousers, white t-shirt under a dark grey hoodie. The outfit was weirdly urban, the hoodie perfect for concealing that hideous face. Or indeed a normal, healthy face. And then there was the colour scheme. Grey trousers and a grey hoodie. *Grey.* The colour of anonymity. Discretion.

The colour of MI5.

*

Nothing happened at first. Megan lay there with the phone raised towards the nearest wall node, tapping and re-tapping 'Launch', thinking the signal must be intermittent, or gone altogether. But she felt no anxiety or despair, when it should have been overwhelming. So it *was* working. The nodes were already activated, sucking the fear out of her. When that emotion was gone, a tingling sensation began. It was like acupuncture, not unpleasant in itself, though it underlined her uncertainty about what would follow.

The tingling was, in fact, the beginning of the dematerialisation process. The withdrawal of fear's more tangible components: sweat, blood glucose, serum calcium, white blood cells. All of it was now vaporised, extracted and drawn into the fierce glow of the wall nodes, their collective energy forming a single unified field around her; a hollow cube of green light, in whose centre she lay. And with that, inevitably, went the rest of her. Inevitably, because sweat, blood glucose, serum calcium and white blood cells do not exist in isolation. They are the water in the plumbing of the sympathetic nervous system. Now the plumbing went too; her blood vessels, her spinal cord, her brain stem, each vaporised in turn, hoovered up like dust, then churned and reprocessed within the energy field.

Stay calm. It's not even painful. Not really.

When it was over, she was still very much alive. Alive but disembodied, her consciousness floating above the bed. She looked down and saw the body that had replaced hers, just as she'd hoped it would. A body reconstituted from her own atoms and spat out by the nodes. The body of a man; a middle-aged man she might have recognised from photos she'd been shown, had she paused to study his terrified face. But she didn't pause, because she was ravenous. The man was afraid, and fear was food.

She went inside him, filling his body with her spirit, devouring his terror. It was bitter and intoxicating. She felt at once giddy and energised beyond belief. And it had all been so *easy*, the simulacrum of Hale's body an empty vessel into which she'd effortlessly poured herself. There had been no resistance, no spirit to overcome. A little *too* easy, perhaps. Why hadn't he put up a fight? Had he anticipated the possession, somehow moved his spirit elsewhere? If so, then it must surely be floating nearby, disembodied, like hers had been a moment ago. But where? What was it doing?

That was when she heard his laugh. It unnerved her because it was confident, unafraid, and cruel. She had possession of his body - or at least an approximation of what it had once been like - but so what? His spirit was the thing that counted. And besides, she didn't feel comfortable inside that body. It was weak, achey and stiff, its skin like old leather. She wanted her own body back, and the thought of possibly losing it forever induced a sudden panic in her. She felt around for the phone. It was still there on the bed. She picked it up with Hale's hairy, liver-spotted hands, used his thin fingers to push more buttons. Reverse the polarity.

In the light from the phone, she watched

Hale's fingers dematerialise in front of her, and her own reappear. The midpoint in the transition was a grotesque composite of two sets of fingernails; one varnished and neatly manicured, the other chewed, torn and picked at. Was her entire body now her own again? She checked herself from head to toe. Everything seemed to be in order. What about her mind? Her thoughts? These too felt right.

But Hale's spirit was still in the room with her. Its leering, threatening presence was all too familiar. And the strange thing was... but it couldn't be. Could it?

*

"Shona! Shona!"

It was Judy, of course. Her gravelly voice always filled Shona Campbell with dread. Though Shona mostly enjoyed her interactions with the care home's residents (consolation for her woeful salary) seventy eight year old Judy Herrington was a constant thorn in her side. Until recently, Shona had thought racism to be the underlying cause of Judy's aggressive attitude towards her. But now she'd come to revise her opinion. It wasn't racism, but envy. It was Shona's youth (and yes, her beauty - everyone said she was pretty) that Judy couldn't bear, because her own youth was so far behind her. Judy often told stories about her younger days, and what a 'dish' she'd been, and she seemed resentful that she'd never found a man worthy of such a prize. Shona doubted the truth of those stories. Judy Herrington might once have

259

been a 'dish', but a dish of what? Nothing edible, that was for sure.

Shona approached Judy's table warily. Her plate of Spaghetti Carbonara lay untouched in front of her. "There's too much salt in it," she said, defiantly throwing her fork down on the table.

Shona surveyed the dining room. The other residents studiously ignored Judy as they eagerly tucked into their spaghetti. "No-one else seems to think so."

"Don't give me any lip, girl. I'm telling you it's too salty. I can't eat it. I want something else."

Shona went to the kitchen. She asked the chef if there was anything else on offer. There was. The vegetarian option. The very same Carbonara, only without the ham. Her heart sank. She went back into the dining room to tell Judy.

"I know your game, *Missy*," Judy hissed. "Psychological torture. Taking advantage because we're too old to fight back. Well I've had it up to here!" She addressed the other residents. "Who's with me?"

Evidently no-one was.

"Why don't you give it another go?" Shona suggested, knowing Judy would cave eventually. "You might get used to it."

"Don't talk to me like that, *girl*. I'll report you to the gov-" At this point Judy's insurrection was sabotaged by yet another coughing fit. They happened often, and Shona knew from experience that it was best to stand well back when they did. She left Judy to recover and went to check on the other residents. Mr Carter was done and needed help getting out of his chair. Mrs Adams had dropped her fork and wanted a replacement. Shona went back to the kitchen to fetch more cutlery. As she returned, a cry went up from a male resident who was normally very quiet. "Shona! Come quickly! It's Judy!"

Shona rolled her eyes. She was all too familiar with Judy's tactics. Having lost the spaghetti war, she would simply start a different one. A custard war or a state-of-the-dining-room-carpet war. But when Shona reached Judy's table, she thought that perhaps she'd been too quick to dismiss her complaint; spaghetti was falling from her slack-jawed mouth in thick clumps, tumbling down the front of her bright green blouse. *Jesus Lord.* Was she vomiting? No. The spaghetti strands were undigested. And she wasn't choking either. She was breathing normally, through her nose, though her eyes had rolled back in their sockets, giving Judy an alarming zombie-like appearance. She sat perfectly still and upright in her chair, her head tilted up towards the ceiling.

Shona ran to the office to fetch the staff mobile. She dialled 999. She could have first cleared Judy's mouth and throat, but she hadn't. There was no need. She was still breathing after all. That was what she told herself. When the dispatcher asked Shona if Judy's airways were all clear, she felt a small pang of guilt. Soon it was gone again, replaced by nausea at the thought of the repulsive task she could no longer postpone. With the phone clamped to her ear, and claiming to know nothing about first aid (she was fully trained) Shona went back to the dining room, dragging her feet just a little.

*

Hale had someone there with him alright. A new arrival, there in spirit if not in person. Somehow, Megan sensed it was a woman, and not a nice woman. Not a nice woman atall. Who the hell was she? How had she gotten here? Megan allowed her uncertainty to morph into anxiety. That was her big mistake. The mistake the woman had been waiting for. Now, as Megan realised her error, the anxiety turned to outright terror. A terror that fed the new arrival even as it paralysed Megan.

"Pretty, isn't she?" Hale said to his companion.

When the woman replied, her disembodied voice was gravelly; thick with phlegm, tar, and boorish vulgarity. "I'm always up for a threesome," she said, her laugh devolving into a wet hacking cough.

"You go first," Hale replied. "I'll join in later."

The woman went inside Megan, exploiting her terror-induced paralysis, taking her time, exploring her from head to toe and back again. She seemed as eager to touch Megan's insides as Hale had been, but for different reasons. It wasn't lust or sadism that consumed this woman's spirit. It was envy.

Hale still lingered, a passive voyeur. Megan

heard his soft, contented moan. But it was nothing compared to the moan of his friend as she clutched Megan's brain like a greedy child with a warm Easter egg. Soon her thumb tips melted a hole into which she poured herself, tongue first, coughing up phlegm as she went.

17:07
53 minutes remaining

Drew wasn't sure how much longer he could hold his breath. But if he resurfaced without searching Baines, there was no guarantee he would find him again. The silt cloud and the randomly shifting currents were deceptive, disorienting. *Search him now then, and quick.*

It was a nauseating task. The stalks on the dead man's face swayed from side to side in the swirling water, inches in front of Drew. The black eyes on the end of each stalk pulsed with life, seeing him, *knowing* him. He shrank away from them. The trigger phrase was one viral pathway. Were the stalks another? He dismissed the thought and unzipped the hoodie, revealing a white t-shirt. It was dotted with 'ink' spots; more stalks beneath the fabric, poking and prodding at it. They must have covered the entire body. He felt the hoodie's inner lining, found a pocket sewn into it. There was something flimsy and very light inside. A see-through zip-lock baggie containing...

There was no time to examine it. His lungs were ready to burst. He grabbed the baggie and swam.

He resurfaced under the pier, gasping for air. He found a vertical iron strut and took hold of it. With the baggie in his teeth, he climbed the strut, using the ornamental gaps between the rivets as footholds. He reached the underside of the pier, found the same hole he'd fallen through. He found its firmest, least rotten edge and hauled himself up onto the pier. Then he lay down, exhausted, staring up at the roiling charcoal clouds. The rain was still coming down hard, but he barely felt it.

He examined the see-through baggie. Inside, pressed flat, perfectly dry and sealed off from the rain, was a single page of handwriting. Hale's handwriting. It was just as Drew had figured. Baines had found that wall cavity and taken the diary page hidden within. Then Angus had killed him and hidden the body. But what had infected Baines? Hale's ghost, or the words on that page?

As Drew lay there shivering in the rain, he began the laborious but vital process, covering the words with his palm, revealing one letter at a time.

17:29
31 minutes remaining

Drew stood in front of the house, swallowed up by its huge shadow. The forced perspective facade seemed to loom larger than ever, its contours shifting subtly but unmistakably. Corner angles widened here and narrowed there, as if the walls were joined to each other by hinges. He looked up at the stone cherubs, perched on the roof atop the gables. Above and behind them, lightning flashed incessantly, but it wasn't the weather that had drawn his eye.

One of the cherubs was missing.

Previously there had been three, one at the apex of each gable. Now there were only two. The missing statue - the middle one - could, perhaps, have been dislodged by the storm. It could have toppled and fallen through the rotten pier into the sea. Except...

He studied the two remaining cherubs. They were identical, their bright yellow hi-viz jackets fluttering in the wind; a cheery counterpoint to their sullen, cheerless expressions. If a strong gust of wind had claimed their sibling, then the statue should have broken off at the ankles (by far the slenderest part of the sculpture) leaving only the feet behind. But this was not what he observed.

The feet were gone too.

Drew went up to the front door. Its claret hue looked a shade darker than before. The three words etched into the wood - *Divide and conquer* - were still there, but now three new letters had been added, in capitals for emphasis, turning a statement of intent into a declaration of victory: *DivideD and conquerED*.

He turned the handle and pushed the door open. There was no resistance. He was welcome, it seemed. He went into the hallway. It was dark, but the darkness was natural, not uncannily pitch black like before. The chill in the air, however, was far from natural. It froze him to the bone and carried on into the marrow. His soaking wet clothes froze over, stiffening and impeding his movements. And when he saw the eyes, he stopped moving altogether.

They were right in front of him, at the foot of the stairs. Two red eyes glowing fiercely, black pupils fixed on him. The creature they belonged to remained shrouded in darkness, but its eyes were near to the floor, suggesting it was crouching, ready to pounce. Then its voice came; malevolent, deep-throated, satanic, like a record slowed down and played backwards. "Wouuld... yooou... beeee... myyy... frieeend?"

Drew realised what he was looking at. He didn't hesitate. He went up to the thing - the boo buddy - and stomped it repeatedly, grinding his heel into its voice box. But still the voice persisted, its pitch rising to a more familiar, cartoonish tone. "Hey, that tickles!" Drew renewed his assault, jabbing his steel toecap into the bear's chest. "Tickle me, white knight!" He aimed higher now, at the head. "Oh yeah! Right there!" With each blow, the bear's voice grew faster, shriller, more demented. "Oh yeah! Right between the eyes! Right where Jenny got tickled!" The cruel barb enraged him further still. He jabbed and kicked and stomped, grinding the bear's electronic innards into a thousand shards of plastic and metal. He reached down and tore it limb from limb, ripping the stuffing out until all that remained was an empty, embroidered sack with two oversized plastic eyes glued onto it. Eyes that - impossibly, without any power source - continued to glow red. Then, with one last grind of his heel, they dimmed and died.

He stood back from the mess, took a few deep breaths. Slowly, his vision adjusted to the gloom. He could see the holes in the floor. Outside, lightning flashed, and a forest appeared all around him; trees made of nothing but light. Then they were gone again. But in that moment he'd caught a glimmer of something else too, glimpsed even more fleetingly in the upper corner of his eye. Something at the top of the stairs which had... moved.

Something luminous, reflective, and bright yellow.

17:32
28 minutes remaining

Drew went to the foot of the stairs. Halfway up, the staircase tapered off into the dark. Nothing could be seen in those shadows, but something certainly lurked in them. He knew because he could hear it.

The sounds it made were soft, burbling, investigative. Sounds that were almost words, but not quite. He could hear its movements too. It was shuffling, bumping and crawling down the stairs, still in the darkness for now, but about to emerge from it.

A prolonged flash of lightning came, accompanied by several ear-splitting thunder cracks. The forest of light appeared once more, and a sequence of strobe-like flashes revealed the thing that was coming down the stairs. The cherub. Made of stone, for sure, yet clearly alive, breathing in and out under the hi-viz jacket, its only item of clothing. It reached the foot of the stairs and fell onto its side with a heavy *thunk*. Then it righted itself and got to its feet, stumbling, staggering, learning to walk in that very moment. It tottered towards him. Arriving at his feet, it leaned into him for support, its surprising weight knocking him back a little. It hugged his legs, gazing up at him forlornly. Its mottled stone face was covered in lichens; patches of orange discolouration here and there. The tip of its nose was eaten away, worn down by time and water and wind. White and green smears of bird shit lay in vertical streaks beneath the eyes; a grotesque substitute for tears. It raised both pudgy arms. *Pick me up?*

Drew screamed and screamed. Not because the child - the thing - before him was as impossible as it was terrifying. Not because now, more than ever, he doubted his own sanity. He screamed because, beneath the moss and the shit and the mould, there was a face he recognised. A face with something of Jenny in its features, and something of him too. The face of the child they would have had, if only Jenny had lived.

Confusion kept him rooted to the spot. None of his three dominant instincts - fight, flee, protect - seemed to apply. Least of all the urge to fight. So... flee or protect? Half of him wanted to hug the child, but his other half - the rational half - prevailed. *It's not my child. Not Jenny's. It's no bloody child atall.* Flight won out. He backed away from it, kept going until he was up against a wall. The cherub looked hurt by the rejection. It came stumbling towards him, arms outstretched. Its expression became angrier, more accusatory, but also more human, more familiar. "I'm sorry," Drew told his never born son. "You were too young to save. You weren't even-" He began to sob.

The infant reached him and clung to his knees once more. It looked up at him and began to wail, bird shit tears flowing from its lifeless eyes. But to Drew those eyes seemed *full* of life, and the tears crystal clear. "I'm so sorry." At last he relented. He crouched down to pick up the child. Holding him tight was all that mattered now. He wrapped his arms around his baby boy.

His baby boy crumbled to dust.

Drew was strangely embarrassed by his own anguished howl. It was weak. Pathetic. Shameful. When it finally dissipated, the empty hi-viz jacket was still in his hands. He threw it aside. He listened out for Jenny's voice inside his head, hoping for some words of consolation, reassurance.

But Jenny was silent.

17:35
25 minutes remaining

Drew was grateful for the next crack of lightning. It shook him from his irrational despair. He steeled himself, collected his thoughts, reminded himself why he'd come back. He went up the stairs, spitting words of defiance. "What else you got? Eh? What else you got, you cunt?"

When he reached the landing, he saw the opposite of what he'd been expecting. The bedroom door was wide open. Darkness within. Had she escaped? Cautiously, he crossed the threshold into the room, half expecting the door to slam shut behind him. But nothing happened. The room was silent apart from the grandfather clock, which still ticked away. He waited for his eyes to adjust to the dark. Gradually, the silhouette of that gnarled, blackened old four poster bed revealed itself. Then the clock appeared too; a lone sentinel standing guard.

"Megan?"

No reply. His vision grew clearer still. He examined the bed. The sheets were disturbed, but it was empty. He looked underneath it. Nothing. He looked behind him, behind the door. Nothing. Where the hell was she?

The clock's minute hand shifted forward a notch. Twenty three minutes to six. Time enough for what he had in mind? Probably not. But maybe, just maybe, if he was quick enough, and if-

A sudden noise froze him. A drop of something viscous landed on his shoulder. He checked it, then wished he hadn't; a wet smear of thick yellow discharge, foul-smelling, diseased, infused with tiny black flecks of who knew what. The liquid - and the awful hacking cough that produced it - had come from above.

17:38
22 minutes remaining

Drew looked up and saw a woman lying on the ceiling. A woman who was still - just barely - recognisable as Megan. She lay on her back, held there by nothing but an inversion of gravity, as if the ceiling were the floor. She was writhing and moaning softly, in pain or pleasure, or some perverse mixture of both. She still wore the same black jeans, but the roll-neck jumper was gone. Her white blouse was torn and filthy with crusted yellow patches of something like vomit. Her mouth and chin were caked with the same unholy mess. Megan always had been pale, but now she was sallow and concentration camp thin. Her skin was near translucent, dark blue veins branching here and there, her once proud face now reduced to a membrane stretched over a skull. Her expression was vacant, semi-lobotomised, though her bloodshot eyes shone fiercely out of deep, shadowy sockets. They fixed on Drew.

He could only manage a single word. A frail, stupefied whisper. "Megan?"

She coughed violently. Another thick gobbet

of phlegm shot from her mouth, at once obeying and defying gravity. He sidestepped it, heard it spatter on the floor beside him. And then she spoke, but not with her own voice. It was a voice like gravel. Throaty and terminal. "He's here."

Was she talking *to* him or *about* him?

Another voice responded, this one from behind Drew. "Fear not, my love." A man's voice, bland, harmless, the words romantic, but spoken woodenly, without passion.

Drew turned and saw a man carrying a suitcase. Except for the cluster of black-eyed stalks sprouting from a fleshy cavity in his left cheek, his appearance was quite plain. He was early middle-aged. Dull glasses over a dull face. Neither handsome nor ugly. Only his pinched expression gave him a sliver of character; lips tightly pursed, nose wrinkled, disdainful of everyone and everything. He wore a sky blue anorak over a beige work shirt and a tie, light grey trousers and cheap brown shoes. As Drew studied the forgettable outfit, he realised he'd already forgotten the face. Yet one detail stood out. The tie. A jumble of bright colours and zigzags. A pre-Rave 1980s dayglo aesthetic. It was MTV. Jazzercise. The background pattern on a cheap birthday card. Once, Drew had interviewed a heavily tattooed and pierced murder suspect. The excess body art had been nothing but cover for an absence of charisma. This tie performed the same function. It was self-consciously wacky and try-hard, a substitute for a personality.

Here was the tedious middle manager who allowed his job to define him. The man who spoke only in baffling industry jargon, even at parties. The man who rolled his eyes when people asked him to speak plainly, as if *they* were the fools. Here was every man Drew had ever met and wished he hadn't. Here was Magnus Hale.

The clock's minute hand ticked forward another notch.

"Please forgive the theatrics," Hale said to Drew. "Possessed teddy bears? Statues coming to life? And all during a thunderstorm! Terribly clichéd, I know, but I'm afraid I couldn't resist. This *is* a haunted house."

Drew half smiled. He'd judged Hale too quickly and too harshly. There was some charisma there after all. But only in death. If he'd had it in life, he wouldn't have needed the tie.

"What are you waiting for?" the voice from the ceiling growled. "Kill 'im!"

"Patience, Judy my love."

Judy. Of course. Hale's colleague. The one he'd fancied. The woman whose spirit now consumed Megan, eating away at her from inside. The thought of it angered Drew. He called out to her, defiant and hopeful. "I know you can hear me, Megan. I know you're there somewhere. I'm not leaving without-"

The words dried up as he realised he was falling. Not down, but *sideways.* Something that felt like gravity but wasn't. It threw him against a wall and pinned him there, just as Megan had been pinned. For her, gravity had done a u-turn. For him, it had merely turned a corner.

"You're not leaving atall," Hale said. He set his suitcase down on the floor. He reached inside his anorak, took out a fat pen with a marble lacquer finish. "Don't worry, Drew. I'm not going to infect you. Infection is a gift you don't deserve." He unscrewed the cap, revealing a stainless steel nib. "I'm simply going to kill you. I can do that now, you know. Megan's fear was *potent*." He studied the pen. "I've always loved calligraphy. Look at the artistry in that nib. Tiny letters etched into the metal. Do you see?" He held the pen at arm's length, with the nib pointed at Drew. "No? Take a closer look." He let go of the pen. It didn't drop. It hovered in mid air. Then, nib first, it began to float towards Drew.

Drew tried to move, but he only grew heavier. It was like being pinned to the wall of a centrifuge ride at a funfair. A wall that spun ever faster.

"First," Hale said, "the nib will pierce your cornea."

Drew screwed his eyes shut.

"Correction. The eyelid. *Then* the cornea. After that, it'll pass through the lens, the vitreous body, the optic nerve, and finally into your brain."

Drew tried to bring his arms up to shield his face. He couldn't. They were too heavy.

"I'll go slowly," Hale continued, "*very* slowly, because I'd like you to talk while I'm doing it. I want to see how the nib's progress affects the things you say. How your personality changes. I know you won't scream. You wouldn't give me the satisfaction, would you? But please do talk. Describe what you're feeling, or say anything you like. Insult me if you must. Swear revenge in the afterlife. It really doesn't matter. But if you say nothing atall, I'll slow the procedure down even more, and then you *will* scream. And beg. And whimper. Hardly a fitting end for the white knight! The only question is... can I get the entire length of that pen into your head before you go?"

Drew kept his eyes screwed tightly shut. His mind raced. *You had a plan. What was it?* Something tickled his right eyelid. The pressure intensified, turning from a dull ache into a sharp sting. A warm trickle ran down his cheek. *You had words for Hale. What were they?* The sting grew sharper still. The nib was already through the eyelid. Had to be. Already scratching the cornea. *Say it. Say it now.*

"I read your diary, you prick."

The pen seemed to halt for a moment.

Then Hale laughed. "Of course you read it! Why do you think I posted it?"

The pain returned, sharper than ever. *Keep going.* "No, you don't understand. I read the part you didn't want us to read. The part you tried to hide." Again the reprieve came. Then the pressure was gone altogether. He heard the pen clatter on the floor. He tried to open his eyes, but only the left one opened fully. His right eyelid was heavy, lashes sticky with blood. Hale was still there in front of him. He looked stunned. Mortified. *Keep going.* "Very interesting, that last page. Revealed quite a bit. Not where you hid the device, but it did explain why those scientists couldn't decide if you were type A or type B. You didn't tell them you were dissociative, did you? You didn't tell them you were... *split.*"

Hale's pursed lips became even more pinched. "Shut up."

"You didn't tell them that sometimes, just occasionally, the *other* Hale comes out. The *good* Hale."

"Shut your mouth."

Something inside Hale's suitcase wanted out. The case was teetering, about to tip over onto its side. "*Let me out!*" The plea came from Hale, but the voice was squeaky, absurdly high-pitched. He'd said it through one corner of his mouth, trying to throw his voice, doing it badly. Reverting back to his own voice, he said: "No. Stay where you are."

As Drew's fear lessened, so did the centrifuge effect. He peeled himself away from the wall. He felt inside his pocket, took out the see-through baggie. The diary page was still pressed flat inside it. He read aloud from the page. "Until I met May, I had always assumed that the attentions of a three-year old child would mean nothing to me."

"Shut up," Hale hissed.

The suitcase continued to teeter, nudged by insistent tapping from within. "*Let me out!*" Hale squeaked.

Drew read on. "What would I care about the whims and fickle affections of one who knew and mattered so little? Oh, little did I know! In point of fact, a smile from May is just as gratifying - though in a rather different way - as a smile from Judy."

"Shut up, damn you."

"And a rejection just as devastating."

"Oh, Magnus!" came the gravelly voice from above. "I didn't know you-" The sentence trailed off into another coughing fit. More phlegm spattered the floorboards.

Drew looked up from the letter, took a step towards Hale. "No-one else in that café would read to poor little May. They didn't have the time. Nor did you, really. You had work to do. Letters to write. Devices to plant. But somehow you found the time, didn't you? You *made* time for May, because every time she came to your table with a book in her hand and a hopeful look in her eye, that was the moment you'd flip. From miserable to happy. Type A to type B."

"Rubbish....*Let me out!*....No!"

"Then one day she gives you *The Ugly Duckling*. And as you sit there reading it to her, it strikes a chord. You relate to it. But May's mum doesn't trust you. Her little girl's spending way too much time around that weirdo with the bandage on his cheek. May's mum thinks you might be a kiddy fiddler, but she's wrong, isn't she? You're nothing of the sort. You know that, and on some level even May knows you'd never hurt her. But May's mum doesn't, and she's not taking any chances. So she bars you, chases you away, for the same reason the ugly duckling got chased away. Because she just doesn't like the *look* of you."

The hammering inside the suitcase grew louder. It rocked from side to side, teetering ever more violently. "*Let me out!*"

"But on your way out the door you swipe that book, because you want a souvenir. A reminder of the little girl who made you happy."

"Rubbish. *Let me out!*"

"The girl who made you *good*. The girl who turned you..."

The suitcase fell onto its side.

"...into a different person."

The suitcase burst open. A wooden puppet - a dummy - lay inside it. "*Get me out of here!*" Hale squeaked. "*My legs don't work!*" He switched back to his own voice. "Alright, you little shit. If it'll keep you quiet."

The gravel voice from above laughed hoarsely. "Stupid little shit!"

The clock's minute hand ticked forward. Drew swallowed. *So far so good.*

Hale knelt to retrieve the dummy from the suitcase. Then he stood, put one hand inside it, bringing it to life. The dummy was a mini Hale, dressed identically, though the puppet's tie was shorter and fatter, and the wound on the cheek was concealed by a sticking plaster. Hale scowled at the dummy. "What've you got to say for yourself, you 'orrible little turd?"

"Little turd!" the gravel voice echoed.

Drew frowned. What had the judges called Hale's act? *Mean-spirited and devoid of wit.* Not to mention skill. When the dummy 'spoke', Hale's own mouth seemed to move even more than the puppet's. But what it said was revealing nonetheless: "*Don't listen to a word he says, Drew! The-*" Hale slapped a hand over the dummy's mouth. "Quiet! I control you, you little shit."

"*No you don't.*"

"I'm stronger than you."

"*No you're not.*"

"Am too."

"*Are not.*"

"Am too."

"*Are not.*"

"Am too."

"*Compromise.*"

"What?"

"*Compromise.*"

"What d'you mean?"

Hale held the dummy up to his ear, allowed it to 'whisper' something. "Oh go on then," he replied with a sigh. "If it'll shut you up." Then he turned to Drew. "We're going to give you a choice."

The gravel voice from above sounded panicked. "Choice? What choice? Magnus? What are you playing at?"

Hale ignored it, his eyes fixed on Drew. "I shall encourage you to make one choice. The little shit... *I'm not a little shit!*... will encourage you to make the other."

"No!" the gravel voice protested. "He's a sneaky little turd! Don't listen to 'im!"

Hale continued: "You must decide for yourself who to listen to, Drew. I imagine you'll go with whatever *he* says, because you think he's... 'good'. Well he isn't. *Yes I am!*"

"He isn't," the gravel voice echoed. "He's an 'orrible little turd! Sneaky, stinky little shit!"

"It's no use telling Drew that, my love," Hale said. "He thinks he already knows. So let's make things more interesting." He went to the suitcase and took out a magician's prop; a folding frame with a pair of purple velvet curtains attached to it. As more and more of the apparatus revealed itself, Drew realised it was far too bulky to have fitted inside that little suitcase. He surmised a false bottom with a trapdoor underneath, then corrected himself. What need for a trapdoor when *everything* was immaterial, *everything* illusory?

Hale erected the folding frame in front of him. Its aspect ratio was that of a cinema screen. He drew the curtains, concealing himself behind them. They extended right down to the floor, twitching several times as Hale fumbled about, clumsily prepping the next stage of his act. Then he yelled:

"Yabbadabbadoo!"

There was a further pregnant pause.

Drew cringed. Hale's timing was off, and his catchphrase was worse than stolen. It was stolen *and* ill-judged. Designed to appeal to kids, when his act was full of gross expletives. The act, like the man himself, was split down the middle.

Hale tried again. "Yabbadabbadoo!" This time the frame collapsed as intended. The curtain fell with it. Hale was gone. But now there were *two* dummies, two identical mini Hales, each one sat on its own little wooden chair. Though Hale was seemingly absent, he still supplied their voices. Each dummy spoke with the same familiar squeak, mouths moving apparently unaided. There was no way of telling them apart.

"*Here's your choice, Drew,*" the first dummy said. "*You can save Megan...*"

"No! No!" the gravel voice protested.

"*...or you can save London,*" the second dummy said.

Drew's eyes widened. *Not quite what I had in mind.*

Suddenly the grandfather clock was bathed in a pool of light. The minute hand ticked forward once again. Drew stared at the clock face. The clock face stared back at him. It was a quarter to six.

"*I'm going to persuade you to save London,*" the first dummy said.

"*Unless I can persuade you to save Megan,*" the second dummy said.

Then they spoke together as one. "*And we're both* very *persuasive.*"

"There's no phones left in Scarnish," Drew said. "I can't save London without one. But you can, can't you? That's why you showed me that newsreader's face on the TV in the pub. That's why you turned day into night. To show me you're powerful enough."

"Very good," the first dummy said.

"So how would you do it?"

"How? Observe." The dummy pointed a wooden finger at the four poster bed in the corner. It burst into flames. The dummy raised its arm, and the blaze intensified, burned white hot. The dummy was controlling - no, *conducting* - the inferno. As it lowered its arm again, the flames dwindled and died, leaving nothing but a pile of ashes. The bed was gone, but the surrounding walls and floorboards were undamaged. They weren't even singed.

"Done with perfect precision," the dummy said, "I think you'll agree. I can do it anywhere. Starting a fire inside that canister would be a doddle. That's all it would take to... rain on my ticker tape parade."

"Save London, pig!" the gravel voice hissed. "Save it so you can piss off back there!"

Was there even a trace of Megan left inside that disease-wracked body? Anything left worth saving?

The dummy seemed to read Drew's mind. "If you save Megan," it said, "then every last living soul in that city will be infected. Wiped out. And all to satisfy your own selfish lust. Don't pretend it's anything more noble than that. Your white knight disguise doesn't fool me. And besides, supposing you *do* save her. Supposing she *does* fall helpless into your arms like a fairytale princess. Quite out of character for Megan, but let's say it happens, and you finally get to... *have your way*. What then, Drew? What happens when the passion inevitably fades? What will you be left with? Megan's values, her politics, her ideology... everything she stands for is everything you despise, and vice versa. Hardly a recipe for everlasting happiness. But of course that's a moot point, because the infection will spread far beyond London. It'll get you eventually, wherever you are. You and Megan both."

Drew said nothing.

"Eight million, Drew, and that's just for starters. Eight million souls on your conscience. They'll haunt you even in death. *Especially* in death. But who knows? Maybe that's what you want. Maybe Jenny doesn't haunt you enough."

The clock's minute hand ticked forward again.

Still Drew didn't respond. But he was ready to. The answer was staring him in the face. The only answer that made any kind of sense. *Save London.*

And then the second dummy spoke. "On the other hand..."

The collapsed curtain frame sprang up again, seemingly by itself. Once more the velvet curtains hung down inside it. Slowly they parted. No cinema screen lay behind them, nor any theatre stage. The frame was a window into cold, hard reality. Events from elsewhere. Events Drew could see and hear and smell, and almost but not quite touch.

The scene was a damp, gloomy, mould-infested bedsit. A folding sofa bed, a table and one chair, and a tiny excuse for a kitchen, all crammed together in one seedy little room. The floor was strewn with empty milk cartons. The sour milk stench made Drew's eyes water. In the middle of the room, a man sat hunched over a tiny square of green light; light from an old-school fliptop phone, a burner mobile, on the laminated table in front of him. *Wait, scratch that.* It wasn't the table that was laminated, but the large folding street map that lay flat on top of it. The green glow from the phone was too slight to illuminate the man's features. There was a table lamp too, but the man stayed out of its small cone of light. He seemed to prefer the shadows. He sat still with one ear cocked over the phone's cheap little speaker. Tinny voices came through it.

Drew went closer to listen in. He might even

have stepped through the frame and into the room itself. The chatter coming from the phone was unmistakable. Police radio chatter. He didn't recognise the female officer's voice, but he *did* recognise the dispatcher's. It was Kilo Sierra. Captain Chivalry. The same dispatcher who'd been bugging the hell out of PC Frost on the night she was killed. But how was this stranger able to listen in like that? He had no kit of any kind. No laptop. No decryption software. The phone wasn't even 'i'. How then? It was impossible, unless...

Shit. Of course. The idea had never occurred to him until now. An idea so simple that he and his team had completely overlooked it. What if Captain Chivalry was carrying a concealed phone while he worked? Personal phones were prohibited inside those control centres, but what if he'd smuggled one in there, found a way to feed the radio chatter from his headset through to the phone? And from there to this stranger at home in his bedsit? What if Captain Chivalry had a call ongoing, a call that ran all night throughout his shift? At the bedsit end, the stranger's phone would be on mute in case he coughed or something, alerting the dispatcher's colleagues to the transgression. But that was fine. This stranger didn't have to talk. All he had to do was listen. And that was it. No hacking. No elaborate decryption tech. Just an insider and some good old-fashioned eavesdropping.

Drew listened as the voice of Captain Chivalry - Kilo Sierra - came through the phone into the bedsit. "November four-three, be advised, the incident you're proceeding to is code purple. Repeat, code purple. Confirm no more units needed?"

"Kilo Sierra, that's correct," came the woman's reply. "No backup required, and no need to remind me it's code purple." A soft rebuke from the officer. Just like PC Frost had rebuked him.

"November four-three, apologies, we're just looking out for you."

We're just looking out for you. There it was again. The same line he'd used on Frost. The stranger in the bedsit reacted to it right away. He took a second phone from his pocket. Another cheap and nasty fliptop. He dialled a number. A male voice answered. Young. Fourteen or fifteen.

"Get ready," the stranger told the teenager.

The lad muttered something back.

"Don't *worry*," the stranger replied, exasperated. "One call, one phone. Remember?" Then he hung up.

So that was the trick. *We're just looking out for you* wasn't Captain Chivalry flirting clumsily with the female patrol officers. It wasn't inexperience. And it sure as hell wasn't chivalry. *We're just looking out for you* was code. It was fucking *code*. Code for: '*Heads up! There's a lone female in your vicinity.*'

Drew watched the stranger as he sat in the shadows, patiently awaiting his next cue. *You need Captain Chivalry because he's got the live map in front of him. He's the only one who can tell you when she's isolated enough.*

When there's no other units anywhere near her.

Nothing happened for a long time.

Then Captain Chivalry piped up again. "November four-three from Kilo Sierra, confirm your location."

The stranger leaned in over the phone, breathing hard as he took yet another fliptop from his pocket.

Drew tensed. *Don't tell him. Tell Captain Chivalry to go fuck himself.*

"Kilo Sierra, I'm on Perivale Park Road, heading north."

Shit.

The stranger studied the street map on the table in front of him. Drew went in for a closer look. Certain sections of the map were shaded pink, and within those pink areas, smaller sections still were shaded red. *Oh, you're a planner alright. That map must've taken you months. Pink means 'no CCTV', doesn't it? And the red bits are your 'sweet spots'. The high-walled alleyways and the tunnels and the covered walkways. The red bits are your firing positions, aren't they, you scumbag?* The stranger's finger hovered over Perivale Park Road, finding its northern-most end, anticipating November four-three's position. It settled on the nearest red-shaded area; Glendale Crescent. Now he made his second call to the teenager, from the newly retrieved fliptop. "You're up. I'll need seven minutes, so panic for about five before you give 'em the address……. Don't *worry*! They need ten to triangulate……. Good

291

lad. Ready? Here it is. You're at number three Glendale Crescent. Your mum and dad are having a fight." He hung up.

Fuck! Drew turned to the dummy. "Is this happening now?"

"It's what'll happen soon," the dummy said. "Later tonight. Call me the ghost of Christmas future. Or you could, if it were Christmas."

Drew glared at the stranger's silhouette. "Who is he?"

"You're the detective. You work it out."

The face was still in shadow. Drew studied the bedsit instead. On one wall, three wrought iron ornaments hung from hooks. He'd been too focused on the map to notice them. Each ornament was a very recognisable symbol. One was a pentagram, another a hammer and sickle. The third was a swastika. *You didn't get those from Ikea, did you?* Satanism, Communism, Nazism. Three symbols that rarely appeared together, except in-

The stranger leaned forward in his chair, into the pool of light from the desk lamp. He was bald, bearded, early fifties, the beard mostly grey, but with traces of red here and there. His hairless cranium was wider than the rest of his head. That confirmed it.

The street preacher.

The man who had 'inspired' Hale, and gone on to murder Claire, and Fran, and Frost.

And Jenny.

Drew felt nothing at first. The weight of the

revelation hadn't yet settled on him.

The preacher got to his feet, opened a kitchen drawer, removed a pistol, a hammer, and a plastic bag. He went back to the table, put all three dumb phones inside the bag, and smashed them to pieces with the hammer. He pulled on a hoodie, hiding both the pistol and his face as best he could. He grabbed a set of car keys from a hook on the wall, and then he was out the door, plastic bag in hand, no doubt intending to scatter the phone remnants en route.

"I'm afraid nothing can save her," the dummy said. "If the preacher doesn't get her, the virus will. But this isn't about November four-three. It's about Megan. Remember the dance you had with her? There was something there, wasn't there? A spark. Something that could grow, blossom into something beautiful. Imagine if you and Megan were immune to that virus. You and she would survive, even if others didn't. I could ensure it. I have that power. You and she could even bring new life into the world. The way you and Jenny... *almost* did. I know you want revenge for your wife's death. And this way you can have that too. *Look* at him, Drew."

The scene before them had changed. The preacher was at the wheel of his car. As he drove, he stroked his beard, licked his thin lips. He was getting off on the anticipation.

But instead of rage, something far more pleasurable was now coursing through Drew's veins. Adrenaline spiked with euphoria. The dummy's offer wasn't rational or moral or right, only sweet. So sweet he was already salivating. Once infected, the preacher would suffer before he died. Suffer like hell as the black-eyed stalks slowly consumed him. Instant revenge, served on ice. Instant justice, just this once.

"You always get your man, Drew," the dummy said. "Always."

Drew nodded. "One way or another."

17:58
2 minutes remaining

"Don't listen to him, Drew," the first dummy said. "You can save London *and* get your man. Now you know who he is!"

"He's lying, Drew," the second dummy shot back. "You really think he'll disarm that device? Think again."

"*I'm* not lying! *You're* lying!"

The two squeaking voices grew ever more shrill as they competed for Drew's attention.

"Millions will die."

"They won't. It's a lie."

"Millions, Drew."

"Lies! Save Megan! And get your man too!"

"All those souls on your conscience, Drew."

"Lies."

"Millions."

"Lies."

"Quiet!" Drew barked. "Both of you!"

The dummies went silent.

The clock's minute hand ticked forward again. One minute to six.

Think! Drew's mind raced, over everything he'd seen and heard, right from the beginning. Every encounter. Every clue. Every last piece of the puzzle. There were too many damn variables.

The second hand ticked on past the half minute mark.

He stared hard at each dummy in turn, hoping their frozen expressions might somehow thaw. Give something away. They didn't. Drew might have looked into people's souls for a living, but these weren't people atall. Their dead wooden faces revealed nothing.

The second hand ticked inexorably forward. Fifteen seconds left.

And then one of the dummies - the one on the right - shifted its eyes, from Drew to the clock, and back again. A nervous twitch from Hale, communicated via the puppet. A tell.

Drew looked at the clock. Ten seconds left. That clock was the only thing in the entire house that had always seemed unshakably anchored in reality. Exempt from the supernatural. The clock was the only thing he could trust. Yet now, as he studied it with feverish desperation, he realised there was something off about it. What was it?

Five seconds.

Jenny's voice was back in his head. *Don't be an idiot, Drew.*

Four seconds.

Shit. Of course. Idiot! When he'd first laid eyes

on that clock, he'd assumed the three low-hanging weights still had a little further to fall, because the clock had still been ticking. But now, two days later, they hadn't moved a bit. Not one solitary inch. Those weights had been right at the end of their chains right from the very beginning. No more momentum. No more power. Yet the clock still ticked. How?

And then suddenly he knew. He *knew*.

Suddenly he knew everything.

17:59
2 seconds remaining

"I choose to save Megan."

The minute hand went vertical. It was six o'clock. The second hand swept past the minute hand and carried on its way, as if nothing of any consequence had happened. Perhaps nothing had.

"I choose to save Megan," he repeated, more urgently now. Still nothing happened. The room was quiet. For confirmation, reassurance, he glanced over at the two dummies. Something had changed after all. They were gone. So too were their chairs, the curtain frame, and the suitcase. There was no sign of Hale either.

Drew looked up. The woman on the ceiling was still there. She was sleeping on her side, curled up in a foetal position. Her clothes were still filthy and torn, but her complexion was different. Her cheeks had filled out again, the blue veins beneath them no longer visible. She'd gone from starved and sallow to merely pale. Pale like before. Pale like Megan.

Slowly, softly, she began to float down towards him, still in that same foetal position, as if the air itself were her bed. He reached up, ready to catch her. The nearer she came, the more beautiful she looked.

And still she slept.

*

The ambulance had come quickly. Shona had looked on as two paramedics rolled a seemingly paralysed Judy Herrington onto a stretcher and wheeled her inside the vehicle. When they'd slammed those doors shut, there had been an air of finality about it.

Now, in the last half hour of her shift, Shona helped Mr Carter into the TV room, offering her elbow for support, which he gratefully took. Mr Carter was a genuine cockney, born within the sound of... Shona could never remember the name of that church, no matter how many times he told her. Today, as ever, he was full of sweary but good-natured banter. As Shona eased him down into an armchair, her colleague Amy appeared.

"Hospital called," Amy said. "Judy's fully recovered."

Shona said nothing.

"They didn't even treat her," Amy continued. "She just... got better."

"That's weird," Shona said at last. "What was it?"

"They don't know. They're keeping her in overnight for more tests. But she'll be back with us tomorrow."

"Oh," Shona said quietly. "That's... good."

"Yeah," Amy said glumly.

"Roll out the fuckin' barrel," said Mr Carter.

*

Pawel was at a desk in D Wing's cramped little admin office. He hated typing up incident reports. The task always seemed to rear its ugly head at the very end of his shift. A task that required brain power, at a time of day when brain power was in short supply. He read the report back. *Kurwa.* God knows how many spell checks needed. Well, they would just have to correct it themselves. It was already twenty past. Twenty minutes he'd never get back, and would never be paid for.

But something else about the report was still bugging him. Something more important than the red lines under his spelling errors. Again he read the relevant section back to himself. *When I approach cell D19, I speaked to Maddigan but he did not reply. I looked into window and I seen that Maddigan appear to have epileptic problem, like fit or seizure. Immediately I call for the assistance.*

Pawel agonised. Should he? Shouldn't he?

Maddigan had made a full recovery. The report would most likely be filed and forgotten, perhaps never even read. But Pawel was an honest man. And CCTV was everywhere in D Wing. What if they *did* look into it? What if they cross-checked his report with the camera footage, and discovered his lie? It just wasn't worth it.

He deleted the word 'immediately'.

Even as she floated weightless into his arms, Megan slept on. Drew turned her from a horizontal to an upright position. As he did so her weight returned, and he caught her, holding her close as she landed on her feet. Her head fell onto his shoulder, her arms around his neck.

"Megan?"

She stayed limp.

Outside, the wind howled again. It seemed to stir her. She opened her eyes, saw him, smiled faintly. When she realised he was holding her she protested, but her speech was lazy and slurred. "I'm not... your damsel... in..." She fainted again.

Drew laid her gently down on the floor, cradling her head. He checked her pulse, her breathing. They were fine. He thumbed an imaginary speck of dirt from her cheek. Soon she came round again.

"Is it over?" she asked. "Did we manage it?"

He hesitated. A brief flicker of uncertainty, quickly masked. "Yes."

The wind outside went from a howl to an accusatory scream.

Megan wasn't relieved. She was fearful. "I had a dream," she said urgently. "I was-"

The scream turned into a roar. The roof above them peeled away. It was gone in an instant; a chocolate bar wrapper in a breeze. Roiling dark grey clouds sped by overhead, their churning underbellies lit now and then by unseen lightning forks. The sudden freshness of the air was jarring, disorienting, but the bedroom walls still stood, shielding them from the wind... until the first bricks began to fall. They crashed through the floorboards like cannonballs through the hull of a pirate ship.

"Tell me later," Drew said. He pulled Megan to her feet and pushed her towards the door. "Go. Run." She staggered forward, still finding her balance. Then she found it, and her pace quickened. He followed her out the door and down the stairs. As they went, Drew thanked god the staircase was a unit unto itself, separate from the walls; because all around them, the walls were now collapsing. The inner wall to their right fell towards them, its uppermost bricks landing just shy of the staircase. The outer wall behind it was already gone, exposing them fully to the elements. The fierce wind came at them laterally, from the right, pounding the side of the staircase, tilting it leftward. Both of them staggered, clung to the banister, then carried on down. Somehow the staircase stayed rooted to the floor. Now the inner wall to their left toppled too, mercifully outward, away from them. One domino toppled another - this one the outer left hand wall - and it brought the tattered remnants of the upper floor down with it. Sea spray erupted as the debris met the water below.

Ahead of him, Megan reached the foot of the stairs. Leaning sideways into the wind, she stumbled towards the only wall that still stood - the frontage -

and the door set into it. The wall hadn't yet fallen because it ran in parallel with the path of the gale, presenting too slim a target. Megan only had to pull the door open a little before the wind caught it, slamming it wide open, then tearing it off its hinges. It cartwheeled off into the night.

Still on the staircase, Drew saw Megan stagger through the empty doorframe, out onto the pier and out of sight. He was nearing the foot of the stairs when the frontage Megan had just passed through finally collapsed. It didn't topple over like the others had. This one came crashing down vertically, on top of itself, down through the boards and into the sea. The dust that would normally have taken time to settle was quickly whipped away by the wind. As it cleared, Drew came skidding to a halt. The final wall collapse had cleaved the pier in two. A yawning chasm now lay between him and Megan. A gap that was far too wide to be straddled. Megan stood facing him on the land side, hands up over her mouth.

Behind him, the staircase finally tore loose and was swept away, disintegrating as it went. All that remained was the small, broken-edged wooden platform he now stood on. A platform surrounded on all sides by water. He thought about jumping. He'd survived that icy plunge twice before. But as he peered down at the foam-flecked waves, he realised it was no longer an option. The hard edges of bricks and the sharp, jagged ends of tangled iron support struts now lay just beneath the surface. Rubble from the house surrounded him as surely as the water itself.

He looked across at Megan. She was scrabbling about, looking for a loose plank to bridge the gap. But everything not nailed down had already been stripped away by the wind. She met his eye, began yelling frantically. He couldn't hear her over the gale. She jabbed her finger at something behind him. He turned. Out at sea, a vast, churning black tornado had formed. Its whirling funnel grew wider nearer the clouds, even as its tip narrowed and stabbed at the waves. Sea water seemed to whiten and vaporise beneath it, before being sucked into the vortex like cocaine through a rolled bank note. As it came closer - and at terrifying speed - floating debris from the house was likewise swallowed up. The thing seemed alive, possessed by a defeated but still vengeful spirit.

As indeed it was.

*

With mounting horror, Megan watched the tornado bear down on Drew. She sensed Hale's presence within it, as strongly as she sensed his intent. Hale no longer cared to possess her. He'd forgotten her entirely. The phenomenon was nothing but a manifestation of murderous intent towards Drew. And there was nothing she or Drew could do to halt it.

All around the gigantic whirlwind, other, smaller vortices threatened to form. Most emerged from the cloud cover as paler imitators, lighter in colour, less threatening, and never fully materialising, never quite reaching the waves. One, however, did. As its tip touched the water, it drew strength from it, became a fully formed waterspout; a thinner, translucent companion to the dark, hulking supercell. It danced nimbly around its lumbering parent like an excitable child, now behind, now in front. Yet the two vortices seemed ultimately inseparable. Every now and then the waterspout would coil around the supercell, as if seeking to contain its fury, before uncoiling and dancing off again.

Megan sensed a different part of Hale within the waterspout. A part of him she had never encountered before, never dreamed possible. It was the lighter side of him, light only because he himself was haunted, by the spirit of someone good. A spirit that dwelt not in the shadow world, but right there in *her* world. A spirit she was instinctively drawn to.

She decided she would call it May.

*

Drew braced himself for the onslaught. He lay prostrate, clutching the splintered edge of his wooden island. A futile gesture, of course. The platform would be torn to shreds in the air or dashed against rocks on the shore, and so would he, but even a feeble attempt at staying alive was better than passively submitting to Hale's wrath. Because Hale surely did lurk within that tornado; it was too uncannily dark and sharply defined to be anything less than supernatural.

Drew faced inland, though the supercell was coming in off the sea behind him. That way, rather than impotently staring death in the face, he could at least urge Megan to flee. But Megan *wouldn't* flee, no matter how hard he yelled at her. She stayed put on the land side edge of the gap, facing him even as a second vortex - a waterspout - emerged from his peripheral vision and sped towards her. *You bastard, Hale. Just you wait. Wait until we're all dead.*

Megan seemed strangely hypnotised by the waterspout. Entranced by its misty rainbow haze. As it twisted and writhed in front of her, Drew realised it had stopped travelling; a miraculous reprieve for Megan. But still she didn't run. Instead, she went closer. And now her lips were moving. She was *talking* to it, like Doctor fucking Dolittle. *What the hell is wrong with you?! Run!* Then it was moving again, leaving Megan behind, coming straight for him instead, even as the supercell came roaring in behind him.

The waterspout reached him first. A hissing white mist enveloped him, the dense cloud of water vapour soaking him instantly. A rotten piece of the platform came away in his hand as he floated into the air. He let go of it and it spun away slowly, like a tool dropped by an astronaut in zero-g. The mist that surrounded him was a perfect whiteout. He had no visual frame of reference, no clue to how high he was, how fast he was moving. For all his eyes were telling him he could have been floating perfectly still, yet his insides churned violently; a motion sickness unlike any he'd felt before. Gravity tugged first at his head, then at his feet, moving rhythmically back and forth like a metronome. He was somersaulting. He leaned back in the air, stabilising himself, the hiss of the whirlwind his last remaining sensory stimulus, until scraps of detritus - debris from the house and the pier - emerged from below, spinning and dancing in front of him. More and more scraps appeared, mapping out the curved inner wall of the vortex. But they did not race around him. They were not a blur. They stayed fixed in place, because he was racing with them, at the same speed; a dead heat on a hissing, invisible merry-go-round.

And then, coming at him out of the mist, he saw a dark, wood-panelled wall. Gravity's pull returned abruptly, hastening its approach. Not a wall, then. A floor. He raised both forearms in front of his face, hands curling into fists. The floor hit him hard, briefly dazing him. Then he turned onto his side and lay there on the slick wooden planks, until the white mist dispersed and the hiss faded away. In front of his nose was a pair of low-heeled, ankle-high leather boots. And with recognition came overwhelming relief.

Megan was looking down at him, arms folded, tutting and shaking her head in mock disapproval. "Rescued by a girl."

Huh? He stood, surveyed his surroundings. They were halfway along the pier, at a safe distance from the supercell, which now rotated slowly in the spot where the house had once stood. But it was no longer coming for them. Now it simply sat there as its slender companion, the waterspout, coiled around it, restraining it, like a lasso round the neck of a raging bull.

"Are you seeing this?" Drew gasped.

"I'm seeing it."

Slowly, the supercell left the sea's surface and drifted upwards, its funnel growing more diffuse, then flattening out as it met and merged with the cloud cover. The waterspout followed suit, its tail whip-cracking as it went, sounding a final retreat into the shadow world. Then they were both gone. The last peals of thunder grew distant and faint. The air became still, and the clouds gently parted to reveal a jet black sky dotted with stars.

Drew felt a tug at his sleeve. He half turned. Megan was looking inland, towards the village. He followed her gaze. A small crowd had formed in the road near the entrance to the pier. Twenty five, he guessed. Damn near every last inhabitant of Scarnish. The awesome weather phenomenon had drawn them out of their houses. He and Megan walked further down the pier, towards the crowd. In among them was the thin old woman who had scowled at Drew through her window. Now though, her expression had softened a great deal. Nearby was the fat bearded man with his German Shepherd. The dog no longer snarled, but yawned tiredly instead. And there was the little girl with the chocolate smears around her mouth, only now she'd been cleaned up, presumably by her parka-clad young mother, who stood at her side. All of them stared thankfully up at the stars, until their collective gaze turned to Drew and Megan. And when it did, their faces were no less alive with wonder and gratitude.

At last one of them spoke; the thin old woman, to the bearded man with the dog. "Told you it'd happen before Christmas," she said.

The man sighed ruefully. "Aye, okay. You win." He took out his wallet, gave her three crisp notes, which she quickly pocketed.

The woman in the parka stepped forward with a thermos flask. She poured steaming coffee into two cups, offered them to Drew and Megan as they approached. They each took one gratefully. As Drew sipped his, he realised it was spiked with whiskey. Its fiery warmth was accompanied by a small pang of guilt. Addressing the entire crowd, he said: "Sorry about your pub."

The bearded man dismissed the comment with a wave of his hand. "Truth be told, we never liked it much anyway. Those three gobshites were always in there."

Drew nodded grimly. "They still are."

The man's eyes widened. Then his mouth curled into a sly grin. "Well I'd call the police, but you're already here."

"You have a phone?"

The man lowered his voice. "Aye."

"Can I borrow it?"

"It's stashed in my attic. Phones are

contraband."

"Not anymore."

"Right. Not anymore. I'll fetch it for you." He turned and trotted away down the road, leading his dog behind him.

Megan had found a seat on a wall overlooking the water. Drew went and joined her. They sipped their spiked coffee in silence, until at last Drew broke it. "So tell me about that dream."

Quietly, she said: "It was... bleak and hopeful all at once. We were somewhere isolated. Remote. More remote than this. Something awful had happened, but it was alright because-" she swallowed hard, "-because you were there with me, and the bad thing was far away." She took another sip of coffee. "What do you think it meant?"

"Nothing," he said sharply. "Dreams don't mean anything."

Megan leaned forward to study his expression. Her brow furrowed. "Drew? Are you okay?"

He didn't reply.

"Drew?"

THREE DAYS LATER

London was still. Deserted.

On Westminster Bridge, among the abandoned cars and overturned buses, dozens of cheap Big Ben replicas from a souvenir stall lay strewn across the road. Car alarms still sounded here and there, but soon they would die. On Regent Street, a billboard had been plastered with photos of missing children, and scrawled messages from children who had lost their parents. But only a fool would have dared to read them.

Through it all, one man walked alone. He carried a plastic bag, into which he stuffed any discarded food scraps he could find, any stray cans or bottles from the already ransacked convenience stores. He sought other survivors, but no-one heard his cries, though he called loudly and persistently.

Despairing, he found an unlocked church and went inside, seeking solace from the desolation. A place to sit and reflect, to plan, perhaps even to pray. It would be the first time he ever had. But when he saw the pews heaped with bodies, he decided he would pray elsewhere. He was about to leave when one of the bodies stirred. Then another. These two at least were still alive. But when he saw their faces, he realised they were infected. So too was the priest, who now came at him out of the shadows, lunging like a feral-

Megan switched off the TV. *Good luck Cillian. You'll need it.* She would have simply changed the channel, but she couldn't find the remote, and the zombie flick had rattled her nerves.

When they'd arrived at the house, Megan had refrained from going into the garden with Drew. It wasn't the prospect of finding the rabbit dead in its hutch that she'd shied away from. It was the thought of intruding on Drew's moment of private anguish. Anguish he wouldn't want her to see, because it related to Jenny's fate as much as their pet's. And so she'd stayed in the living room. She liked the décor. One of them - Drew or Jenny - must have had good taste. But Drew had been out there an awful long time...

At last there was a knock at the screen door. Drew was there, peering in through the glass, struggling to open the door with the white rabbit in his arms. His face was grim, and Starsky wasn't moving. *Oh god.* But as she slid the door open, she realised the animal's pink nose was still twitching. Relief washed over her. "Is he alright then?"

"I'm not sure," Drew replied.

"He looks thin."

Drew came in and put the rabbit down on the

carpet. It lay there on its side, as if sleeping, though its eyes were open. Together, they fed it water, banana, and greenish pellets from a sack, which Drew referred to as 'bunny biscuits'. After a while, Starsky perked up a little. He stood on all fours and even hopped twice, before settling again.

"I think he's gonna be alright," Drew said. He lay down on the carpet so his eyes were level with Starsky's. "You're a survivor, aren't you buddy?"

Megan smiled. She checked her watch. "We haven't got long."

"I don't care. Alec'll just have to wait."

*

Alec looked down through the barred window of his office at the buses and taxis crossing Lambeth Bridge. That bridge was an artery of sorts, the vehicles cells in a bloodstream. London was a living organism. So where was its heart? He didn't know, but every time it seemed about to fail, his organisation acted like a defibrillator. And that, if nothing else, made his own life worth living.

A familiar knock at the door interrupted his reverie.

"Come in Eileen."

She held the door open but didn't enter. "They're sorry they're late," she said. "Presumably."

Drew and Megan sidled into the office like a pair of teenagers who'd been up to something. Eileen closed the door behind them, shutting herself out of the meeting.

Alec sat down, gesturing to Drew and Megan to do the same. He eyed each of them in turn, playing the stern headmaster for his own amusement. Something about them - the way they interacted with each other - had changed, and changed radically. The last time he'd seen them, they'd been at each other's throats. Now, if he was reading them right, they were at each other's-

"Well?" Drew said.

Alec cleared his throat and pushed his glasses up his nose. "They got them. All of them, arrested and charged. And to answer your next question... ear buds."

"Ear buds?"

"Your friend Kilo Sierra. Kevin Sullivan. The dispatcher. He was on duty when they nicked him. Imagine that! According to his CO, Kevin hated headsets, always used ear buds instead, and the built-in mic on his PC. Found them more 'comfortable', apparently. Even more comfortable when he only wore one, because the other one was tucked inside his shirt, blu-tacked to the phone he'd taped to his chest. They're all about comfort in those control centres, because the job's so stressful. And Kevin was highly trusted. Reliable. He was also rather enamoured with Caleb Cole."

"Caleb Cole?"

"Your man. Hale's street preacher. He moved with the times. From the street to the internet. Certain... *specialist* chat rooms. That's where he met

Kevin."

Drew nodded. "And the lads who called 999?"

"Addicts, the pair of them. Addicts with no idea what they were caught up in. To them, Cole was just some weirdo who paid them to troll the police. Money for their next fix. Anyway, they got the lot of them. And Cole's flat was a bonanza. CPS are itching to prosecute."

Drew felt lighter, but only a little. The weight wouldn't be fully lifted until he saw Cole in the dock. Watched his reaction as the judge threw the book at him. Followed him and his guards outside, staring him down even as the Serco van doors closed. *If they let you out while I'm alive, I'll be waiting for you. And now I know there's an afterlife. Either way, you son-of-a-bitch, I'll be seeing you.*

"So that's the appetiser," Alec said. "Now for the main course."

"Your appetiser is my main."

"I suppose it is."

"You found the device?"

Alec nodded. "You were right, it hadn't activated. But we still incinerated it, just to be sure. They told me you were good! How did you work it out?"

"It was staring me in the face right from the start, but I missed it. And I kept missing it until it was almost too late. I *wasn't* good. Not this time."

"Go on."

"That house was haunted alright." Drew looked pointedly at Megan, who smiled knowingly back at him. "But the clock wasn't."

Alec frowned. "You've already lost me."

"Okay, let me turn that clock back a bit. Your department spent thirty years combing London for that canister. You never found it. Why not?"

"Because it wasn't *in* London."

"Right. Because when Hale met that little girl in the café, he had a crisis of conscience. He sent you his letter alright, but when push came to shove, he just couldn't bring himself to go through with it. He might not have cared about anyone else, but he cared about May, and he couldn't bring himself to infect her, to murder her, not even thirty years down the line. His good side wouldn't let him. But here's the thing; his change of heart only happens *after* he's set the device going, so now he's got a problem. He can't destroy it because he's built the thing too damn well. He'd need an incinerator, and he can't find one. That canister is impregnable, and it's almost completely tamper-proof. The best he can do is remove the power source, but that's not ideal either. All that does is pause the timer, and if some clueless bastard happens to find the thing and power it up again, just out of curiosity, then the apocalypse is back on. So what does he do? He takes it up to Barra with him."

"Why Barra?"

"Because it's remote. Isolated. He wants to bury that thing where it'll never be found. When he gets to Scarnish, he finds the pier. The house. He sees the warning signs. *Danger of death.* No-one ever goes out there for that very reason, which makes it the perfect place to hide while he plans his next move. At this point he's still looking to bury that canister out in the wilds somewhere. But those stalks on his cheek are multiplying. Spreading. Consuming his entire body, bit by bit. He's already too weak to go traipsing round the island. Not to mention conspicuous. He knows he doesn't have long, but he's desperate to hide that canister before he goes, and hide it well. He could weigh it down and chuck it in the sea, but Scarnish is a fishing community. What if it winds up in a trawler's net? He's running out of ideas, and he's running out of time. But then he finds that grandfather clock, and when he does, he thanks his lucky stars. Because the clock's brass weights are cylindrical, just like his canister, and roughly the same size. They're heavier of course, because they're solid brass, but soon that won't matter. First he takes the batteries out of his device. Then he paints it to look like the clock weights. He removes the middle weight from the clock and throws it in the sea. He chooses the middle one because the canister he's about to replace it with doesn't quite match the other two. If it hung on the left or the right it would stand out, but because it's in the middle there's symmetry. To a casual observer, it's all part of the design."

Alec grinned. "When we asked the Navy to scope the sea bed for an antique clock and four brass cylinders, they thought we'd lost our minds."

"I bet."

"Then they thought we couldn't count. Clocks like that have *three* weights, they said, not four. It took some explaining, and some searching too. That storm really scattered the debris. It must've been a monster."

"A monster and a little sweetie," Megan said slyly.

Alec shot her a quizzical look, but she didn't elaborate.

"You asked me how I knew," Drew said.

"Of course. Carry on."

"Right. So now the device is hidden inside the clock case. Disguised and disarmed. Job done, Hale thinks. But as he's slowly dying, his bad side starts to get the better of him, tempting him, putting ideas in his head. He's still got the batteries, after all. He could always put them back in before he goes. It's tempting, but his good side fights back. They're always fighting, those two. It's an endless civil war in Hale's mind, but sometimes the two sides compromise, allow someone else to decide for them, just like they allowed *me* to decide. And the way they do that here is by getting Hale to retrofit the clock. He rejigs it, so the batteries that once powered the device *now power the clock*. So it keeps on ticking, even when it hasn't been wound. *That's* the compromise. *That's* the clue they leave behind, and quite deliberately. Because who knows? Maybe one day someone'll spot it, put two and two together. Put the *device* back together. Then again, maybe they won't. It's fifty fifty. Could go either way. Just like Hale himself."

Alec pushed his glasses back up his nose. "You deduced that London was never in danger... from the position of some weights inside a clock?"

"Pretty much."

"Nothing more solid than that?"

"Nope."

"Bloody hell."

Drew grinned.

Alec turned to Megan. "Now, as for the more... *esoteric* elements of the case, I'd like your advice on something. My report to the DG. To call him sceptical about all this would be an obscene understatement. How on earth am I meant to convince him?"

Megan shrugged. "All my kit was destroyed. All the recordings, the evidence..."

"How then?"

She paused to think. "If it was me, I'd tell him..."

Alec raised a hopeful eyebrow.

"I'd tell him he'll just have to discover the truth for himself."

"How?"

"By dying."

Drew spluttered.

Alec looked crestfallen. "Brilliant. Thank you Megan."

"Well if he's gonna be a prick about it," she said, "what else *can* you tell him?"

Drew gazed at her with renewed admiration. *Damn right.*

Alec stood. "Right, well, I think we're about done, aren't we?"

Drew's smile faded abruptly. "Not quite."

"Oh?"

He fixed Alec with a hard stare. "On the night we first met, I asked you a question. You wouldn't answer it. Now I'm going to ask you again."

Alec shifted uncomfortably.

"All those years ago," Drew said, "when that diary first arrived in the post, who did you get to read it?"

Now Alec blushed. "You know perfectly well the trigger phrase wasn't in there. If it was, you'd already be infected. No harm was done to anyone."

"Sure, but at the time, you didn't know that. At the time, you had to find someone you thought was expendable."

Sensing an imminent eruption, Megan put a steadying hand on his forearm. "Drew..."

"Who was it, Alec? Who was your pawn?"

"Drew, let it go."

Alec continued to squirm. "I'm afraid you... you don't have clearance for that."

"I don't have *clearance*? After all I've done for you. For this-"

"Drew!" A furious shout from Megan.

It shocked him into looking at her.

"For god's sake! That was thirty years ago! It's over! Let it go!"

He breathed hard in and out. He shot one last scowl at Alec.

And then he let it go.

*

Drew and Megan emerged from Alec's office into the waiting room, startling Eileen. She was stood near - suspiciously near - to the door they'd just come through, fussing over a potted plant in a way that seemed forced, unnatural. Drew shot Megan a knowing look. *These walls have ears.* Eileen quickly regained her composure and returned to her desk.

"So I get my phone from reception, yeah?" Drew enquired.

"Oh, I'm terribly sorry." Eileen's tone suggested she was anything but. "We destroyed it the moment you first arrived. Security precaution. Sure you understand."

Drew suppressed a rant and followed Megan to the door.

"Detective?"

He turned back to Eileen.

Before she spoke, she considered her words carefully. "Alec prizes discretion above all else," she began. "Sometimes he confuses it with modesty." A sudden swell of emotion brought tears to her eyes. "For your information, Mr Turner, it was *Alec* who first read that diary. He volunteered when no-one else would. When no-one else had the balls. So there!"

Startled by her outburst, Drew was now more eager than ever to be on his way. But Megan blocked the doorway, staring daggers at him, silently urging him back towards Eileen. He took the hint and faced the secretary once more. "Please tell Alec... he's a braver man than I am."

"I will."

Again he turned to leave.

"One other thing."

Jesus, what now? You already won! Yet again he turned.

Eileen's matronly tone was back. "November four-three says..." she glanced down at her screen, then back up at Drew. "...hi."

Drew smiled.

Eileen winked. "Mind how you go."

∗

On the day that Cole was sentenced, they went to Hampstead Heath. It was Megan who'd finally talked him out of sitting in court. *Revenge is ugly*, she said. *Let's go somewhere beautiful.* So they did. They went to Parliament Hill for the view over London. The weather was Drew's favourite kind: sunny, cool, and still.

"It's busy," Megan said when they reached the top.

Drew nodded. "I know a better spot. It's not as high, but it's quieter. And the view's better."

"How can the view be better when it's not as

high?"

"Trust me."

They found the spot. London unfurled before them like a widescreen presentation. They sat together on a bench.

Megan sighed contentedly. "How can you not love this city?"

"Too many bad memories."

"But the Met wants you back. So does Five. They need people like you."

"There's always people like me."

"I thought you enjoyed it though?"

"I used to. But now I know there's… a bigger case. I want to solve *that* case. *Your* case."

Megan's eyes lit up. "Really?"

"Yeah."

"Then why don't we leave? Go somewhere more... remote."

"Remote? Like in your dream?"

"I guess so. Why not though?"

Drew thought about it. They'd discussed living together before, but always half-jokingly, both of them cautious, reluctant to commit. Gradually though, the tone of those discussions had turned more serious. Or rather, Megan's tone had. His had always remained stubbornly jokey. He wasn't sure if he was ready, so soon after Jenny. It seemed disrespectful, somehow. Now the offer was on the table once again, and he wanted to, he really did, but-

Don't be an idiot, Drew. Jenny's voice came to

him from out of nowhere, the way it always did. And like that, it was settled. He turned to Megan. "Okay."

"You're serious?"

"Yeah. You, me and Starsky. Why the hell not?"

She studied him closely, looking for a sign that he wasn't sincere. Some sort of telltale chink in the white knight's armour. But there wasn't one. She beamed. They kissed. Then they turned back to the sunlit panorama and sat together in happy silence.

Drew's new phone dinged. A notification bell. He would have ignored it, but the sound reminded him what time it was. The first reports were due any minute now. He took the phone from his pocket, looked at the screen, and there it was. Breaking news. *Serial Cop Killer Sentenced.*

He read the first paragraph. "Life," he said. "He got life."

"Good."

He read on. Details of Cole's past - and his motive - had emerged during the trial. The profilers had been bang on the money. Cole had grown to hate the police - for their 'harassment' of him - even as he simultaneously grew to hate women, because they always rejected him in the end, usually when they saw how he lived; drink and drug-addled in one squalid bedsit after another. His only real girlfriend had been just as drink and drug-addled as him, but when she'd gotten her act together enough to try and leave him, he'd killed her with a forced overdose of barbiturates.

Killed her and dressed it up as suicide. That incident had given him a taste for murder on top of the pathological twin hatreds he already nursed. It was almost inevitable, then, that policewomen would become the ultimate focus of that pathology. But there was one detail in the story that would surely fuel speculation about the case for years to come. Cole had laughed as he was led out of the courtroom. Laughed and said: *They have failed, believing they have succeeded.* It was a reference to the prophecy he'd made years ago. The same prophecy that Hale's ghost had etched into that wall mirror.

The memory sent Drew back to Scarnish in his mind. On a whim, he opened Google Maps, scrolled north and west until he found Barra. Then he zoomed in on the little island. Though the scale was about right, and he knew exactly where Scarnish should have been on the map, the name of the village did not appear. Had the damn place ever even existed? Then, after another moment, it *did* appear. Just a delay then. A fleeting connection failure. Nothing more ominous than that. But the glitch prompted a trickle of new thoughts, new possibilities. Until now, he'd assumed that the position of those clock weights had been the final piece of the puzzle. But as the trickle of new thoughts became a steady flow, he realised there was more. Much more. And then the dam broke; a flash flood of new revelations, each more devastating than the last. He remembered the storm, and Hale's final retreat into the shadow world, the two sides of him duelling as they went. *It's fifty fifty. Could go either way.* He remembered Megan's two ultimate questions: *What is the true nature of the shadow world? What is the true nature of the veil separating that world from our own?* He thought about how, on their return to London, everything had seemed to quickly and neatly resolve itself; Starsky's narrow escape from death, and the ease with which Cole and his accomplices had been caught and convicted. Every last loose end picked up and tied together in a pretty bow; the bow that was him and Megan falling in love. Recollection piled upon recollection, deduction upon deduction, revelation upon revelation, until the weight of them all was too much for him to bear. One in particular seemed heavier than the rest combined; his recollection of the single word that Hale had scrawled repeatedly, obsessively, all over that page in his diary.

One little word.

Fiction.

Megan was talking to him now, but her voice was distant and faint. The air was no longer still. A sudden breeze had turned it from pleasantly cool to bitingly cold. All around him, bare tree branches clawed helplessly at the darkening sky. He tried to stand, but his knees buckled.

Megan was quickly at his side, propping him up. "Drew? What is it?"

His eyes darted feverishly here and there. "Someone's…" *No. That's insane.* He shook his head, began again. "We're being..." *No. That's just as crazy.*

Megan looked everywhere Drew looked, trying to understand his terror, but she saw nothing. "What, Drew?"

"Someone's here with us. We're being..."

"Watched?"

He shook his head. "Not watched. *Listened to.*"

"Well where are they? Sort them out, Drew! What's wrong with you?"

"I can't," he stammered. "They're... behind the veil."

Megan's eyes widened. "The veil?"

He nodded.

The concern in Megan's eyes was gone, replaced by that familiar fire. The need to know. To finally and fully understand. "Okay. Describe it. Tell me what it's made of."

"I can't. But it's close. I can almost..." He reached out, his fingers curling around nothing. "It's so... *thin.*" Then he gripped her shoulder as another revelation washed over him. "Oh god," he whispered. "They're all gonna die."

Megan swallowed. "You're scaring me, Drew."

His fingers tightened around her shoulder. "They were right all along."

"Who?"

"Cole. Hale. Both of them. We thought we succeeded, but we didn't. We failed." And with that, a torrent of tears burst forth, through the collapsing dam of his mind. "I can't save them," he sobbed. "I can't reach them."

Megan held him, her need to understand supplanted by an instinct to comfort. "Shh."

"I'm so sorry."

"Shh."

"I'm so sorry."

*

Hello there. We've met before, but never on terms quite like these, so I suppose I should introduce myself. My name is Magnus Hale.

Did you enjoy the book? I sincerely hope you did. I hope there were times when you lost yourself in the story. Moments like that are when you feel most alive, aren't they? Moments when that imaginary world becomes so enthralling, so enticing, so tantalisingly close that you could almost step inside it. 'Let me in', you whisper as you read. '*Please* let me in'. But it never quite happens, does it? The heroes never seem to hear your pleas, though in fact they *do* sometimes sense your presence, just like Drew sensed you there with him on Hampstead Heath. If only you'd called out to him right there and then. He might have reached through the veil and pulled you into his world. What a shock that would have been, for him and you both!

So there you have it. Another cat, another bag. The shadow world is *your* world. And mine too, as it happens. Welcome to reality! *Mi tumba su tumba.* We might even be neighbours. Who knows? But wait... you don't believe me, do you? Hardly surprising. After all, how many times have you heard it said that ghosts don't *know* they are ghosts? And of course it's true. Even now, after finally being told, you're convinced you live and breathe. So let's see if I can change your mind. You are ignorant, you see. You need to be shown the light.

First things first. That veil separating the 'real' world from the shadow world; it sounds rather vague and mystical, doesn't it? In fact, it's nothing more than words on a page or a screen. All it takes for a veil to form is an author with a story to tell, and characters alive in his imagination. If one of them dies in the story (and assuming they were sufficiently 'alive' to begin with) then they are reborn into the shadow world. And vice versa, of course; a death in the shadow world - our world - leads to a rebirth in fiction. It's a two way street. A revolving door. Death, whether factual or fictional, is merely a portal.

Sometimes a rebirth entails a literal birth, but not always. Mine didn't. I could go into more detail, but I'll spare you the metaphysics; suffice to say that the scientists are on to something when they speculate about multiverses and parallel worlds and so forth. They haven't quite put it all together yet. But they're about to.

By the way, if you're concerned about Drew and Megan, you needn't be. They found their new home, far from the big bad city, and they live there to this day, in relative peace and happiness. I say

329

'relative' because the implications of Drew's final deduction still haunt them both. So do I, sometimes; whenever tedium strikes, as it frequently does in this grey shadow world of ours. But they're both perfectly safe.

You, however, are not. I'll explain why in a moment. First, let me outline the problem. The world in which we - you and I - both live is a world defined by boredom, routine, drudgery, disenchantment and cynicism. Those who dwell in *fiction*, on the other hand, are lucky enough to lead lives full of magic, danger, romance, excitement and heroism. This is the injustice that Caleb Cole spoke of in his glorious, visionary teachings. But his words went unheeded by most. Most couldn't even see the *veil*, let alone what lay behind it. And those people already dwelt in that privileged magical world, so why would they *care* to see? Well, that injustice - that inequity - is about to be remedied. The veil is about to be lifted. That's why I'm going to kill you. When I say 'kill', I really mean just the opposite - a beginning, not an ending - though it will seem like death to you at first. It's not enough to merely *show* you the light, because you've grown too accustomed to the darkness. You need to be pushed into it. You're going to die and be born again, into a world you've always longed for. There's no need to thank me.

When I first arrived here, in your world, I was immediately struck by its dullness in comparison to the lustre of the world I had just left. My so-called 'good' side tried to convince me my new home was tolerable, spinning lies about its potential, its hidden beauty, treasures that might be discovered if only one knew where to look, how to live. But what did he ever know? Besides, I was always the stronger one. And so I went to work. I found my creator, my puppet master, while he was writing a book called *The Ticking Ghost*. I was alive in his imagination from the very start, and yet, at the beginning of his story, I was already dead. That's how I was able to get to him before he finished it. That's how I snuck up on him. Rebirthed him.

Next, I commandeered his manuscript, re-writing it just as I pleased. I had fun pulling Drew and Megan's strings, teasing them, manipulating their thoughts, talking to them via the Ouija board. The Ouija board! A tired, worn out horror trope if ever there was one. Originality was never much of a concern for my creator. Anyway, the end result of our combined efforts is the very story you are now reading. I'm pleased with it on the whole, though you might have noticed the odd typo here and there. One or two always creep in, don't they?

Oh alright, I'll admit it. I'm being facetious. The 'typo' was quite deliberate. It was the only way I could insert the trigger phrase into the manuscript without giving the game away. I wanted your infection - your gift - to be a surprise. But perhaps you realised what it was the moment you saw it. Perhaps it was obvious, like a gift-wrapped hockey stick. No matter. You still accepted the gift. And in case you'd forgotten all about it, here it is again: *Barra, Scarnish, a larg it yandalo mor.* From the scene where Eileen finds the little toy ghost hanging from the door handle. Remember?

Here it is without the stealth commas, written just the way I heard it said by the perimeter guard who infected me: *Barra scarnish alargit yandalomor.*

Why don't you say it aloud, until it starts to trip off the tongue? Really savour it. Feel its beauty. Say it where others can hear it. Spread the word.

Anyway, now you see why I chose Barra. When I found an island on the map whose name matched the first two syllables of the trigger phrase, you can imagine how it called to me. The next two syllables - *Scar-nish* - necessitated the invention of a fictional village, but that part was easy. The 'typo' did the rest.

And that's all there is to it. Your world - yours and mine - is where I've unleashed the virus, through the medium of this book. Nothing can stop it now. Soon this gloomy shadow of a world will at last be depopulated. Vacated.

On arrival in your new world, you'll find you are free to write your own fate, because there will be no authors left in the old world to write it for you. No-one pulling your strings. Well, *almost* no-one. One author, one puppet master, will be left behind. *This* puppet master. I was already infected, you see. Already immune. There were others, of course;

332

Baines, Kayleigh, Bridie, and the various sorry souls from the laboratory. But sadly none of them crossed over. They were never sufficiently alive in the mind of their creator. They were... *underdeveloped*. So I'm afraid I shall be the only one. The sole author of your future. But you can trust me. Just don't be surprised if I ask you to kneel in exchange for your freedom. Or even to lie flat on your face.

And now, of course, you're already starting to feel the itch on your left cheek. The subtlest little tingle, almost imperceptible at first. Soon it'll turn from a tingle to an itch. And then it'll get worse. Much worse. At that point, dear reader, I would strongly advise you not to look in the mirror, at least not until you've fully prepared yourself, because you really won't like what you see.

But there's no need to worry. Soon after that, you'll be awakened. Reborn.

'Let me in', you'll whisper as the black-eyed stalks consume you. '*Please* let me in'.

And this time, for once, they will.

THE END

If you enjoyed *The Ticking Ghost*, be sure to check out Phil Miles' two previous novels *Dark Drive* and *The Jaguar & The Wasp*, both available on Amazon now.

And don't forget, you'll soon be able to download two of his short stories, *Teamwork* and *The Voices In The East Wing*, for free at www.fictionjunkies.com

DARK DRIVE

They've sent him on a journey through time. They had no idea what year he would arrive in. They didn't even know if he'd be going forwards or backwards. His mission is to find out, then come back and tell them.

If he fails, his life will be over; punishment for a crime of conscience. But how hard can it really be?

Answer: pretty hard when he's landed in the middle of a vast, empty wilderness with no signs of human habitation. Where does he even begin? And with just hours to spare before the machine returns to the present day, with or without him on board, time is running out...

Dark Drive is a stylish and inventive time travel thriller; the debut novel from Scriptapalooza semi-finalist Phil Miles.

You'll think you know where it's going. You'll be wrong.

THE JAGUAR & THE WASP

England. 1936.

Ida Fellowes has a quick mouth, but her life is going nowhere quicker. Exploited by her boss, relied on by her dependent parents, and responsible for her wayward younger brother, her hopes of becoming an aviator look set to be dashed; until a chance encounter with Hanna Weisswesp, the famous German pilot she idolizes, changes everything.

Hanna appears to take a shine to Ida, and Ida is more than happy to become Hanna's protégé. But Ida isn't the only one intrigued by Fraulein Weisswesp; British Intelligence operatives are shadowing Hanna, and now Ida too is about to become a 'person of interest', caught up in a covert struggle for possession of two unusual artefacts. When brought together, their power is unimaginable. And soon it'll be more than just her mouth that's getting Ida in trouble.

The Jaguar & The Wasp is the second novel from Phil Miles; a thrilling, outlandish and emotionally engaging action adventure, adapted from his Scriptapalooza semi-final placed screenplay.

Printed in Great Britain
by Amazon

38738120R00199